MW01594962

THE GOOD SAMARITAN

ROB MACLAINE BOOK 2

LES HASWELL

1

SIR ANDREW SAVAGE, CEO OF SAVAGE GUIDANCE SYSTEMS (SGS) was a modern, forward thinking manager. He believed in the Steve Jobs management philosophy, *"It doesn't make sense to hire smart people and then tell them what to do; we hire smart people so they can tell us what to do."* On that basis he hired the best people he could find and let them tell him what they could potentially do with Laser Guidance Systems. He listened to their dreams and ambitions, took their advice and made business decisions based on what he heard from his team and what he considered commercially viable.

When his technical team talked at a weekly management meeting about modifying their existing technology used to guide missiles to their targets, giving the potential to guide a "smart bullet" fired from a light drone to its target, he sat up and took notice. He engaged with an innovative UK manufacturer of drones he had previously met on a Department of International Trade sponsored trip to the US. They had agreed that such a product would present a huge opportunity for both companies, if they could interest a suitable ordinance manufacturer in developing a remotely operated device to fire such a "smart bullet."

Drones were a given, readily available and in constant use for a wide variety of applications, from big boy's toys to surveillance and mapping. They were even under consideration for delivering parcels by a large internet retailer. An arms manufacturer had already recognised the potential for a drone mounted rifle and had done some early development work following initial feasibility studies. They had continued their development programme after an approach from Sir Andrew, as they had always believed the guidance system for such an application to be the stumbling block to commercialising their product. Eighteen months later, a prototype smart bullet firing drone mounted weapon was ready for demonstration to a small hand-picked audience of potential clients.

Sir Andrew had already spoken to his security consultants, Harper MacLaine Security about providing protection and safe transport for these select few. Now Joe Harper and Rob MacLaine were sitting with him in the conference room in the Savage building in Chiswick, discussing arrangements for the day, allocating operatives to specific roles and getting Sir Andrew's approval for the arrangements.

"There will be parties of three, from both the ordinance and drone manufacturers. They are going to provide names and other details by Wednesday" Sir Andrew explained.

"Kasia, can you coordinate that, make sure they are forthcoming with the information by the due date," he added, looking at the small, attractive, dark haired young woman to his right.

Kasia was a recent addition at SGS, replacing Sir Andrew's niece, Justine, who had left to join Rob MacLaine in running the highland estate Rob had taken over after the death of his brother. She and Rob were recently married, which delighted Sir Andrew as he had come to regard Rob as a good friend since they had met when Rob left the military four years earlier and with Joe Harper, had set up Harper MacLaine Security. Rob and Joe had been with Sir Andrew's son Chris when he had been killed in Iraq and Rob had become almost a surrogate son in his eyes, one of the few people allowed to refer to him as Andy, albeit, no one would ever replace Chris in his affection. At six foot four, powerfully built, with blond hair and piercing light blue eyes, Rob MacLaine, didn't resemble Chris physically, but shared the same determined nature and droll sense of humour. Nor did Chris have the prominent white scar which ran diagonally across Rob's right cheek. Joe Harper resembled Chris more closely physically, five foot ten inches, wiry, dark complexion, very like Sir Andrew himself. Rob had the physical presence that Chris had had, the charisma, the charm, which was why in most instances Rob took the customer facing role at Harper MacLaine, the salesman, the networker, the relationship builder. Joe was the sensible, pragmatic man in the background, who managed the business on a day to day basis, who made the business work from a practical point of view and allocated human resources to clients dependant on their needs.

"There will be a junior minister from Defence there on the day and someone from QinetiQ. We need to find out his travel arrangements, but the minister will have his own transport and close protection officer from the Met with him," Kasia pointed out in an easily detectable Eastern European accent.

Rob raised his pen and interrupted, "That's fine but we take over all security at the gate Kasia, make sure everyone knows that, I don't want any discussion about that on the day. I know what some of these Westminster security people can be like".

Kasia looked at Sir Andrew for approval.

"Agreed," Sir Andrew nodded. "Now that brings us neatly to potentially the biggest problem of the day, the Americans." They were adamant that their people override all other security arrangements. They are providing their own transport from and to their airbase and will have a full complement of security personnel who would operate separately from all other security arrangements. They also confirmed that their security would be armed."

"I spoke to the MoD about this, it's their range we are using and they went ballistic. They said no personnel will be allowed on MoD land with unlicensed weapons, full stop, no argument. I put this to the Americans and they said they would take it up with MoD, which they have done and they have been told, categorically, no unauthorised, armed security people will be allowed on site, end of!"

"That won't please them," Joe chipped in with a wry smile.

"Will your guys be armed, Joe?"

"Yeah, side arms. We've cleared it with MoD and police in the usual fashion. Filled in a mountain of paperwork, presented CVs and permits and photographs and inside leg measurements," Joe replied theatrically.

"What's the agenda for the day Andy?" Rob asked

"Well, after the greetings and niceties we are going to have a recognised sniper take pot-shots at a target with a normal rifle and ammo, then repeat that with a handheld rifle and a smart bullet, but at a much increased range, basically to prove the smart bullet. Then we move on to the drone mounted weapon, show them what it can do, even let some of them fire the thing, just to prove how poor a shot can still hit a target. Then a few drinkies and nibbles and off home," Sir Andrew explained.

"We need to find a good sniper, Rob. MoD said they could find us one but apparently that has been vetoed by the powers that be at the last minute. Left us a bit in the lurch," Sir Andrew added with a frown

"I know a guy who might be able to help you" Rob said brightly "And he is undoubtedly one of the best snipers the modern army ever had. You met him at my wedding, six foot seven inch, two hundred and sixty pounds of gentle giant called Iain MacDonald. Better known as Big Mac."

"I remember him, we talked a bit. He said he ran an outdoor activity centre on Arran. Didn't say he was a sniper though, that's interesting."

"Well, like me, he's been places and done things that he didn't do, 'cause he was never there," Rob explained to Sir Andrew's amusement and Kasia's bewilderment. Joe nodded.

"He gave me his card, tried to get me interested in sending some of our people on one of his courses. Women would love it but it would frighten the hell out of my male technical wizards. Yomping around muddy highland hillsides getting midge bites and sprigs of heather stuck up their arses, God no, they would freak!" Sir Andrew laughed, Kasia frowned at him. "Sorry Kasia, bottoms."

"Give him a call then, I'm sure he would love to get involved. Give him a chance to show off, great Scottish child that he is," Rob suggested

"Eh, excuse me, my son is Scottish," Joe interjected

"So am I!" Rob protested

"Oh yeah," Joe shrugged and they all laughed.

They discussed a few more of the details for the demo day and allocated people and deadlines to all outstanding tasks, thus drawing the meeting to a close.

"I'll stick you through a final costings for the day, Andy," Joe ventured as they walked back to the lifts. "Rob said not to include his time as he is there as an invited guest, but for ease of access on the day, I will include him on the Harper MacLaine list for site security, if that's OK."

"That's very good of you Rob," Sir Andrew replied

"Well you did invite me along to meet the drone people, I could hardly charge you for coming to talk business with them."

"Speaking of which, I met one of their software guys when I

was out there. He works with them part time as a contractor. He's ex Special Forces, like you guys, only he didn't fare as well as you two did. Came back in a wheelchair, paralysed from the waist down as a result of a gunshot wound. I've had him look at a few things for me of late and my guys say he is pretty hot stuff at what he does. Identified and sorted out a couple of glitches in our software which were causing my own team problems. Told one of our techies he could hack into just about any system given time and just loves trouble shooting system problems. You might want to talk to him, I think you'll get on," Sir Andrew offered as they reached the lifts.

Joe looked horrified, he turned to Rob, "My flabber has never been so ghasted, Rob. Is our esteemed client suggesting that we would do something illegal?"

"Absolutely not, he knows us too well to suggest that we would do that, Joe!" Rob echoed Joe's horror.

"It's because I know you two so well that I suggest you meet this guy," Sir Andrew laughed. "What you would use him for would be totally up to you. I also know that if you pair had stuck to the rules in the past, at least one of you might not be alive today, so don't give me the holier than thou act. Watch these two Kasia, I tell you they're a couple of chancers!" Sir Andrew laughed with Rob and Joe, his hands on their shoulders as they entered the lift. Kasia appeared to be unsure as to whether Sir Andrew was serious or not and this showed on her facial expression as the two men waved from the back of the lift before the doors closed.

Sir Andrew looked at Kasia's perplexed expression. "Only joking, Kasia. I'd trust these guys with my life. Come to think of it, I do, frequently. If you're ever in a spot of bother you could do worse than call Batman and Robin there."

2

THREE WEEKS LATER, ROB WAS SITTING IN ONE OF THE HARPER MacLaine cars, a black BMW X5M which developed 575 bhp from its powerful 4.4 litre twin-turbocharged V8 engine. But most importantly, sitting in a car park overlooking Salisbury Plain on a chilly Spring morning, with the frost covered grass sparkling in the early sunshine, the car had heated seats and a heated steering wheel. That trumped the sheer power of the vehicle.

Rob had been one of the first on site and was watching the various factions arrive, be checked in by his team and greeted by Sir Andrew and his people from SGS. Rob was a thinker. Some of the soldiers he commanded in his Special Forces group said he thought too much, while others reminded them that on occasions it was Lieutenant MacLaine's quick thinking, that had kept them all alive in dangerous, life threatening, situations. As Rob sat in the warm cabin of the BMW, waiting for the others to assemble, he thought back over the last few, life changing months of his life. He looked at his reflection in the rear view mirror. Rob had a face that turned women's heads to look twice. Once to admire the handsome tanned face, short blond hair and piercing blue eyes, which could either melt a woman's heart or send a shiver down the spine of someone who'd got on the wrong side of him. Twice to stare at the vivid scar which ran diagonally across his left cheek.

Ten months ago, Rob had bumped into – literally bumped into, Justine Fellows, an intelligent, beautiful, tall, blonde woman of around his own age and simply, fell in love with her and she with him. Although not directly linked with that meeting, it marked the start of a series of events which literally changed Rob's life for ever. He was summoned in mysterious circumstances to return to the island estate, his family home where he spent his early years, before being banished by his father at the age of eighteen. That fateful return saw Rob reunited with his childhood soulmate Lorna Cameron. He broke up a people smuggling operation his brother had been involved in, saw Justine and Lorna kidnapped by his brother and witnessed his devious brother's murder. Through a second series of events, Rob had been reunited with his mother and his elder brother, neither of whom he had seen for sixteen years. He negotiated to buy full ownership of the family's estate on the island of Achravie, which he and Justine now ran with the help of Lorna Cameron and Fraser McEwan, the estate ghillie. Ten weeks ago he and Justine were married in the church on Achravie. Boy! You couldn't write it,"Rob thought to himself as he looked back across at the reception marquee.

He felt the growing need for a coffee so he switched off the car's engine and walked over to the hospitality marquee where the parties were gathering. The warm air fan heaters were working away quietly in the corners, keeping the ambient temperature at a comfortable level, despite the just above zero outside. Sir Andrew Savage saw Rob approaching and signalled him to join a small group of people he was with. He introduced Rob to the group which consisted of the CEOs of the Drone manufacturer and the munitions supplier who, according to Sir

Andrew, would actually manufacture the smart bullet which would incorporate SGSs guidance software. They were joined by their Sales Directors and one of their senior technical people. As they talked, Ian MacDonald, "Big Mac" to those who knew him, arrived in a Harper MacLaine car. He and Rob greeted each other with the gusto of long lost friends and Rob introduced him, firstly to Sir Andrew and then to the wider group. As they talked, the two technicians excused themselves and moved over to the coffee station where a young man sat in a wheelchair, he had arrived in the marquee just before Big Mac. Sir Andrew saw Rob's attention move to that corner and excused himself, taking Rob's elbow as he did.

"Let me introduce you to Ryan, I mentioned him to you the last time we met. Interesting chap," he said as they crossed the marquee.

"Ryan, good morning, sorry I haven't had a chance to say hello yet. Truth be told, I was waiting for this man to arrive and thought I would kill two birds with one stone," Sir Andrew shook Ryan's hand as he spoke.

"Ryan, this is Rob MacLaine, CEO of Harper MacLaine, I think I mentioned him to you. Rob, this is Ryan Hughes, he has done some software development for both the Drone control system and for our guidance system."

Just then, the Junior Defence Minister arrived, driven in a dark red Jaguar and accompanied by a close protection officer from the Metropolitan Police.

"Can I leave you to chat," Sir Andrew said "I'd better meet and greet."

"Hi Ryan, Andy speaks very highly of your work. He was keen for us to meet."

Ryan Hughes shook Rob's hand firmly and smiled, "So, a real live Laird. I've never met one of those before."

"Oh!" said Rob slightly taken aback, "You know about that"

"Yes, in fact I know quite a lot about you. Sir Andrew said

he would introduce us today, so I did a bit of research on you and Harper MacLaine for that matter. Old habits die hard. Don't know what's more impressive, the work you did with the Regiment or Harper MacLaine's track record."

"My work with the Regiment?"

"Yeah, you've been to a few places for Queen and country that you shouldn't have been anywhere near, Lieutenant MacLaine. Don't look so shocked, the information is all out there if you know where to look." Ryan laughed, "Promise I won't tell."

Rob looked at Ryan and frowned "I might have to kill you if you know that much about me," he said quietly, then smiled. "You can really find your way into information like that? Andy said you were an interesting character."

"Oh yeah. Although, the way I get there is just as off the books as some of your activities, so I guess that means we might have to kill each other" This time they both laughed.

"We need to talk, Ryan. I take it you wouldn't be averse to picking up some work with Harper MacLaine?"

"Sounds right up my street. You haven't mentioned my wheelchair Mr MacLaine"

"You didn't ask about the scar on my face so it seemed a bit unnecessary," Rob smiled "and it's Rob. Mr MacLaine was my father and I didn't like him very much."

"Not surprised," Ryan countered, "Oh yes, I know about that too, you've had an interesting life Rob" he laughed.

Rob shook his head, with a wry smile and handed Ryan a business card, "Seriously Ryan, call me. I think we would work well together."

"Despite the wheelchair?"

"I don't see the wheelchair, Ryan. I see a guy whose skills and attitude impress me."

3

JUST THEN, A BLACK S CLASS MERCEDES PULLED UP OUTSIDE AND immediately two large men got out. Both were dressed identically, black suit, crisp white shirt, dark tie and dark glasses. They looked well-muscled and sported short buzz-cut hair. They looked exactly like archetypal US Secret Service agents. They swaggered into the marquee and their attitude told Rob these two would be troublesome.

"Who's in charge here?" the smaller of the two demanded from no one in particular.

"I'm Sir Andrew Savage, gentlemen I take it you.."

"Where's your security? We were told you would have tight security here. I don't see your people" the larger of the two butted in.

Rob stepped toward them "They're all around you. I take it you are with Senator Wade"

"I don't see them. Who are you anyway?" the bigger agent demanded.

"I'm Rob MacLaine. I'm in charge of security today and my staff don't advertise their presence"

"I don't think so buddy," the smaller of the two, came

forward. "We are in charge of Senator Wade's safety here, not you, so show me your security, Mr MacLaine."

"And make it snappy, Senator Wade doesn't want to be sat in his car all day."

"Of course not," Rob smiled "Follow me gentlemen," he replied moving to the entrance of the marquee.

Rob touched his lapel and said quietly, "Gentlemen, raise your right hands if you will please"

At once eight men at various positions around the area and all wearing dark padded jackets raised their right hands.

"Thank you."

He turned to face the two agents. "Now, let's be perfectly clear about this. When I said I am in charge of security here, I mean all security and that includes Senator Wade. The safety and security of everyone here is in my hands and for that to work to maximum efficiency I cannot and will not divide that responsibility. In the event of an incident of any kind, all subsequent actions must be coordinated by one person. Do I make myself clear?"

"Bullshit!" Mr Big retorted threateningly. "We will not relinquish our responsibility to the Senator. Do I make myself clear?" He stepped forward to stand directly in front of Rob, but found himself looking up at the man who stood six foot four in his stocking feet.

"In that case I would have you both removed from site," Rob countered

"Oh yeah, you and whose army buddy?"

"My army," Rob nodded to the eight men in padded jackets fanned out just behind them. "I would have thought that even two Secret Service agents would have more sense than to challenge nine highly trained, armed personnel," he added. The eight man army lifted their jackets slightly to show the side arms they carried.

Sorry make that nine", Rob corrected himself lifting his own jacket to display the Heckler & Koch SFP9-SF he carried.

"Eh, make that ten wee man," Big Mac growled in his ear as he stood cradling his sniper rifle in the crook of his arm.

"Thanks Mac, how could I forget you?"

"Now, what's it going to be gentlemen, stay and accept our hospitality and excellent coffee or leave now?"

"They stay!" came a rather irritated voice from the car. At some point during this confrontation, Senator Robert B Wade had buzzed down the darkened rear window of the Mercedes and was now looking directly at the two agents. You stay and you do what this man tells you to do, or *I'll* have you removed. Now, will someone let me out of here, this goddamed door must be on child lock for God's sake"

The two agents just beat the driver to the Senator's aid.

As the Senator got out he turned to the driver "Pick me up again in three hours. That should be enough time?" he looked at Sir Andrew

"Yes Senator, that fits in perfectly," he replied.

"OK," the Senator added, nodding to the larger of the two "You stay with him, make sure he gets back here in time. Don't want to miss my next meeting."

"Yessir!" came the reply accompanied by a brisk salute. The agent got into the front passenger seat of the Mercedes and signalled the driver to move off.

The Senator turned to Sir Andrew's party who had all watched the proceedings with surprise and mild amusement.

"Sorry about that, gentlemen and my apologies for being late. My car turned up at my hotel twenty minutes behind schedule, hence his child minder to get him back in time. My escorts today are not Secret Service, they're MPs who have been commandeered for the day. My visit, as I explained to Sir Andrew is very much off the books so I have no real call on official resources." He looked at the remaining MP who was looking more than a little uncomfortable, "Too many *"Men in Black"* movies by the looks of things" he smiled and the MP looked even more uncomfortable as the others laughed.

The Senator was introduced to the rest of the party and after a coffee, as they made their way down to the demonstration area at Sir Andrew's request, the Senator walked next to Rob.

"You got guts to stand up to these two the way you did, son, I agreed with you by the way, one man in charge, knows what's going down, takes charge, gives the orders. Good leader, I like that and I apologise for their behaviour."

"No need Senator, they were doing their job as they saw it. Their big mistake was not knowing when they weren't going to win. That gets people killed in a hostile situation."

The Senator smiled, "You're right, son, like Kenny Rodgers sang *"You've got to know when to hold 'em, know when to fold 'em, know when to walk away, and know when to run"*

"Senator, sorry to interrupt, can I ask you to take a seat, just over there in front of the monitors," it was Kasia

"Hi Kasia," said Rob with a tone of surprise in his voice, "I didn't expect to see you here. How are you?"

"I'm very good Mr MacLaine. I'm organising the catering and the logistics for today. Making sure everyone gets food and drink and sits in the right place. Like an usherette, I think you say, in the cinema?" she laughed and pointed out a seat for Rob.

As he made himself comfortable, Sir Andrew walked down to the front and stood just to the right of the large LED monitors.

"Good morning once again everyone and welcome to our demonstration of what we think has the possibility to add a new dimension to modern warfare. The three companies represented today have collaborated to produce a weapon which we know has been on a few wish lists for quite some time. Together we have developed the technology, both hardware and software, to make that weapon a reality. We would like to demonstrate to you today a remotely operated drone, coupled to specially designed ammunition. By using a modified version of SGS's proven real-time optical guidance system we can track and direct a .50-calibre "smart bullet" at targets by compensating for weather, wind, target movement and other factors that can impede conventional hits. We can demonstrate rounds manoeuvring in flight to hit targets that are moving and accelerating.

We will begin with a live-fire demonstration from a standard rifle showing how a conventional sniper operates at present, with a standard bullet. We will then demonstrate the vastly superior ability of that sniper to hit moving and evading targets with extreme accuracy at sniper ranges, unachievable with a smart bullet. Finally we will show that it is now possible to successfully bring down a target just as accurately but at a much greater range by the addition of drone technology.

We at SGS are convinced that introducing our guidance capabilities into a small .50-calibre size projectile is a major breakthrough and opens the door to what could be possible in future guided projectiles across all calibres."

"I am acutely aware that you came here today to see a demonstration, not listen to me, so let's get the show on the road. We'll start with the here and now scenario, sniper with a rifle and a conventional bullet. Iain will be looking at a target at a range of 1,200 yards. He will make four shots, gentlemen and you will be able to witness the result on these monitors"

Ryan Hughes spoke into a headset microphone and instructed Big Mac to commence firing at will. Big Mac took eight minutes to register 3 kills out of four, much to the delight of his audience.

"Iain will now fire "smart bullets" at a target at a range of 2,000 yards, just over a mile," Sir Andrew explained

Again Ryan Hughes spoke into his microphone and Big

Mac responded, this time taking five minutes to record four direct hits with four "smart bullets". The audience applauded what they saw as outstanding marksmanship.

Sir Andrew took the microphone, "And now gentlemen, we come to the main event. If you look at the monitors, you will see a man shaped target mounted on the back of a pick-up truck, which has been mounted on rails, courtesy of the MoD. That guy is just over three miles from here. After this introduction, Ryan will bring up the drone where you will be able to see it then fly it off in the direction of our truck. When the drone is about a mile from the target he will then detect it using an on-board camera and lock on to it with a laser. Once he has done that the "smart bullet" will pick up on it and Ryan will fire the bullet at the truck which by this time will be accelerating down the tracks. Take it away Ryan."

Ryan Hughes took a few seconds then brought the drone into line of sight for the audience. He turned it to face the small marquee where they were all sitting and suddenly, much to everyone's amusement, the monitors lit up with images of the audience sitting watching.

"Smile please, you're on Candid Camera," Sir Andrew joked and everyone laughed.

Ryan then spun the drone and it flew off in the direction of the target. The on-board camera came back on and the audience watched Ryan zoom in on the target as he approached to within about a mile of the pick-up, which was starting to move down the track. He picked out the man with the laser and released the "smart bullet". Seconds later, the target exploded and the audience cheered and broke into animated chatter.

"Now, Ryan is just downloading the on-board video of the strike and will add a couple of lines to it to illustrate the straight line which a conventional bullet would have followed had it been fired and the actual trajectory of the "smart bullet" which was fired." There was a moment or two of hush as Ryan did his work "There," Sir Andrew picked up as an image came on the screen. "The red line is a straight line trajectory and the yellow line is the actual trajectory of the bullet we fired. It is not a straight line because the bullet was following its target."

"Now, our snipers will say in their defence, that they would make allowance for the movement of the vehicle by aiming ahead of it and firing to where they calculated it would be when their bullet reached it. That's true, provided the target didn't change speed or direction in the few seconds before potential impact. With the "smart bullet", it doesn't matter what their man does. The bullet is locked on to him and is following him as the monitors show. Also, that "smart bullet" was fired from a range of about a mile. So in conclusion, we have just hit an accelerating target, from a range of just in excess of a mile. Also, we have done it with a weapon mounted on a compact drone, which on impact of the bullet, would be flown back to the controller, complete with film of the hit and could be packed away and carried safely from the scene with no more effort than a conventional weapon. Up until now, if we had a target we needed to take out, we either sent in men, or, if that was not possible, or was too dangerous, we deployed something like a "Hellfire" missile, which did the job, but also caused no end of collateral damage to innocent people and property and I have to say, is a dammed sight more expensive than a "smart bullet".

The audience were obviously pleased with what they had seen and watched video re-runs of the event, asked questions and put suggestions. They exchanged business cards and contact details over coffee, drinks and sandwiches back in the main marquee. Kasia fussed around in the background, ensuring the guests were well catered for. Rob ensured that his operatives were on their toes, doing what they were there to do and satisfied that they were, he grabbed some food and a soft drink. He was about to walk back outside when he encountered the junior minister from the Ministry of Defence.

"Mr MacLaine, good to meet you. I'm George Bigglesworth, junior minister at the Ministry of Defence, but you probably know that already." Rob put his drink down to shake the man's offered hand. "Did a bit of research on you and your company before we came out today. Very impressed by what I found on both. Harper MacLaine comes very highly recommended and your military record, or to be accurate, lack of it speaks volumes. You've obviously been a naughty boy for Queen and country in a few highly deniable places"

"You may think that, but I couldn't possibly comment, as Francis Urquhart said on numerous occasions" Rob smiled in response.

"Ah yes, House of Cards, Ian Richardson as Francis Urquhart, brilliant, brilliant," Bigglesworth mused. "Speaking of Urquhart, Tony asked me to pass on his regards when I spoke to him the other day. Went to school with Tony, he went into the military and I opted for politics. He knows your history and I'll be diplomatic. He's doing very well at NCA, bit of a rising star is our Tony. Very impressive display today, very impressive. I'll take back an extremely positive report to the minister. He wanted to see this for himself but he's in the Middle East with a high ranking trade delegation, so he asked me to come instead."

"Thanks", Rob replied "I know Tony well. He was my CO in the Regiment and I've worked with him a couple of times since"

"Yes, Tony said you pulled him and his chaps out of a rather deep hole in Afghanistan a few years back. Got yourself a DSO, for that one, well done you. Ah, here comes my driver, must dash. Good to meet you Rob," Bigglesworth shook Robs hand vigorously and strode over to his ministerial car which departed swiftly.

"You met Biggles then," Sir Andrew smiled

"Biggles! Oh please, don't tell me he gets Biggles!" Rob laughed.

"Um, 'fraid so. I mean, what else are you going to call someone with a name like Bigglesworth? He knows everyone calls him that. Loves it, plays on it. Once told an Italian trade delegation that he tried to get into the RAF, by telling them he was related to Biggles. But, don't be fooled by the "old school, old chap, hail fellow, well met" act, because that's exactly what it is, an act. He's a pretty switched on guy, very astute, one or two have been rather badly caught out by underestimating our Biggles."

4

"Gentlemen, please excuse me for interrupting, but my driver should have been here to collect me twenty minutes ago," Senator Wade interjected. "I've tried calling both him and Max the big guy I sent away with him, neither are responding and the hire company haven't heard from him either. I know cell phones can be dodgy in some areas, so they may well get back to me if they are having signal problems. In the meantime, I guess I'm looking for a "Good Samaritan" to help a traveller in trouble." Can someone drop me off at the Holland Park Mews Hotel in London?"

Sir Andrew looked at Rob and raised an eyebrow

"Eh, sure. Yeah, I can do that," Rob replied

"You sure, Rob" the Senator asked

"Yeah, no problem. Let me tell my guys what's happening and I'll be right with you Senator"

"You look just like Rodger Moore when you do that," Rob smiled at Sir Andrew

"Do what?"

Rob raised an eyebrow theatrically and laughed as he turned away.

Senator Wade sat in the rear of the car while his remaining security guard sat in the front passenger seat of Rob's BMW as he accellerated out of the main gate of the site, heading to the A36.

The Senator was calling the hotel and his aide to confirm last minute arrangements for a party he was hosting at the London hotel later that week and to arrange meetings for the week he was to be in London.

After a few miles of silence Rob's passenger turned to look at him. "Look, I'm sorry about earlier, Max and I, we're not used to doing this kind of work, we're military police, not body-guards and we were told to look after the Senator's safety today as a favour to our commanding officer who is an old buddy of the Senator's. I guess we got a bit carried away."

"It's OK, you were doing your job as you saw it, you just approached the problem the wrong way," Rob responded.

"I'm Kevin by the way"

"Good to meet you Kevin."

"I'm worried about Max, it's not like him just to drop off the radar like this,"

"Why was there no formal security arrangements put in place?" Rob asked

"Because my visit here was off the books. I wanted to see this demo for my own information, Sir Andrew can explain when you talk to him," Senator Wade interrupted from the back seat between calls. His phone rang and he took another call.

"See what I mean, there is no problem with cellphone signals in the area" Kevin said quietly

Just at that moment as if on cue Rob's Bluetooth headset buzzed telling him he had an incoming call.

"Rob MacLaine!" he answered.

"Rob its Ryan Hughes, your friendly eye in the sky. I've been following you with the drone, just to see how it fares for reconnaissance, I think you may have a problem"

"Go on."

"The black Merc that brought the Senator is behind you."

"OK so they found their way back."

"No, that's not the problem. The problems are sitting in the back seat. I had a closer look and there are two passengers in the back, one in the front. I can't see the one in the front but the two in the back are holding what looks like assault rifles. They have been sitting about a mile back from you since you left the site. These guys are following you, Rob, they are making no effort to catch up with you."

"Are you sure it's the same car?"

"It is, same registration and I'm sure it's the same driver. Tall thin guy looks to be of Middle East, North African origin."

"Sounds like him. Are any of my guys still around?"

"No, they're all escorting their allocated guests back to wherever.

"OK," Rob thought for a moment. He looked at his satnav screen.

"Right, there's a road to my left just up ahead, I'm going to turn up there, see if they follow, maybe try to get a look at them."

"OK, I'll keep watch. I can maintain surveillance for about fifteen minutes more"

"Sounds good, here we go."

By this time both Kevin and the Senator had picked up that there may be a problem. Rob explained quickly as he took the left turn. He drove slowly for about quarter of a mile and just beyond a tight left hand bend, stopped, reversed into a field entrance and drove back out on to the road facing the way they had just come stopping just short of the bend.

Rob had put the Bluetooth on to speaker so that everyone could hear his conversation with Ryan.

"They've turned in after you. They must have a tracker on your car or following your GPS" Ryan's voice came into the car.

"OK, can you see us?"

"Yeah."

"OK, as they approach the bend in the road that I'm looking at, let me know."

"OK."

A moment or so later Ryan's voice filled the BMW.

"Approaching now."

Rob gunned the BMW towards the bend just as the Mercedes rounded the bend at speed. The Mercedes driver saw the big SUV late and as Rob had expected took evasive action. The black Merc shot across the narrow road just missing the BMW and with a crunch and crash of shattered glass, smashed through the wooden fence. The front end dipped over the edge of an almost sheer embankment, the momentum of the big heavy car taking it all the way over and it began to somersault, end over end, down the steep incline. The Mercedes finally crunched into a large conifer tree near the bottom of the embankment, hitting the tree trunk about eight feet above the bottom. It fell to the ground and came to rest.

Rob kept his foot on the accelerator as he rounded the bend and sped back towards the main road."

"Report, Ryan!" Rob called.

"The Merc is sitting on its roof against a big tree near the bottom of the embankment. The guys in it? I don't think they're going anywhere. Problem is, I think there is a silver Audi stopped by the road end. I wasn't sure till now but they may be part of the same party. Look out for it, no one has got out yet."

"OK."

Rob powered the BMW down to the end of the road. The big SUV seating gave Rob enough height to allow him to see there *was* a silver Audi sitting just before the junction, but no other traffic around. He steered the BMW into a left hand turn on to the main road, the large tyres squealing as they struggled for grip and Rob steered into a four-wheel drift, taking the full width of the road. He floored the accelerator again as the 575 bhp from its V8 engine translated into rapid acceleration pushing his passengers into the backs of their seats. Rob looked into his mirror and saw the Audi rapidly accelerate after them. Rob was familiar with the silhouette of an Audi RS4 from the one Joe Harper drove. These guys had chosen their cars well.

"We're not going to outrun those guys on roads like this, gentlemen," Rob explained the RS4 would match the performance of the heavier BMW X5M.

"Ryan, have you called this in?"

"Sir Andrew has called Joe Harper and let the MoD know that there is a problem and they are responding, they have also told the Americans," Ryan replied

"I've called my people as well," Senator Wade shouted from the back seat.

"Good, we may need back-up eventually," Rob said

The Audi was slowly gaining on the BMW and Rob knew they would soon be right behind them. As the Audi got close Rob expected to see assault rifles appear from the side windows and when one did, the shots were aimed at the tyres.

"He's wasting his time trying to burst these babies" Rob informed his passengers, "but the fact that he isn't shooting at the windows suggests they want a prisoner rather than a body. That changes things slightly."

The Audi was now right behind the BMW and Rob eased off the accelerator slightly. The Audi pulled level with the BMW for a second.

"Hold tight!" Rob slammed on the brakes, the alloy wheels locked sending plumes of smoke from the tyres and the Audi shot past them, the driver, caught totally off guard, braked hard when he realised what had happened.

Rob slammed the BMW into reverse and floored the throttle. The big car shot back the way it had come the engine howling in reverse gear at revs it was not designed for and could not sustain. Rob continued the rapid reverse away from the Audi whose driver was taking it through a three point turn.

Without warning, Rob took off the power, throwing the not inconsiderable weight of the armoured BMW onto the rear wheels and spun the wheel of the BMW. The vehicle reacted by sliding through a 180 degree spin. Rob disengaged reverse, paused momentarily in neutral then slammed the car into a forward gear. His foot now hard on the throttle, the BMW accelerated down the road at speed. The Audi was some distance behind, but Rob knew it would quickly catch them again. All he had done was bought time.

"Jeez, man, where the hell did you learn to do that?" Kevin stared straight ahead, his legs braced against the bulkhead, his hands holding the passenger grab-handle and seat squab so tightly his knuckles shone white. His eyes looking as if they might pop out of their sockets at any moment, his face ashen.

"Afghanistan. I've never tried that on tarmac," Rob quipped, "It's easier on sand though"

Again the Audi was gaining as Rob had expected, the extra weight of the armouring on the big BMW working against Rob in this instance by taking the edge off the performance of the car. Closer and closer the Audi came until again it was right behind the BMW. Too close! Rob stood on the brakes without taking his foot off the power and the reinforced rear bumper of the big SUV went over the top of the lower Audi front bumper. The impact crumpled the front grill of the Audi, pushed the electric fan into the radiator and sent up a cloud of steam from the now punctured radiator. Rob accelerated again as the Audi driver, realising that with a leaking radiator he had to do something quickly, set about overhauling the BMW and pulling out to overtake it. Rob looked at his speedometer as the Audi drew level, they were hitting just over ninety miles an hour, the Audi probably ninety five. As the Audi rear wing drew level with the BMW front wing, Rob steered into the side of the Audi, pushing the back end out. As the Audi driver steered to compensate for the side force, Rob let it go and the Audi rear end fishtailed out in the opposite direction. The Audi driver tried to correct again and as the Audi fishtailed back Rob hit it again, to help it on its way. The Audi broadsided for a second then rolled, once, twice, three times and came to rest on its roof.

Rob was out of the BMW in a heartbeat and unholstered his Heckler & Koch SFP9-SF

"Stay in the car, Senator," he shouted back.

As he neared the Audi the driver stirred but didn't move. The rear passenger also stayed inert, still hanging upside down, held there by his seatbelt. The front passenger was slowly climbing out of the window on the far side and began to raise an AK47 assault rifle to aim at Rob. The man was still groggy and didn't quite make it as Rob calmly pulled the trigger of his pistol twice and sent two bullets into the man's face. He was dead before he hit the road.

Rob checked the other two, the rear seat passenger was dead. His head at a strange angle suggesting a broken neck, the driver was still unconscious, blood dripping down onto the Audi's roof from a head wound.

As Rob surveyed the scene, Kevin and Senator Wade got out of the BMW, walking towards him.

Kevin spoke first, "Hey soldier, you could kill someone driving like that," he said with an embarrassed grin on his face.

"I think I just did," Rob responded nodding at the rear seat passenger, still hanging upside down.

"I take it you've got a pilot's licence?" Senator Wade asked

"A what?"

"A pilot's licence. You weren't driving just then, you were flyin' low son!" the Senator chuckled

Just at that moment the drone hovered above them, then landed just beside the BMW. Rob went back to the car.

"Ryan, are you still there?" he asked the Bluetooth microphone.

"Can I have my drone back, mister" Ryan asked in a child-like voice.

"How much of that did you film?"

"Every last second," came the reply. "That was awesome, can I come and work for you?"

"I thought you already were" Rob replied with a smile and as the adrenalin started to fade, Rob started to laugh.

Senator Wade walked back to the BMW and put his hand on Rob's shoulder.

"Cavalry's on its way son, we got to stay here till they arrive," he made to walk back to the Audi but turned around. "Thanks Rob. I don't often say this, but you saved our lives this afternoon and I'll never forget that. You really are one cool son of a bitch!"

"Do you know where the guys from the Merc went Ryan?"

"Last time I looked they were still with the car. I think at least one of them is hurt."

Within minutes of each other, two military police cars arrived from Salisbury Plain, one of Rob's cars arrived having delivered its occupants to the railway station and a Sikorsky UH-60 Black Hawk helicopter landed on the road which had been closed off by the MPs. Having been told by the Senator of the second car, the MPs went to search for the wreckage and check out the occupants who, Ryan said, were still in the car. As they left, a local police unit arrived to take over as they said it was civilian jurisdiction not military. They seemed not to know what to do about the Black Hawk which had landed on their road.

As the disarray grew, phone calls were made to more senior officers and politicians from both countries and decisions were made in high places which allowed the Black Hawk to take

Senator Wade and Kevin to a safe site. From there the Senator would return to his London hotel, albeit with somewhat beefed up security. They looked on these events as a serious attempt to kidnap a US Senator and wanted him out of harm's way as soon as possible. They also allowed Rob to depart the scene with the now damaged but drivable BMW. The Security Service (MI5) would take charge of the prisoners and interrogate them to try to find the source of threat to the Senator. At the same time they would try to find out how they knew about a private visit by the Senator to the Salisbury site. Rob's operatives took charge of the drone to ensure its safe return to Ryan Hughes and then to its rightful owner.

5

ROB DROVE HOME TO BOURNE END IN BUCKINGHAMSHIRE TO THE house which he and Justine had bought from her parents and she had renamed "Achravie". The Harper MacLaine office had also been moved there to a suite consisting of a conversion of the large double garage linked to the original office/study and a first floor conference room.

Joe and Justine were waiting for him in the conservatory.

"Rob, are you OK, darling," Justine rushed to meet him and threw her arms around his neck.

Rob kissed her forehead and smiled at Joe Harper.

"I'm OK, yes, I'm safe and sound but hungry, I haven't eaten in hours."

"And what about this afternoon, what happened Rob?" Justine pressed him.

"A few guys tried to kidnap Senator Wade, we made sure they didn't get to him. Did some fancy driving and only two shots were fired. Neither of them at me, although I did put a dent in the Beamer, well, two dents actually. But the police have got all the guys involved and Senator Wade is on his way back to his hotel in London, even as we speak, so mission accomplished."

"How did the BeeEm get damaged?" Justine wanted to know.

"Em, a slight coming together with an Audi. There's not a lot of damage, the reinforced bumpers took most of the impact," Rob said, nodding at Joe.

As Joe started to say something, Justine turned to Rob

"Are you going to tell me about the man you shot?"

"Yes, we always said no secrets, Tina. The guy was lifting an AK47 assault rifle to shoot either me or the Senator, I had no choice. You know I don't shoot people lightly, but given a choice of, them or me, I shoot them, I won't hesitate," Rob replied

"I know Rob, I'm sorry. It's just, every time I hear stories like these, I wonder when it will be my turn to grieve. You know I'll never get used to the killing. Can you not take more of a back seat on the operations side of the business, Rob? Joe?"

"To be fair," Joe said, coming to Rob's defence "Rob hasn't been on an active contract in over a year Tina, and certainly not since he met you. I don't have a problem with that, we have enough good guys capable and more than willing to take the risks. They get well paid when they do and that's what attracts them."

"Joe's right, Tina. The only times I've had a gun in my hand in anger have been on Achravie, just after we met and today. This started out as a simple chauffeur job as a favour to Andy Savage and it all kicked off from there. I was only at the site to meet some people and talk about drones. Neither of these involved Harper MacLaine contracts.

"By the way" Joe interjected, "the MP who went missing, they found him at the scene of the crash. He'd been in the boot of the Mercedes but was thrown clear when the car crashed. Few broken bones but otherwise, OK."

"Oh, I'm sorry guys. I just get so uptight when I hear about you getting involved in a shooting. I suppose military wives must feel like that every day their husbands are posted to a combat zone," Justine sank down on a settee.

"Well, there's your answer Tina, join a choir!" Joe ventured tongue very firmly in cheek.

"Argh, you!" Justine laughed and threw a cushion at Joe. "You're as bad as each other, really, I don't know why I ever let you seduce me in the first place Rob MacLaine" and threw the matching cushion at Rob.

"Me seduce you? I think if you'll recall..," Rob started

"Too much information, I have tender ears and I'm easily embarrassed," Joe interrupted as he stood up and tossed his car keys in the air. "Must fly children, family calls."

Joe turned at the door, "You know, Suzi asked my crying Scottish son the other night, do you want to be fed then, and I'm sure he said "och aye the noo".

"Good night all," he waved and disappeared into his Audi, leaving Rob and Justine laughing on the doorstep.

As they closed the door, Rob slipped his arms round Justine's waist and pulled her close.

"So, wife, Lady Laird, how do you fancy a weekend on Achravie?" he teased.

"You know the answer to that. Which weekend are we talking about, husband?"

"This one, fly up tomorrow first thing, back down Sunday evening, I've got a meeting with Andy on Monday morning to go over today with him. He's not using the Agusta, so he said we are welcome to use it."

"Are you serious? Tomorrow?

"Yeah, Pete Hall will pick us up at 8.00 at Wycombe Air Park. It's only 15 minutes from here. If you want to get all your stuff together from the architect and the contractors, we can go over it on the way up".

"What about Fraser and Lorna, do they know we're coming?"

"No, I wanted to check with you first, just in case you had a hair appointment or meeting the girls for lunch"

"You sexist pig, Rob MacLaine!" Justine countered, throwing another cushion at him.

Rob ducked and laughed. "I'll go call them to let them know"

6

The grey, yellow and white liveried Agusta 109S Grand rose into the air at 08.10 the next morning with Pete Hall at the controls. Rob and Justine were sitting in the rear passenger cabin surrounding themselves with drawings, specifications and draft marketing materials.

With a cruising speed of 180 miles per hour and a journey distance of 350 miles, Pete Hall had estimated an arrival time of 10.00. The Agusta was built as an executive, mid-range people carrier and was much quieter and smoother than the military Chinooks and Bell UH-1 "Hueys" Rob had experienced in Iraq and Afghanistan. With their minds firmly on the documents around them, the journey passed quickly and they were soon banking around Hillcrest House and descending onto the helicopter landing pad which Fraser had proudly constructed for Rob and Justine's wedding.

Pete Hall switched off the twin engines and as the rotor speed slowly decreased, Rob and Justine alighted from the Agusta. They were gathering their bags, laptops and paperwork when a white Achravie Land Cruiser rounded the gable end of Hillcrest House and crunched to a halt on the gravel surface, well out of range of the main rotor. The two front doors swung open in unison and as Lorna Cameron jumped down from the driver's seat, Fraser McEwan alighted from the front passenger's seat and both made their way forward to greet Rob and Justine. Lorna stood in front of Rob and eyed him warily, Rob wrapped his arms round her waist and lifted her off her feet as she put her arms round his neck and pulled him tight to her.

"I wasn't sure if I was still allowed to hug my big boss," she laughed, "Evidently I am." She patted his chest playfully.

As she turned to Justine, both women held out their arms and hugged each other warmly.

Justine touched Lorna's dark hair which she had grown to just below her shoulders. "You've let your hair grow Lorna, it really suits you, don't you think so Rob?" she turned back to her husband.

"Yeah, looks good Lorna. What about you Fraser. You not growing yours?"

"Nae hair to grow, son."

Rob shook his offered hand, then to Fraser's surprise, Rob hugged the older man.

"I think we've passed the handshake stage old friend," Rob laughed.

"I agree," Justine added and gave Fraser his second hug of the day, much to his embarrassment. Fraser's face by this time was bright blush pink.

"A'll tak these bags for ye," Fraser fussed

"Thanks Fraser, I'll help you," Rob lifted his own and Justin's luggage into the tailgate of the Land Cruise.

"Right, let's get some caffeine and maybe a wee biscuit if we're lucky Tina," Rob added as he held the car door open for Justine.

"Play your cards right you just might" Lorna answered as she pulled away in the Land Cruiser, turning toward the court-yard behind the house.

Lorna was as good as her word and produced a tray of bone china mugs filled with hot, fragrant coffee and a plate of assorted biscuits.

"OK, let's first of all get an update on where we are with the sites," Rob suggested as he picked up another biscuit.

"Well, I thought if we leave the adults only area for the minute and concentrate on the west site, we can go over things here first then go down and have a look before lunch. Pop back here for a bite of lunch then go up to the other site in the afternoon. How does that sound?" Lorna suggested.

"Sounds good. Yeah, let's do that and we can finish off with dinner at the Red Lion tonight."

"OK, that sounds good, I'll give Lizzie a call and book a table for four."

"Oh, you want me there too?" Fraser enquired.

"If that's OK with you Fraser, sure, why not" Justine replied.

"Good, that's settled then. Now, west site, what's the state of play," Rob asked.

"West site, East site, can we not come up with something better than that? We're going to need to for marketing and advertising" Justine questioned.

"Yes, I've been thinking about that Tina. The West site overlooks the Kintyre peninsula and the East site overlooks Arran, so what about Kintyre and Arran?" Lorna suggested.

"Funny you should say that," Justine replied as she pulled out a map of Achravie with the site positions shown and the names Kintyre View and Arran View written in followed by question marks.

The four looked at the map for a moment and nodded in agreement.

"I like that, it sounds good and it's self-explanatory. So, that's agreed," Rob inked out the question marks on the map.

"The site itself is pretty much on schedule, although we're having to pull out all the stops with the lodges. You know the ferries don't normally carry heavy goods vehicles and we need to be able to get the lodge modules across from Arran. We had to do a deal with the ferry operators to run some night-time trips with two trucks per trip to get the modules across. Thankfully, Fraser knows the area manager and was able to persuade him that the project would bring a lot of traffic on to Achravie when it was finished so he talked a reasonable deal out of him. Tina knows about the extra cost."

"I've made adjustments for it Lorna, it's not a big impact in the scheme of things because I had already allowed for transportation costs of some kind, so well done Fraser"

"What about the landscaping on the site?"

"All in hand and making good progress, although they need a lot more supervision than the contractors on the other site"

"OK, listen," Rob suggested, "why don't we head over to the site and have a look. That'll tell us more than sitting here doing a Q&A."

7

It was a ten minute drive from Hillcrest House to the newly re-named Kintyre View site. The sun had just appeared from behind a large grey cloud as they parked the Land Cruiser beside the site office and compound.

A large low loader was offloading one of the lodges just beyond the compound as they walked into the site office. A stocky, weather-beaten man wearing a Hi-Viz jacket and hard hat was on the phone as they entered. He huffed and swore at the phone slamming the receiver down as he turned to face his visitors.

"Lorna, Fraser, wasn't expecting to see you today"

"What was that all about?" Lorna asked the obviously furious man.

"That truck outside, the driver's been told not to unload that lodge there, we have no easy way to move it to where we need it to be, but he won't listen, he's intent in just dropping it there."

"Oh is he," Lorna bristled, we'll see about that. Oh, sorry Matt, these are Rob and Justine MacLaine, the site owners. Rob and Justine, this is Matt Smith our site manager and a good one at that."

Rob and Justine shook hands with Matt and exchanged greetings.

"Right, Matt let's see if we can sort this truck driver out," Lorna said walking out of the site hut followed by the others and crossed to where the driver was using a truck mounted hoist to lift the lodge modules from the truck then stacking them on the ground.

"Excuse me, I think you've been asked not to offload here, we need this lodge at the back of the site and we've got no way of moving it if you just leave it here. You need to take all this to the back of the site, to its own plot," Lorna shouted up to the driver.He looked down at Lorna, a heavy set man, with a large paunch and a shaved head.

"Not my problem darling, I don't get paid to handhold you lot. I get paid to deliver to site and that's what I'm doin', so why don't you just naff off and let me get on with my job."

"First of all, I'm not your darling and secondly, I'm not going to naff off because I'm the boss lady on this site and what I say goes. Right now I'm saying we need that lodge at the back of the site, not just dumped here."

"In your dreams, lady. I'm offloading here and then I'm back on the next ferry out, I don't have time to handhold you, much as I might like to if I had time." He leered at Lorna.

"Oh, you think so. Well listen up Romeo, you've picked the wrong lady to argue with. It just so happens that I make up the manifests for the return ferry crossing and trust me, your truck won't get a look at a ferry until you drop that lodge off where you were asked in the first place. Do I make myself clear?"

Lorna turned to walk back to the site hut and as she passed the truck driver he jumped down from the truck bed and stood in front of her.

"You try stopping me getting on a ferry lady and...."

"And what?" Rob interjected, having listened with rising amusement to the confrontation and Lorna's tough lady stance, a side of her he had never seen before today.

The driver looked at Rob, "What's this then, cavalry to the rescue?"

"I don't see anyone who is in need of rescue here. As the boss lady says, she makes up the manifests for the ferries, so maybe it's you that's going to need rescuing if you don't comply. If I were you I wouldn't push her too hard, fella"

"Move, before I move you," the irate truck driver demanded, stepping a pace closer to Rob.

Fraser moved up beside Rob. "Son, you're fighting a losing battle here. That lady means what she says about the ferries. She pays for the them so if your truck's not on the manifest, you're going nowhere. Now, this big lad here, I've seen fellas he's hit. Bigger men than you, son and you wouldnae want to end up looking like them, broken bones an' awe that. You'd be better doin' what's being asked and getting hame tae yer wife in one piece."

"Oh yeah, I don't think so." The truck driver lurched at Rob, who caught his right arm as he swung at him and twisted it fiercely against the joint. The man howled and tried to take the pressure off his elbow by twisting away from Rob, but Rob kept the pressure on.

"Now, see what a mean son," Fraser stepped up. "He moves that joint another half inch, it'll break and then where will ye be. No' be able to drive for a kick off. What would you dae then, ye'd be stuck here. Nae ferry, nae work for weeks. Better jist dae whit needs to be done, eh?"

"OK, OK," The driver grimaced. Rod let his arm go and moved back as Lorna stepped forward again.

"Sorry it came to this, but I'm serious, we don't have the

equipment here to move a lodge once it's been offloaded, it'd been a real problem for us. I'm not just trying to be awkward. Just take it up the back of the site to where we need it and once you get that done, you'll get on the ferry and get home"

"OK, OK, point taken," he glowered at Rob, but moved back to his truck and started to reload the lodge modules.

In the meantime, Matt Smith took Rob, Justine and Lorna round the site. He showed them the good progress that was being made in erecting the second tranche of lodges. The ones being delivered now were the third and final phase. The first phase, which had already been built, was almost completely fitted out and furnished. The décor and furnishings had been chosen by Justine and Lorna together, Rob was impressed. When they got back to the site hut, he left the three of them to discuss a couple of problem areas and possible improvements to the original plans then went for a walk to have another look at the site.

He walked past the lodges, up into the woods behind the third phase site. He turned and looked back over Kintyre View. It was well named. The panoramic aspect beyond the site was to the north of Achravie Village over the stretch of water known as the Kilbrannan Sound and onward to the Kintyre peninsula. On a clear a day like this, Saddell Castle, a historic 16th-century castle on the shore of the Kilbrannan Sound in Saddell Bay was clearly visible. Rob remembered spotting it in the video for Paul McCartney's 1977 Christmas number one hit "Mull of Kintyre", with the Campbeltown Pipe Band marching along the beach.

Rob's reminiscing was interrupted by Justine and Lorna waving from the car park at the site hut and he started down the hill. He was about to pass the lorry driver who by this time had finished offloading the lodge and was making ready to leave. Rob caught sight of a small tattoo on the man's shoulder.

"So you were in the Regiment?" Rob commented.

"What?" the man started, not having heard Rob approach.

He followed Rob's eyes to his tattoo, "Oh that, yeah. Did my bit for Queen and country. Not supposed to have the badge but not many people recognise it, unless... You were in the Regiment?" the man straightened to face Rob.

"Yeah, did my bit for Queen and country, as you say."

"Bloody 'ell mate, small world. How long you been out?"

"Came out after Afghanistan"

"What you come out as?"

"Lieutenant"

"I did Afghanistan, sergeant . Andy Mackie" he extended his hand and Rob shook it.

"Rob MacLaine."

"Look sir, sorry about earlier, that's just me since I got back from Afghanistan, slightest thing I lose the rag."

"S'OK, listen, got to go, take it easy." Rob started to walk away as Justine and Lorna appeared round the front of the truck.

"Hang on *Lieutenant* Rob MacLaine! - *Musa Qala!* - that was you, you got these guys out? Bloody 'ell sir, you're a legend, I was in Bastion when that went down. We couldn't believe it, we thought they was gone for sure, but you got them out."

"Everything all right, Rob?" Justine asked with a frown.

Rob laughed, "Yeah, all good. Andy's just reminiscing and getting a bit carried away. Cheers Andy, stay cool" He turned toward the car park and lunch at the Red Lion.

Rob Followed Lorna, Fraser and Justine into the Red Lion, a last minute decision. The bar was moderately busy with a smattering of tourists as well as the regular locals. Rob was also pleased to see a few of the men from the site having lunch in the bar. The murmur of chatter quietened slightly as they entered and were recognised, in particular by the regulars.

"Lorna," Lizzie Allen shouted from behind the bar as she poured a drink for a customer. She pointed to a table with a reserved sign and four place settings already laid out. "I've kept you a table, take a seat. I'll be with you in a minute. Hi Robbie, hi Justine!"

"Who said Robbie?" Hamish Allen's head appeared round the corner from the kitchen.

He waved to the foursome. "Quick Lizzie, hide the decent wine, I've still got that bottle of cheap Rioja Robbie was drinking the last time he was here, cannae hae it goin' to waste lass".

"Ignore him Robbie, I tell you, he gets worse," Lizzy laughed, as Hamish disappeared back into the kitchen.

The four sat at the reserved table as directed and perused the menus. After a few minutes, Lizzy came over to take their food orders while Rob went to the bar to get drinks.

He returned with a beer for Fraser, two glasses of New Zealand Sauvignon for the ladies and a glass of Hamish's "cheap Rioja" which Rob knew from experience was actually a rather palatable Rioja Reserva.

"So how come you and Andy are best buddies all of a sudden, I thought you were going to pull his arm off earlier," Lorna teased

"The guy was in the Regiment, SAS to you. He apologised for his behaviour in the carpark, said he's been like that since he came back from Afghanistan. Sounds to me as if he's got PTSD issues, a lot of guys do and sadly very few of them get any help."

"Who or what is Musa Qala?" Justine asked, "I heard him say 'that was you'?"

"Musa Qala is in Helmand Province, lot of fighting went on there. At one stage, after a siege of the town, a group of British soldiers got trapped in a so called safe house. I led a small group into the town and helped get them out. It was a bit haram scarum but we managed it without loss and it was celebrated quite widely the next night in camp. That's how Andy Mackie, your truck driver, knows about it. He was in Helmand at the time apparently."

"Aye lass, and he got a DSO, a Distinguished Service Order, an operational gallantry award given for highly successful command and leadership during active operations, but he'll no tell you that." Fraser interjected .

"Don't ask me how I know that lad, 'cause I'll no tell ye," he smiled mischievously, tapping the side of his nose.

"You shouldn't know that, Fraser," Rob blustered.

"Cannae help whit a know, lad" the older man smiled, "Cannae help whit a know."

Justine stared at Rob. "Would you ever have told me that?"

Rob shifted uncomfortably in his seat, "No."

At that, Lizzy appeared with a tray of food and saved Rob further embarrassment.

"So, what's the plan for the rest of the day?" Rob changed the subject.

"Finish this, head up to Arran View, have a look at the site there" Lorna explained, "We can have a look at the golf course. All the prep work has been done, the design and modelling is complete and the groundwork is underway, but still a long way to go. Paul has done a really good job on the design, I'm glad we went with his idea of an eighteen hole par three course. It's much more compact and interesting than a par three eighteen tee set-up and because of the natural shape of the landscape, it's going to be really challenging."

"Plus, as Lorna says, using the existing rise and fall of the terrain, every hole has a spectacular view over to Arran"

"I know you'll be impressed" Justine added.

Rob's mother's husband Richard, was a keen, low handicap

golfer and had been asked for his opinions at various stages in the design process. He had been very enthusiastic about the par three, eighteen hole concept, sighting a similar course he had played regularly at Ampfield, near Romsey in Hampshire. Rob had been convinced and was now looking forward to seeing the reality, albeit at a fairly early stage.

8

Rob surveyed the emerging holiday village; most of the
lodges were complete. These were slightly smaller in the main,
than the Kintyre View site which was aimed more at a family
clientele than Arran View. They were top end lodges with built-
in hot-tubs on the verandas and rights to the golf course
included in the cost.

On arrival, Lorna, Fraser and Justine went into a huddle
with the site manager in the office while Rob excused himself
to go for a walk around the site. He strolled around Arran View,
went into one of the completed lodges and admired the quality
finish and range of technology on offer. He saw some earth
moving equipment working up on the golf course and decided
to investigate.

The steep incline from the lodges took Rob up to what
would, in a few months, be the first tee. The designer had, in
the main, used the natural contours of the ground to form the
course. Fairways, greens and tees needed to be reseeded,
greens, bunkers and tees had to be formed. Rob was aware that
building a new golf course was a two year, £3 million project.

He had not realised the complexity of the undertaking until after an enlightening conversation one evening with the course designer at the office in Bourne End. The project was going ahead because Rob's brother Angus had asked for only £2 million for his share of Achravie, thus allowing Rob to undertake the investment in the course.

Rob surveyed the groundworks and envisaged the finished course. Slowly he turned round to look back down the hill over the Arran View site with Arran as a backdrop. Lorna had been right, it was absolutely spectacular and would be visible from pretty much the whole course. The vista took in Arran, with Goat Fell, the highest point visible and part of the Kintyre Peninsula towards Carradale. The warm glow of the late afternoon sun highlighted the subtle rise and fall of the countryside and accentuated the sheer beauty of landscape. Rob looked down to see Justine walking up the hill to meet him.

"Look at that, Tina, isn't that just beautiful and that's only part of it" he said wrapping his arms round her as the two of them looked across to Arran.

"Mmm, I've never really seen this part of the country before."

"I remember sitting in a freezing command tent out in the desert in Helmand one night, chatting to a Colonel about home and we got to talking about the West Coast of Scotland. 'Rob' he said 'I've been all over the world with this job and I thought I'd seen it all, till we holidayed in Scotland. But the only word I can use to describe the scenery on the drive from Kilcreggan up to Oban is magnificent'"

"Tell you what, Tina, looking at that, he was right."

"It's absolutely beautiful, Rob. You're a very lucky man."

"Yes, I am, considering where I was at one point in my life. Blamed for the death of one of my friends, disowned by my father, thrown off the island, away from all my other family and friends. Forced into the military, whether I wanted it or not, hadn't a clue what was going to happen to me. I had a Sergeant Major, when I arrived at my first training camp, he was a psycho, made my existence a living hell. There were times when I could have just ended it, times when I thought I'd had enough, couldn't go on. But I did go on, if for no other reason than to prove to Sergeant Major McCall that I was a bigger man than him. Eventually, the more he pushed and goaded me, the harder I fought back and just stared him in the eye, almost daring him to push me further."

"I met him, years later, I was in the Regiment, had just passed my exams and made Lieutenant. He marched right up to me, 'Sergeant Major McCall, Sir, very proud of you if I may be so bold, Sir.' And he smiled at me for the first time ever. 'When I first met you I saw a boy who was just about functioning and I knew if I hounded you, you would either buckle, in which case you were no use to me or the Army, or you would push back at me and you did. Everything I told you to do, you did more. I knew then you would become a soldier I would be proud of one day, Sir'. He saluted and turned to walk away then over his shoulder said 'Regards to Sergeant Major McEwan, Sir' and marched off.

I'm pretty sure that's how Fraser knew about Musa Qala, the sly old devil".

"Now, I have my family and friends back and thanks to Angus, we own Achravie, the home I was forced to leave." He pulled Justine closer, "And, I have you. What more could a man ask for?"

"A child to leave all this to?" Justine asked sadly.

Rob cupped Justin's face in his hands and tilted it up to look directly at her.

"If I ever need an heir, it will be because I have departed this life. I will be the former Laird of Achravie and Angus's boys can fight over who the next Laird will be. I've told you before, you're the important one, you and me. Look what we're achieving here, we have the house in Bourne End and we have each other. I started all this from nothing, an army wage and if I had to go back to nothing, but had you, I'd be a happy man Tina." He kissed her and they wrapped their arms around each other, Justine with tears in her eyes.

9

FOR THE SECOND TIME THAT DAY ROB AND THE OTHERS IMMERSED themselves in the warm, welcoming glow of the bar in the Red Lion, this time being looked after by landlord Hamish Allen.

"First of all Laird, may I welcome you and your party to my humble village hostelry. It may not be what you are used to down south but its home to me"

"Hamish, should you really be waiting tables?" Rob enquired

"Certainly, your highlandness, why should I not be?"

"Because you're so full of bullshit Hamish you must constitute a health hazard."

"No, I washed my hands yesterday, so you'll be OK."

"Now, can I get you some drinks? We have a full range of beers, all passed by the management of course and some elegant wines, the grapes for which I trampled with my own dainty feet. Or you can have your usual Sauvignon Blanc, ladies, pint for you Fraser and some more of that special Rioja Reserva we import from Spain especially for you Laird."

The four laughed and shook their heads at Hamish's usual

theatrical antics but agreed on the second suggestion from the landlord.

Hamish took their food orders and disappeared into the kitchen to give the order to the chef. He reappeared behind the bar, beside his daughter, Lizzie, and began pouring their drinks.

They were enjoying their drinks when Lizzie appeared with chef in tow, carrying a tray of food for their table. He stood as she took the plates and distributed the food.

"Chef's Chicken Caesar Salad ladies, well done, sirloin steak, Fraser."

"Aye, a dinnae want it biting me back, lass."

"And last but not least, Scampi and Banana Curry for you, Rob."

"Thanks Lizzie. How're you tonight, looks busy" he waved around the bustling bar.

"I'm fine, Rob and aye we're pretty busy tonight, even for a Saturday."

"Eh, Justine, Rob, you'll no have met Calum," she said, with a hint of embarrassment.

"A lot of the biz is down to Calum. He's been doin' the evening cooking for a while now and adding a bit more variety to the menu. Dad's fine wi basic pub food but he's wanting to do less cooking, not more, and wi the Lodges goin' to be here soon, we thought the time was right to bring in a chef to take over from him. So, Calum!" she allowed Calum to rest his hand on her shoulder as she introduced him.

Calum smiled," Hi folks, good to meet you. Heard a lot about you. Hope you enjoy your dinner". He and Lizzie turned away and headed for the bar and kitchen.

Rob looked quizzically at Lorna, "Do I detect a little more than just a working relationship there?"

"Yes, I think you do, Hamish thinks they are getting quite serious. He's dead chuffed."

"Not a local though"

"No, he's from the mainland, Prestwick, I'm told. He was in what used to be the Army Catering Corp, then did agency for a while before he came here and I'll tell you what, he can cook!"

"Mm, I didn't expect to be tucking into Scampi and Banana Curry tonight, it's not very Hamish."

"No but it's very Calum."

They picked up their cutlery and began to chat as they ate and drank, Rob catching up with the local gossip over desserts and coffees.

Rob strolled over to the bar to pay the bill and caught Hamish's eye.

"Hamish, that was a lovely meal, compliments to the Chef, if I may."

"Oh, no, his heid's big enough," Hamish shouted in the direction of the kitchen, with a laugh and got the reaction he had expected"

"So, I hear there might be a bit of a romance in the air as well as a working relationship."

Hamish leaned across the bar and dropped his voice, "Oh, yes and all joking aside, Lizzie could do a lot worse than Calum. He's a lovely lad, really good chef and got a bit of ambition about him. They make a crackin' couple, Robbie. Fingers crossed."

"Good, I'm pleased to hear that. Lizzie deserves someone a bit special. Speaking of the future is there any chance we could have a meet-up tomorrow before Tina and I disappear off again"

"Aye, what do you want to talk about, am assuming you've an agenda?"

"Yeah, I said when we took on Achravie Estate that I wanted all the projects we were undertaking to support local businesses, not create competition. Wandering around the two lodge sites today, I realised that there is a fairly limited number of restaurant tables on the island and these sites could potentially see an influx of close on a hundred extra mouths needing to be fed in the height of the season. A lot of these will self-cater in the lodges but a fair percentage could be looking to eat out, at least a few nights. Do you see where I'm going with this Hamish?"

"Aye"

"OK, I just wanted to get your take on what, if anything, you might want to take the benefit of the opportunity. Have a think about it and we can talk tomorrow, I'll bring Tina and Lorna if that's OK."

"Aye, that'd be fine, Robbie, and funnily enough, I've already had a few thoughts about the subject, so a'll get Lizzie and Calum to sit in fur a while if that's OK. They're mair the future o' this place than me."

"OK sounds good. Why don't we come down for a late breakfast and we can talk after that?"

"Sounds like a plan, young Robbie".

"OK, see you about nine. Night Hamish," he waved over his shoulder.

Rob caught up with the others in the car park and brought them all up to speed with his conversation on the way back up to Hillcrest.

10

BREAKFAST THE NEXT MORNING CONSISTED OF EGGS BENEDICT for the ladies and a full Scottish, including black pudding for Rob, toast and marmalade and a large pot of coffee. They ate in the little snug at the back of the main bar where they were joined by Hamish, Lizzie and Calum, once the plates had been cleared and the coffee pot replenished. The kitchen, by this time had closed for breakfast, so the group would have privacy for their discussion.

Rob started "Seeing as I asked for this meeting, I'd better kick it off". Firstly, Hamish, did you fill these guys in on our brief conversation last night?"

"A did lad, aye, and as I said, we'd already talked about the effect these lodges would have on our business here. We know they're a wee bit away from bein' finished and open but we still need to start planning now"

"Good..."

"Just let me finish Robbie. My Dad ran the Red Lion and when I took it over it wisnae in great shape because my Dad, God rest him, didnae move wi the times. A changed it, expanded it, we've built the four rooms in the courtyard. Lizzie came into the business when she left school and now we've got Calum on board and it's a good business, busy and profitable. Whit am trying to say is that, I'm no the future o' this business Robbie, these two are." He motioned to Lizzie and Calum. A want to make sure that what they take over is a business that's movin' wi the times and provides a good livelihood for them. So that's why a wanted them here this mornin'."

"Lizzie, dae you want to...."

"A thought ye'd never ask!" Lizzie replied, slapping the palm of her left hand down on the table, her third finger sporting a brand new engagement ring. "Calum asked me to marry him last night and as you can see..." she waved the ring in front of everyone.

"That's brilliant, Lizzie, congratulations" the two women shrieked in unison and hugged her with great gusto.

Rob waited his turn and picked Lizzie up as she wrapped her arms around his neck. He put Lizzie down and held out a hand to Calum.

"Congratulations Calum. You do know if someone gets on the wrong side of her, I am the first one she tells?" Rob joked.

"I do not, you big lump," Lizzie thumped Rob's arm.

"I've no intention of getting on the wrong side of her, she scares me even more than you would, Rob, trust me," Calum replied with a smile.

"OK, so this really is a family business going forward."

"Aye, lad, it is." Hamish replied.

"So, the future. What's on your minds, Rob brought everyone back to the table.

Hamish began, "We weren't sure what your plans were for the sites Rob, whither you planned to build a restaurant or a café or something of that ilk on the sites. So maybe if you'd answer that yin for us, it'd be a good start.

"I said right at the very beginning that I didn't want to harm any existing business on the island. I think I added the caveat that depended on existing businesses being willing to give the guests what they needed. But in essence, I have no plans to include a catering outlet on the sites. The west site, now called Kintyre View, by the way, is close enough to the village to walk into the Red Lion or the Four Seasons. The other site, Arran View, is a bit further away, so maybe we need to think about some sort of transport up and down if any guests want to come down. Does that answer your question, is that what you expected?"

"Aye, pretty much. As a said, we've talked a lot about this in the last few months. The first thing was to get a commitment from Calum to stay on for a while to help us build the business into something more than just a village pub wi village pub food and a few months back he agreed to stay. A said to him that we've the coach house next to the pub and it's a fair sized space when ye tak awe the junk oot o' it. We looked at that and Calum did a floor plan and we reckon that we could get five tables for four, one for six and a table for two into that withoot a squeeze."

Calum pushed a sheet of paper into the middle of the table, "We would take down the wall between the bar and the coach house and move it back into the bar area, there, leaving an access from one to the other, plus form a door from the car park into the coach house, that way diners can get access to the coach house without coming through the bar area, if they want."

"Not very original, but it would be the "Coach House Restaurant." Lizzie chipped in.

Justine, Lorna and Rob exchanged looks,

"Did you know about this idea?" Rob smiled at Lorna.

"No, I didn't. You kept this under your hat, Miss Allan," Lorna nudged Lizzie.

"Well, we didnae know whit your plans were. If you were planning a restaurant at either o' the sites, we would have looked pretty silly comin' oot wi a plan like this, so we didnae see the point in trumpetin' wur plan," Hamish explained. "Lizzie did say she didnae think you would build, so we thought we needed to have a plan o' oor ain."

"I'm impressed guys, really. I think it's brilliant. Can I be really cheeky though? Have you any idea of what it could cost? If you're going to do it right, it won't be cheap."

"A spoke wi Boab the Builder...."

"Who?"

"Boab the Builder, Robert Anderson, the builder frae Brodick who did awe the work on renovatin' the buildin's at the outdoor centre that yer pal runs and did the work on the court-yard bedrooms for us. Boab gave some advice and some estimates. To dae it right and that means re-roofin' it, Boab reckons tae dae the renovation and kit it oot, aboot £100,000. The buildin' itself is in good condition, he says, but we'd need to inject a damp course as well as the roof.

"And that doesn't frighten you?"

"It scares the shit oot o' me lad, but it would be a great investment for the future. A've got some money tucked away for a rainy day and Lizzie tells me she has too and is happy to put in up. When Calum and I talked aboot this, months ago, he said he has money put away from when he left the Army and wid be happy to invest it for a share o' the business. That was one of the reasons he was happy to stay. The ither reason is sat beside him. So we can raise aboot eighty percent o' it and the bank have said they'd look favourably on us once we had a completed business plan, but we couldnae dae that till we knew whit your plans were."

"You've obviously done your homework guys. How would your local bar trade react to the bar area being cut down like that?"

"Well, if they're nae happy they can drive doon the harbour, get a ferry to Blackwaterfoot and go to the Blackwater Inn for a pint, but bein' as the last ferry back is at half eight at night in the winter, A think they'd pit up wi a wee bit less elbow room at oor bar," Hamish laughed.

Justine looked at Rob and nodded slightly.

"OK, guys, you know the set-up we have to run the Achravie Estate project and the estate itself. We run the whole thing as a limited company and I suggest you guys do the same to protect yourselves. If you are happy to do that, Achravie Estate would put up the final twenty percent, either as an investment in return for equity in the business and you can repay the investment and our share diminishing to zero on repayment or keep us as a shareholder or as a straightforward interest free loan."

Hamish's mouth dropped open and Lizzie and Calum simply stared at each other.

"Have a chat about it among yourselves over the next few days, let Lorna know what you want to do and we can work out any detail later."

"Ladies, we need to get going. We've still got a few things to go over and Pete's picking us up this afternoon about three o'clock." Rob stood, Justine and Lorna followed suit.

The three said their goodbyes leaving a still stunned Hamish, Lizzie and Calum to somehow prepare for lunches.

Back at the office in Hillcrest House, the three were joined by Fraser where they had a final discussion and decision making session, interrupted only by a sandwich lunch.

Justine and Rob packed their overnight bags, laptops and paperwork and as arranged, Pete Hall picked them up in the Agusta just after three o'clock.

11

NEXT MORNING JUSTINE STEPPED INTO THE SHOWER BEHIND ROB.

"Am I too late to soap your back," she teased.

"Even if you were, I just might let you do it anyway, so feel free" Rob replied passing the shower gel over his shoulder.

"Olive Oil & Aloe Vera" Justine read the label on the plastic bottle, "is that the stuff we bought in Corfu when we were there?"

"Yep, almost finished now."

"Maybe we need to go back and get more."

"Nope, get it off the internet."

Justine slapped Rob's back. "Spoilsport!"

"That's me, and even worse, I need to get going. I've got a meeting and lunch with Andy over at Chiswick this morning to do a debrief of Friday" Rob said, turning round to wrap his arms around his wife.

Justine pouted "You really are a spoilsport aren't you."

"In that case, take me with you, buy me lunch too then I can get to meet my replacement," Justine added wrapping her arms round Rob's neck and kissing him lightly. "I'll drive," she added as an extra incentive.

"Kasia? You'll like her, she seems very organised," Rob said.

"Of course, I'd forgotten you'd met her."

The two finished showering and got dressed, Rob in a mid-blue three piece suit and Justine in jeans, a white silk blouse and knee length tan boots, They had just finished breakfast when Joe arrived as Rob picked up what he needed for the meeting from his desk in the Harper MacLaine office.

"Morning," Joe greeted Rob with a smile and a wave as he entered the office.

"Morning Joe, I was just going to call you and tell you I was off to meet Andy this morning for a debrief on last week."

"Oh, OK. When will you be back?"

"Mid/late afternoon, I would think, we're taking Andy for lunch."

"We?"

"Yeah, Tina wants to come, feels the need to meet her replacement in Andy's office."

"Kasia?"

"Yeah"

"OK," Joe laughed

Rob turned as he reached the door.

"I'd like to talk to you when we get back. I met a guy Friday, he was piloting the drone for the demo. A guy called Ryan Hughes, Andy made the intro. Ryan's ex-military, came back from Afghanistan in a wheelchair, unfortunately. Andy said the guy's an absolute wizard with electronics and software and he certainly showed that yesterday, plus he rode shotgun on me yesterday with the drone, really helped. He told me I had a tail when the big Merc was behind us and then he alerted me as to the Audi waiting at the end of the road. I think we could use him, but I'm not sure how it would work. Maybe just part time or ad hoc at first, see how things progress. But obviously we need to talk about him."

"Sounds like a useful guy. Bear in mind, we use software in

the office as well. Put that together with what you just said and he might just be what we need, but didn't know we needed. These drones really fascinate me Rob, it's a shame I couldn't make the demo, I think we could make good use of these things." Joe replied.

"I agree, it's a real shame you didn't get along. I was really impressed with this drone, it's not the sort of thing you would buy in the local electronics store to amuse the kids. This is a serious piece of kit with some very sophisticated software driving it and we would need to get permits etc. So yeah, let's talk about it when I get back" Rob turned to go back through to the house where Justine was waiting. "Oh, by the way, I'll arrange for the coachworks to pick up the Beamer this morning and assess the damage for us. The spare keys are in the Keysafe, just use them, Joe."

12

_____

"Good Samaritan, he said, next time someone says "Good Samaritan" remind me to turn the other cheek, slope my shoulders and generally look disinterested," Rob laughed as he, Justine and Sir Andrew Savage walked towards Sir Andrew's office.

Sir Andrew looked sheepish, "Sorry, I kind of got you into that one, Rob," he apologised

"No, not at all Andy, I'm only joking. Neither of us knew what was going to happen. We all thought it was just a simple lift home for a stranded Senator."

"Having said that, if you hadn't been there, who knows what the outcome might have been. Another driver wouldn't have reacted the way you did. You probably saved his life and as a total aside, saved my presentation day into the bargain. Nice J turn by the way, I've got it on video from the Drone," he added with a smile

"Eh, excuse me," Justine interrupted with a playful slap to Sir Andrew's back. "Do you mind not encouraging my husband to do his Sir Galahad act at the drop of a hat? He seems quite capable of getting himself into trouble without you egging him on."

"He's also very capable of getting himself, and others, out of trouble. Which is why we do business with Harper MacLaine," Sir Andrew replied, puting his arm affectionately round his niece's shoulder.

"Mmm, I suppose," Justine conceded. "Anyway, why don't you introduce me to Kasia while you two talk big boy's talk?"

"Sure, Rob have a seat in my office, there's coffee and biscuits on the table. Help yourself and I'll introduce these two," Sir Andrew invited, "Although, Kasia has been in a bit of a mood recently, so be warned!" he added to Justine as they crossed the hall to Kasia's office.

"Kasia, I'd like you to meet my niece, Justine Fellows she.."

"Sorry, Justine who?" Justine interjected

"Oops, sorry, Justine MacLaine, I do beg your pardon, madam!" Sir Andrew replied theatrically. "You've met her husband, Kasia, Rob MacLaine from Harper MacLaine"

"Yes, of course, I remember." Kasia stood shyly to greet Justine.

"Can I leave you ladies to talk shoes and handbags for a while?" Sir Andrew joked and headed back to his office.

Rob and Sir Andrew spent the next hour or so going over the events of the day in question, discussing the attempted kidnapping of Senator Wade. They contemplated what the reason behind the attempt might be and concluded that the Drone demonstration could provide a plausible link.

"That reminds me Rob, Senator Wade asked me to pass on these invitations to a reception he's hosting at his hotel on Friday night." Rob picked up the two invitation cards from the coffee table where Sir Andrew had tossed them. "He's got your name printed on one and Justine's on the other. Boy's obviously done his homework. Looks like a pretty high level guest list from what I was able to glean. Sharon and I are going, might be good for business if you and Tina went along, never does any harm to be seen in that sort of company. Senator Wade is a very influential man, on both sides of the pond. Fingers in lots of pies, all very legit I might add."

"Yeah, impressive. We're not doing anything this weekend so, unless Tina has other ideas, it might be interesting. It's about time Mr and Mrs MacLaine hit the town," Rob picked up the invitations and tucked them into his jacket pocket as he stood up from the comfortable armchair.

"Sorry I can't make lunch Rob, but the drone demo has set a few hares running and they need to be chased down as soon as possible, as I'm sure you appreciate. Hence the last minute meeting arrangement," Sir Andrew laid his hand on Rob's shoulder as they walked across the corridor to Kasia's office.

The women were deep in conversation as the men entered the smaller office. Justine stood quickly to face them.

"Give us a couple of minutes Kasia" she said.

She squeezed past Rob and Sir Andrew into the corridor and gestured toward Sir Andrew's office. "Can we....?"

The two men looked at each other, frowning, but followed her into the office.

"Yes, dear, as I learned to say very early in our marriage," Rob quipped as Justine closed the door.

Justine turned to Sir Andrew.

"Remember you said Kasia seemed a bit distracted of late?"

"Yes, mind not on things as it should be sometimes."

"I've just found out why. She burst into tears when you guys disappeared. She didn't expect me to be with Rob today and she wanted to talk to him, said you told her if she was ever in trouble she should talk to Rob or Joe"

"Trouble, what trouble, Tina? You're worrying me now?" Sir Andrew frowned

"Her sister is missing, kidnapped, she thinks. She phoned Kasia about three weeks ago and said that she was coming to the UK and that she would see her in a week or so, but not to tell anyone she was coming. Kasia says she tried to get more information from her but she said she didn't have time to explain but she would tell her more when she saw her. She hasn't heard from her since and their parents haven't seen or heard from her either." That's why she seems distracted, Uncle Andy, she's worried sick, the poor girl."

"Why didn't she say something, Tina?"

"Apparently you told her if she was ever in a spot, she should speak to "Batman & Robin" at Harper MacLaine and she was waiting to speak to Rob or Joe. She knew Rob was coming in today and was going to try to speak to him. All of a sudden I'm here too and she thinks she isn't going to get a chance to talk to Rob and just broke down when you two left her with me to chat to"

"I don't like the sound of that, I think she's right to be worried. Go and get her, Tina," Rob interrupted.

"Where are they from, Andy, Kasia and her sister?"

"Mostar, in Bosnia, its south of Sarajevo."

"OK, yeah, I know where that is."

As Justine came back with Kasia, Sir Andrew and Rob heard her sob, "I get fired?"

Sir Andrew immediately stepped forward.

"No Kasia, you won't get fired. If you've got troubles, you're among friends, we can help. Now, sit over here" He pointed to one of the big armchairs.

Rob sat opposite her in the other chair and took her hand.

"OK, start from the beginning Kasia, what makes you think your sister has been kidnapped?"

For a few seconds Kasia said nothing, then she looked at Justine, a look of despair on her face. Justine nodded to her and quietly said,

"Go on Kasia, if Rob is going to help he needs to know the background."

Kasia looked back at Rob and took a deep sobbing breath.

"When I come to UK, my family pay for my tickets and my visa and I tell my father I will pay him back when I get job. It take me 4 months to find job and start to send money back to my father, but since then, every month I send money back to family. Soon I pay back all money to my father, but I still send some money back to family. I can live here comfortably and still do this. Half a year ago, my father say that Magdalena, my sister, leave home to find work in Hamburg in Germany. She work in architect's office in daytime and find work in bar at night, so that she can also send money to home.

One month ago she phone one night and say she will come to UK and that she see me in one week. I ask her why and how she will get here. She tell me that her boyfriend will bring her, but she cannot speak for long and that she will speak to me when she get here. I hear nothing for one month. She does not answer mobile, or phone in flat. My father, he say he know nothing about her come here and she send no money for two months. He worries too. I think something bad happen" Kasia shook her head and began to sob quietly.

"OK," Rob said, "Have you told anyone else, have you spoken to the police, immigration, her employers in Hamburg, anyone?"

"No"

"Can you let me have a photograph of Magdalena?"

"Yes, have one of both of us."

"What age is she?"

"Twenty four."

"Does she speak English?"

"She speak English, German and French."

Kasia composed herself for a second or two.

"Sir Andrew, say that you are good man when I am in trouble. He say you can help. Please will you help me find sister?"

Rob looked at Sir Andrew Savage and then at Justine both of whom nodded in turn.

"I'll do what I can Kasia, that's all I can promise. I'll do my best to find out where she is and see that she's safe. OK?"

"Thank you," Kasia sighed.

She turned to Sir Andrew as a tear rolled down her cheek.

"I can keep job?"

Sir Andrew smiled, "Of course you can keep your job Kasia. You're very good at what you do and I wouldn't want to lose you. If you need time off till this is sorted out, just let me know and take what you need. Family always comes first."

Kasia smiled back weakly, "Thank you, I think maybe you are good man too."

Rob interrupted, "Kasia, I need that photograph as soon as possible. I need your sister's mobile number if she has one. I need her address in Hamburg if you have it. I need to know when she was last in touch with both you and your parents and what she said. Does she have friends she might have been in touch with? Who was she working with in Hamburg? When was she last seen at work or where she was living? I know that's a lot to take in but think of anything you believe might help. Work, friends, family, communications, anything at all, no matter how insignificant you might feel it is. Here's my card, email me the information and if you can, the photograph and do it quickly. The longer she is missing the harder it will be to find her."

"Two last questions and don't take this the wrong way, Kasia." Rob looked intently at the girl. "Has Magdalena ever dropped off the radar for a few days before, gone off with a friend or a boyfriend?"

"No never."

"And on a scale of one to ten, how likely is she to do that?"

"Zero. She would never do that, she would not want people to worry."

"OK, send me everything you know about her recent life and ask your parents what they know and send that too. I'll do what I can Kasia."

Rob closed Justine's driver's door and walked round to the passenger's and lowered himself into the cream leather seat and closed the door. Justine looked over at him quizzically.

"Do you think you can help her Rob?" she asked.

"I can try. Not sure where to start till I get all the information from Kasia and we'll see where we go from there. It might just be a case of sister gets distracted and forgets to call, or it could be something more sinister. From what Kasia says, I tend to think it could be the latter and like I said, the longer she's missing the more concerned I'll get."

"I hope you didn't mind me getting you involved. She was breaking her heart Rob and she seems like a genuinely nice person." Justine glanced over at Rob as she drove.

"Not sure how much help I will be, but I will do my best to find out what has happened to her," Rob replied, as his phone pinged to tell him a message had arrived.

"It's from Kasia, she has sent me the info I asked for and a jpg. Which I assume is the photograph. I'll have a good look through this when we get back to the office. She hasn't wasted any time," Rob commented, slipping the phone back into his pocket.

13

———

Sitting in the Harper MacLaine office, Joe had joined Rob and Justine as his curiosity got the better of him, listening to the conversation the two were having about the files Rob was bringing up on his computer monitor.

"What's this then, Sir Rob to the rescue of a fair maiden?"

"No, this might just be a bit more," she added and started to explain the turn of events at the meeting with Sir Andrew that afternoon.

"That doesn't sound good, guys" Joe answered, a worried frown on his face, having listened to Justine's and Rob's version of their discussion with Kasia earlier and having looked at some of the files Kasia had sent over. "Her sister looks just like a younger version of Kasia. In fact if they weren't *both* in that picture, you would almost think it was just an old photograph of Kasia."

"It was taken about six months ago, just before Kasia started with Andy," Justine explained.

"Where do we start Rob? How do we find her?" Justine asked.

"Well, let's be clear, *"We"* don't start anywhere or anything.

You have enough to do with Achravie at the moment. I need you to concentrate on that, you're due a trip up there. When are you looking to go?"

"Tuesday next week," Justine replied, "and I still have stuff to do before I go, so, OK you carry on but keep me in the loop. Rob, that poor girl is worried sick and talks easily to me"

"Of course I will. I'm not trying to cut you out, I just know you've got a lot on, plus, I don't like the sound of this. You saw the kind of people we were dealing with on Achravie with my brother's little venture and if this goes into the same sewer as that did, I don't want you anywhere near scum like that again."

Magdalena Petric was a very beautiful young woman. Her dark hair and high cheekbones were typical of the region, her wide smile and large hazel eyes set off a perfectly proportioned face. She was as Joe had said, a slightly younger version of the undeniably beautiful Kasia. She and Kasia had lived much of their lives with their aunt in the Austrian town of Salzburg, the Balkan Wars having done nothing to improve the education infrastructure in their home town of Mostar in Bosnia. Their parents sent them to Austria to give them a more settled and complete education. Living so close to the German border, both girls had become fluent German speakers and Magdalena had used this to good effect by gaining a place in Ludwig-Maximilian University of Munich where she studied for and attained a Bachelor degree in Business Management & Accountancy. She later moved to Hamburg having found a relevant job hard to find locally. She went to work as an accountancy assistant with an established architects practice in Hamburg, later augmenting her daytime income by taking on a part time bar job in a local night club. Now she was missing.

"Good morning, Savage Guidance Systems, how may I help you?" the pleasant voice at the other end of the phone replied when Rob speed dialled Sir Andrew's office.

"Good morning, my name is Rob MacLaine, can I speak with Kasia Petric, please."

"Certainly Sir, I'll put you through".

A few seconds later Andy Savage's unmistakable voice came on the line, "Rob, Andy here"

"Hi Andy, I asked for Kasia, they must have misdirected me, sorry"

"No it's fine, I am taking all Kasia's calls till we get this thing with her sister figured out. Is it something I can help with or do you want Kasia?"

"I'm looking for Magdalena's address in Hamburg, if Kasia knows it and a few other things which might help."

"OK, hang on Rob, I'll put you through. Good luck with this and thanks, Rob, I hope this Good Samaritan act doesn't get you into any trouble like the last time"

"Don't even joke about that Andy."

"Putting you through Rob, Cheers."

"Mr MacLaine, have you found something?" Kasia's voice sounded apprehensive, not knowing what to expect.

"Hi Kasia, I'm sorry, I haven't found anything yet and if we are going to be talking like this, Mr MacLaine was my father and I really didn't like him so please call me Rob."

"Do you have an address for Magdalena in Hamburg and do you know where she was working in the evenings?" Rob enquired

"Yes, we share flat for two months before I came here. I still have key. I email you address now Mr... Rob."

"The night club?"

"Luftballon", Air Balloon in English. I will email you that address as well," Kasia replied

"Kasia, can I pick up the keys from you first thing Wednesday morning?" Rob asked

14

ROB HAD LEFT SAVAGE GUIDANCE SYSTEMS' CHISWICK OFFICE
earlier on what had been a pleasant but chilly Wednesday
morning, with the keys to the flat Kasia had shared with her
sister, Magdalena, and driven to Heathrow. He parked at "Meet
& Greet" on level 4 of the Short Term car park at Terminal 5
and headed for the comfort of the BA lounge for coffee and a
snack before boarding his flight.

As the Airbus A320 rose from the runway at London's
Heathrow airport and turned into a heading which would see it
arrive in Hamburg some one hour and forty minutes later at
16.10 local time, Rob reflected on how much he had hated early
morning flights, which usually meant getting out of bed at
around four o'clock or a similar ungodly hour. These early
flights were usually filled with eager business people all doing
their best to maximise their day with clients at their destination. He had used the excuse that he had to pick up keys from
Kasia to book the later 13.30 flight.

Having checked his Google maps, Rob booked a hotel on
Bugenhagenstrabe in the Altstadt area of Hamburg. Magdalena's flat was in Davidstrabe and the "Luftballon" club was in

Spielbudenstrasse, both in the St Pauli district and about a 10 minute taxi ride from the hotel.

A fine drizzle fell on Hamburg as the taxi from the airport dropped Rob at his hotel. Having checked in, he took the lift up to his room, which in common with most hotel chains, was identical to any other hotel in the chain anywhere in the world. He settled himself in, found where everything was, then made himself a coffee while he read and answered his emails. Late in the afternoon, he put on his coat, retrieved Kasia's keys from his overnight bag, picked up a taxi outside the hotel and made his way over to St Pauli. He had decided to go to the flat first as the "Luftballon" would not yet be open. The flat was on the second floor of a three storey, traditionally built terrace. It had a keypad entry system for which Kasia had given him the four digit code. Rob quietly and slowly climbed the wide stone stair-case, listening for sounds and watching for movements. On reaching the second floor, He picked out the green painted door of flat 2C. He rang the doorbell, not wanting to just walk in, in case Magda had a flat-mate or a friend staying with her, or for that matter had given up the lease of the flat and it had a new tenant. There was no response so Rob inserted a key in the mortice lock and turned it. The lock opened easily so Rob tried the second lock. The door opened and Rob entered the flat.

He stood in the hallway for a minute there was no move-ment to be detected so he closed the door and walked down the hall into the lounge. It was quite large as was typical of many older properties, comfortably but sparsely furnished. There were no pictures on the walls and no ornaments except for a vase on the fireplace mantle and a framed photograph on top of the television in one corner of the room. Rob picked up the photograph, it was similar to the one Kasia had shown Rob, possibly taken the same day. A couple of magazines lay on a coffee table beside the settee. A layer of dust covered every-thing in the room.

Rob walked through to the bedroom. It was tidy, again frugally furnished and decorated. A digital alarm clock sat on a bedside table and a photograph of Magda and Kasia, with an older couple sat on the other bedside table. The bed was made neatly, but again there was a film of dust everywhere. Rob opened the wardrobe, it was full of a young woman's clothes and shoes. He checked the drawers, they were filled with a young woman's underwear.

The kitchen cupboards, when Rob checked them, contained tins of food and some dry goods, pasta and pulses. They were well stocked. The fridge contained juices, yoghurts and semi-skimmed milk, all out of date and a few wilting vegetables, now only fit for the bin which was almost empty but gave off a sour smell which said it had not been emptied recently.

The whole flat had a musty, not used smell, which made it obvious to Rob that the flat had not been lived in for quite some time. Magda was not living here and nor was anyone else.

As Rob approached the front door of the flat, he heard voices and the sound of shoes, probably high heels coming up the stairs. The footsteps stopped on the landing outside the door. Rob stepped back behind the door ready to surprise anyone entering the flat. A few seconds later he heard the jingle of keys and a lock being turned. Not the lock on Magda's door, the one across the hall. Quickly Rob moved back to the door and opened it slowly and quietly. He looked out and saw two young women about to enter the flat across the landing. One was tall, well dressed, attractive with short blond hair, the other was short, petite her shoulder length blond hair also well groomed. They chatted animatedly as they opened the door.

Rob stepped out onto the landing as they entered their apartment and they looked across at him in surprise. He dangled the keys to Magda's apartment in front of him. "Sorry, just viewing the flat he explained. Oh sorry, do you speak English?" Rob asked

"Only a little", the taller of the two young women replied, smiling apologetically. Her accent sounded local, German, at least to Rob's ear.

"Oh, OK," Rob smiled back. "I was viewing the flat, thinking of renting it," he explained.

"Do you know how long it has been empty?"

"About four maybe five weeks, two girls were in it. Eastern European I think."

"Did you know them at all" Rob enquired

"No, not very well," the tall girl replied

"They were Irena and Magda" the other girl offered "but that is all I know about them.Irena left and then, one month, maybe more, Magda."

"Sorry, we need to go," the tall girl said and closed the door as she stepped into their flat.

Rob started down the stairs again, he would learn very little else at the flat at this stage. "Four or five weeks," Rob mused, that tied in with Kasia's not having heard anything for a month.

He hit the street and started back to his hotel.

15

ROB PULLED THE COLLAR OF HIS JACKET TIGHTER ROUND HIS NECK to keep out the cold wind which was blowing down David-strabe. Rob knew that "Luftballon" would not come to life till close on midnight so decided to find somewhere to eat, before having a look at the nightclub.

Rather than walk back toward Spielbudenstrasse, Rob had decided to head for the riverside area to find a restaurant over-looking the river Elbe where it flowed through Hamburg. He found a steakhouse he had checked out on TripAdvisor and having secured a table overlooking the river, ordered some warm breads with oil and balsamic vinegar while he waited for a rare fillet with sautéed asparagus and a bottle of mineral water.

He watched the light evening traffic passing up and down the river, contemplating how to approach the staff at Luftballon and how best to glean information about the missing Magda. As he waited for his food, he pulled her photograph out of his jacket pocket and looked at the face of a younger version of Kasia. She was, like her sister, a beautiful young woman, ideal fodder for the cruel people traffickers such as the ones his brother had been involved with. Rob hoped that he was being overly pessimistic and that there would be a simpler, explanation for Magda's disappearance.

"Sir?"

The waiter brought Rob back to the present by offering his main course.

"Danka" Always say "thank you" in the local language Rob had learned.

Rob adjusted his plate and examined the large juicy steak with the side of sautéed asparagus, both of which met with his approval. As he ate he again thought about the task of finding Magda and from there to the invite he and Justine had to Senator Wade's reception in London at the end of that week. Rob's Thames-side apartment was occupied by a tenant so rather than try to drive back to Bourne End that night, Rob had booked a room in the same hotel and was rather looking forward to meeting the Senator again and getting to know him better. A good, well connected Stateside contact, could be very beneficial to Harper MacLaine and the Senator seemed to fit that bill. Rob ate heartily, enjoying the tasty, well-cooked food and having cleared both plates he paid his bill and left the restaurant to make his way to Luftballon.

He used the taxi rank outside the restaurant, asked to be dropped off just round the corner from the club. He let the taxi driver drive off before slowly wandering round on to Spielbudenstrasse, stopping in an alleyway just down from the club on the opposite side of the road. He stood in the shadows for a while, watching the comings and goings around the club entrance to Luftballon, which was large and well-lit by red and blue neon lights indicating all concerned that this was Luftballon . Two large bouncers dressed in dark suits, jackets and bow ties stood one on each side of the doors eyeing up the people entering the club, speaking to some, waving others in. The clientele was of mixed age, some looked to be in their twenties and thirties, others slightly older. Most were well behaved and those that weren't were refused entry to the club with the two large doormen ushering them away from the entrance and the other customers.

Everything looked normal with all the doorway activity very much as Rob had seen in nightclubs everywhere. He crossed the road and walked along the wide pavement to the entrance, doing his best to blend in with the other clubbers seeking entry. No suspicious moves, no eye contact with the doormen, hunched over slightly to hide his stature, just another punter intent on a good night out. He walked up the steps, passed the doormen and into the club foyer. To the left of the entrance was a cloakroom and two toilet doors. On the opposite side two small booths marked "Members" and "Non Members" where member's cards were checked and scanned and non-members were asked to sign in and pay an entrance fee. Rob approached the Non Members booth and paid the required fee which he was informed, by a well-dressed young man, included his first drink on presentation of his ticket at the bar.

The club was typical of most high-end nightclubs, a bar stretched almost the full length of one wall, with a small area in one corner housing a DJ with his equipment. The other three walls laid out in booths, including on either side of the entrance. Small round tables and chairs formed a second line of seating around the room. The rest of the space was taken up mostly with a dance floor. The ceiling was low, the music loud and the multi-coloured lights flashed and moved in time with the beat of the music.

Rob approached the bar and sat on a high, swivel stool. He signalled one of the three barmen and ordered a small beer. There was a large full width mirror behind the bar and Rob used it to have a cursory look round the room. It still wasn't busy. As Rob had imagined, it would probably fill up in the next hour or so and stay that way into the early hours of the morning. Most of the booths however were occupied as were some of the tables. Four or five girls were circulating, chatting to the customers, taking drinks orders and delivering them back to the tables. Rob turned to face out into the room and have a closer look at the girls and the customers they were serving.

The girls were dressed in short black skirts, white halter tops and walked on black stiletto heeled shoes. They were all young and attractive, obviously chosen for their eye appeal and looked as if they enjoyed the admiring glances and wanton stares of many of the male customers, whose attentions the girls were doing nothing to discourage. The customers were pretty much as Rob had seen from the shadows in the street opposite. Most of them, late twenties to mid-forties, good mix of gender and all looked to be enjoying the atmosphere of the club.

As Rob scanned his surroundings, he became aware of someone standing at the bar beside him. He turned to his left to see one of the waitresses smiling at him. An attractive girl, as they all were, with short blond hair and the regulation short black skirt and white halter top with "Luftballon" printed on the front

"Hi, can I get you a drink?" she enquired.

"No, thanks, I'm fine for now."

"Can I get you something else," she asked, resting her hand on his arm as she spoke.

"Actually, yes, maybe you can help me," Rob replied as he pulled the photograph of Magda from his inside jacket pocket. "Do you recognise this girl, her name is Magda."

The girl looked at the photograph and then back at Rob for a second before returning her gaze to the photograph.

"We are not allowed to talk about other girls. It's for their safety and privacy. I am sure you understand, Sir."

"She is the sister of a friend of mine, who hasn't heard from her for a while," Rob explained

"Still – sorry," the waitress replied and she turned away to speak to another customer.

Rob summoned the barman who had served him earlier and ordered a second small beer. As the man placed the drink in front of him, Rob pushed the photograph across the bar towards the barman.

"Do you know where I can find this girl, Magda, does she still work here?"

The young barman shrugged and turned away.

As the man moved up the bar, Rob noticed the blond waitress talking to one of the doormen who looked over in Rob's direction. He nodded and said something into a microphone attached to the lapel of his jacket before heading in Rob's direction.

"What's the problem, sir," he growled. He stood back slightly from Rob and shouted slightly to be heard over the sound of the loud music.

"No problem, just trying to find this girl," Rob shouted back as he held out the photograph of Magda.

The doorman took the photograph, looked at it, then crumpled it up in his large hand and let it drop to the floor.

"I think you need to leave, sir."

"Hey, I was just trying to do a favour for her sister, see that she's OK."

The doorman stared at Rob.

"I think you need to leave, sir," he repeated "we don't like men asking questions about our girls."

The big, well-muscled doorman stood to the side and gestured towards the door, inviting Rob to leave in no uncertain terms as the other lump of door muscle started to take an interest in the conversation. One thing Rob had learned working undercover was not to get yourself noticed by getting involved in a public fracas, so he slowly stood up hands in the air to signal that he wanted no trouble and walked to the exit and out on to the street.

He noticed a taxi rank further up the road and started to walk towards it. He would learn nothing more by hanging around the club so was going to head back to his hotel.

There was only light traffic on Spielbudenstrasse which made a speeding, silver Audi noticeable as it approached and did a fast U-turn, stopping at the kerbside just ahead of Rob. Two men got out of the car and stood across the pavement in front of Rob. One was almost as tall as Rob and just as broad, the other was of average build and height. Their facial appearance led Rob to imagine that they could be eastern European. When the smaller man spoke he confirmed that to Rob. The driver who Rob couldn't see, stayed in the car and kept the engine running.

"You ask about a girl, Magda, in Luftballon. Why you doing that?" he demanded. His accent definitely Slavic, Eastern European.

"What's it to you? Rob replied.

"My boss own the club and he want to protect staff from unwanted attention from customers."

Rob gave the appearance of relaxing.

"Oh, right, yeah, I can understand that, Sorry, I am a friend of Magda's sister and when she heard I was going to be in Hamburg she asked me to look in on Magda. She hasn't heard from her for a few weeks and was a little concerned. You know what young girls can be like, no concept of time. She does still work for you I take it?"

"No, she steal money from club and disappear one month past, so we are keen to find her, like you."

Rob had no interest in arguing with these guys, any altercation at this stage might not be helpful to Magda if they had her somewhere.

"Sorry to hear that. I don't know Magda, her sister is a friend of a friend. But at least now I can tell my wife that she has done a runner with some money. Not very good is it?" Rob shrugged.

"Look guys, I'm sorry if I caused any trouble and thanks for letting me know. It's getting late so I'll head for my bed if you don't mind. Thanks again" Rob moved to pass the two men, but they both moved to block his path.

"Why don't you let us drop you off at your hotel, as we take so much of your time?" the smaller man who had done all the talking so far suggested.

"No, it's fine, I'll walk, it's just round the corner," Rob lied

"We insist," the large, silent ox of a man said and held the rear door of the Audi open, a cold smile appeared on his pock-marked face.

"No, thanks," Rob repeated and again tried to pass the two who now stood directly in front of him blocking his way.

The large thug lunged at Rob and shaped up to swing a massive right hook at him but was way too slow and predictable. Most people will sway back out of range when having a wild punch thrown at them. Rob surprised his assailant by moving inside the punch with a perfectly delivered "Glasgow Kiss" head butt. The man's nose and forehead took the full force of Rob's attack. His now broken nose spurted bright, crimson blood, his eyes rolled and he fell backwards, hitting the back of his head on the Audi's door pillar. Rob swung round to meet the other Eastern European as he hesitated, stunned by the speed and ferocity of Rob's counterattack on his partner. Rob swung a hard kick at the man's groin, landing a debilitating blow to his genitals. The man collapsed slowly to the pavement, trying hard to breathe, emitting a low moaning sound. Rob kicked him hard on the side of the head and he passed out lying in a heap on the pavement.

At that moment, the driver of the Audi punched the car into

drive and with a squeal of tortured rubber shot away from the kerb, in the process, driving over the left hand of the victim of Rob's head butt. Rob looked around the street but there was nobody there. He crossed the road walked briskly up Spielbudenstrasse and into a narrow, dark alleyway. He stopped in the shadows, to look back down the cold, windy street for any sign of anyone following him. The coast looked clear, one or two passers by were showing some interest in the two figures lying at the side of the road, but passed by after an initial, cursory look. Rob continued down the alley, out the other end onto a road which ran parallel to Spielbudenstrasse. Not keen to hang about in case people came looking for him, he walked quickly round to the taxi rank he had seen earlier and got into the first taxi on the rank. As the car pulled away, Rob could see that both men were still on the ground but conscious and about to get up. There was no sign of the silver Audi. At Rob's request, the taxi dropped him a couple of blocks from his hotel, at a smaller establishment and he walked into the foyer where he stood till the taxi was well out of sight. Once sure that the taxi had gone he went outside and walked the two streets to his hotel.

In the morning, rather than risk being seen in the dining room by anyone looking for him, Rob ordered a room service breakfast, although he imagined he was safe enough from further engagement with someone from Luftballon. He ordered a hotel limo rather than take an unknown taxi to the airport and arrived just as his flight was closing, again as a precaution. By 10.40 British Airways flight 962 was airborne, climbing into a heavy, cloudy rain filled sky, and he was on his way back to London, arriving ten minutes ahead of schedule.

Rob retrieved his car at the Meet and Greet heading to the Savage Guidance Systems office in Chiswick to bring Kasia up to date with the little he had found out. He tried to sound positive with his synopsis but in reality ended up by saying he wasn't much further forward but had established Magda had links to Luftballon and had not been in her apartment for about four weeks. He made light of the altercation after he left the club and assured Kasia that he and Joe would keep digging.

As he was leaving the building Sir Andrew Savage was stepping out of his silver Jaguar. Rob quickly brought him up to speed.

"Thanks for doing that Rob, I really appreciate your help. Invoice me for your time and expenses when you are done," Sir Andrew offered as he shook Rob's hand

"No, that's fine Andy, I don't mind helping a damsel in distress" Rob chuckled.

"Oh now, be careful, remember the trouble you got into the last time you did your Good Samaritan act," Andy Savage laughed as he made for the automatic doors to his office building.

"Tell you what!" He called back, "Are you and Tina still going to Senator Wade's bash tomorrow night?"

"Yeah, looking forward to it actually, haven't had a good night out in ages."

"OK then stick your room on my account, can't say fairer than that."

"OK, you're on!" Rob called after Andy as the doors closed.

16

ROB SPENT FRIDAY MORNING BRINGING JOE UP TO SPEED WITH HIS
Hamburg trip and the fact that he had only managed to
confirm that Magda had disappeared from the flat around the
time Kasia had last heard from her. He related what he had
been told by the guys he had had the altercation with outside
the club and told Joe that he didn't believe a word of their accu-
sation. Had he elected to go with them in their car, it was
obvious their intention was to further discourage him from
making enquiries about Magda's whereabouts. The whole
scenario suggested very strongly that Magda's disappearance
was not going to end well if she could not be found. The fact
that his assailants had been Eastern European and not German
rang alarm bells in view of his experience with his brother and
the Bosnians on Achravie. He had not mentioned this to Kasia
when he visited. No sense in worrying her until he knew more
facts and was relying less on assumptions.

"I will need to do a bit more digging though" Rob suggested

"Maybe I should come with you. If these guys know you
and recognised you, you could be in big trouble. They don't
know me so I could nose around while you kept a watching

brief in the background, just in case things kick off," Joe suggested.

"That sounds like a good idea."

"OK, let's have a think over the weekend and we can have a talk on Monday" Joe suggested rising from his desk. "Suzy and I have to take young Harper for injections this afternoon and I'm sure you'll want to powder your nose for this posh "do" that you and the lovely Mrs MacLaine are attending tonight."

"I've already powdered my nose *and* plucked my eyebrows, not that I would expect you to notice such sartorial detail, sitting there in a scruffy old sweater and a pair of jeans."

"Anyway, where did you get that awful sweater?"

"You gave me it for Christmas!" Joe huffed

"Oh, right, so I did, I'd only worn it a couple times, if I remember"

"Honestly, you two. You're like a couple of kids!" Justine had just appeared in the doorway.

"It's a pity you and Suzy can't come with us, it looks like a good night and you two haven't hit the town for ages."

"Joys of parenthood," Joe shrugged as he picked up his jacket and made for the door. "Enjoy tonight children and remember, if you can't be good, be good at it," He kissed Justine's cheek lightly and punched Rob's shoulder on the way out.

"Right, you all packed and ready to go?" Rob enquired swivelling round in his comfortable leather high back chair.

"Just waiting for you," came the response.

"Oh, good, will we take my car or do we need the Beemer for your cases?"

"Sarcasm is the lowest form of wit, as you should know. I'm taking my usual small overnight bag and a hanger for my dress. So yes, we can take your car, but don't even think of putting the top down. The sun may be shining but it is only March"

"Spoilsport" Rob huffed and followed Justine into the house to gather their things for the Senator's reception.

Fifteen minutes later Rob had stowed their overnight bags in the limited boot space of his beloved Maserati before heading to central London and the Holland Park Mews Hotel.

The journey took just over an hour with traffic and Rob eased the Maserati up to the hotel entrance at a little after 3pm. The reception started at 7pm in the Kensington Suite so Rob and Justine had a few hours to relax in their accommodation and enjoy the bottle of Moet that Sir Andrew had ordered for them, sipping on the Champagne and just relaxing in each other's company away from the constant demands of work.

At one point, Rob was aware of a change in Justine's breathing rhythm and realised that she had dozed off in his arms. He slowly unwrapped himself, finished his glass of Moet and headed for the bathroom in preparation for the evening. As he showered, he became aware of a presence behind him, He opened his eyes and there was Justine shrugging off her robe and wearing only a mischievous smile she stepped into the shower.

"You called master?" she asked

"No"

"I thought you called for me to soap your back"

"Oh yes, that," Rob laughed, slipping his arms round her slim waist and pulling her to him and kissing her gently.

Rob didn't get his back soaped. They made love slowly in the shower then towelled each other dry before putting on their respective underwear. Rob pulled his pale grey Armani suit and Delsiena shirt out of the wardrobe and dressed while Justine dried her hair and applied her usual light makeup before finally slipping into a simple, sleeveless, v-necked red silk cocktail dress with matching elegant, high-heeled shoes. Rob finished tying his tie and turned to look at his wife.

"Wow! Look at you, if I weren't a married man..."

"You'd what?" Justine interrupted crossing the bedroom and making a small adjustment to his tie.

"Best you don't know."

"What, would you spill another drink on me, whisk me away to your man cave overlooking the river, make mad passionate love to me then tell me you need to go."

"Dammit, you guessed!" Rob laughed, "lets go."

17

Senator Robert E Wade had a physical presence and bearing which said ex-military, self-assured, and assertive. A born leader, who knew what he wanted and was prepared to do whatever was necessary to get it. Standing just over six foot his broad shoulders and narrow hips suggested that at over sixty years of age he was still in good physical shape. He wore a hand tailored dark blue, two piece suit complemented by a white cotton shirt and a brightly coloured patterned silk tie. His black leather shoes shone is if straight off the parade ground. He had kept his military style buzz cut hair, his face had the tanned appearance of someone who lived in a warm sunny climate.

The MP, who Rob knew only as Kevin, from the dramatic events following the Salisbury presentation, stood just outside the entrance to the Kensington Suite checking guests against his list, before showing them into the room.

"Mr MacLaine, Sir, good to see you again," Kevin shook Rob's hand vigorously.

"Kevin, good to see you too. Please call me Rob. Mr MacLaine was my father. You're still with the Senator I see, that's good. This is my wife, Justine."

"Good evening Ma'am, I'm pleased to meet you. This is quite a guy you're married to. Boy can he drive a motor vehicle!"

"Um, not sure I want to know what he gets up to when he's working, but yes, quite a guy as you say," Justine slipped her hand into his as she spoke.

"Please go through, sir, ma'am. Enjoy your evening, Rob, Mrs MacLaine"

Senator Wade stepped forward to greet them, with a broad grin and hand held out to welcome the couple.

"Rob, good to see you again." He shook Rob's hand firmly with both hands and turned to Justine.

"You must be Justine. I've been looking forward to meeting you. I imagined you to be quite a lady to partner this young man and I was right by the looks of things."

"Pleased to meet you too Senator, I've heard a great deal about you from Rob."

"Some of it good, I hope!" the Senator laughed

"My, but you complement each other so well," said the Senator, looking from one to the other. He sounded genuinely delighted to have their company. "Please, go and get a drink and meet some of the others, you'll know a few of them. Once everyone has arrived we can have a chat. Andy and Sharon are here somewhere. I'll catch up with you later."

As the couple moved into the room, almost as if on cue, Justine felt a light touch on her arm. She turned to see Sir Andrew Savage at her right shoulder and his wife Sharon waving as she crossed the room to join them.

"Tina, you look beautiful, my darling" Sir Andrew said, "Marriage to this man must be suiting you"

"Hello Tina," Sharon Savage added, kissing Justine's cheek. "Rob, how are you?"

"The better for seeing you two," Rob greeted her.

"Quite a turnout Andy," Rob gestured across the room.

"Oh yes, the good and the great of this country's defence industry, Rob. If you were only attending one bash this year, this would be the one to be seen at. Good contacts here for both of us."

"Oh dear, Tina, sounds like we've been dragged along to a well-dressed business meeting," Sharon laughed as she summoned over one off the waiters circulating with a tray of drinks.

"Champagne? The young man offered and the four helped themselves to drinks as he passed.

"Let me introduce you to a few of 'the girls', Tina, while these two talk business" Sharon suggested leading Justine across the room to an assembled group of ladies.

"So, Rob, you must know some of these guys, but why don't we take a wander, see who we can introduce you to," Andy suggested, with a hand on Rob's shoulder.

"You met Biggles at the presentation we did at Salisbury, didn't you?"

"Yeah, briefly."

"George" Sir Andrew greeted George Bigglesworth "How are things at the MoD?"

"Andy, good to see you. Rob, this is twice I've caught you with this man. You're keeping bad company, sir, always a good idea in this world. Saves learning the hard way, old boy!" Rob felt a firm handshake from the man who's bonhomie Rob knew from Andy's earlier comments was not to be confused with incompetence.

"Hi George, good to see you again. If I can't learn from my best client, who can I learn from," Rob replied with a broad smile.

As Sir Andrew was greeted by another guest, Rob felt a hand on his shoulder.

"Rob MacLaine, long time no see," the short, stocky figure of Tony Urquhart smiled up at Rob.

"Tony, good to see you. Yes, it has been a while. Is that a good or a bad thing I wonder?"

"Bit of both probably," Tony chuckled

"So what exalted position to you now hold in the National Crime Agency?"

"I'm Deputy Director, Organised Crime Command, as of last year, soon be earning as much as you, Rob" Tony joked, "Although from what you drove up in this afternoon, I might still have a way to go!"

"What?" Rob exclaimed.

"A Maserati Grancabrio is what!" You always did like your cars."

"Still don't miss much, do you!" Rob joked.

"Speaking of which.." Tony lowered his voice and steered Rob to a quieter corner of the room.

"You were er, spotted in Hamburg the other day."

"Really?"

"Apparently you made rather a mess of a couple of Eastern European thugs in Spielbudenstrasse. Be interested to know why."

"What interest would you have in my being in Hamburg, Tony?" Rob replied in a more serious tone of voice.

"From what I am being told, you and I may have shared interests in Hamburg, but this isn't the time or place to go into detail. Why don't you pop round to Citadel Place on Monday? We may be able to help each other."

"You always did know how to get a guy's attention, Tony. OK, can we do early afternoon?"

"Sure, I'll ask my office just to confirm a time if that's OK."

"Sounds like a plan, Tony, see you then." They shook hands and parted company.

Rob looked around to check on Justine. He found her in a huddle of ladies chatting and laughing in a corner alcove. Satisfied that she was in good company, he accosted the nearest waitress and opted for what he found to be a very fine red wine rather than more bubbles. The Senator obviously new his wines.

Rob wandered round the room, stopping occasionally to chat with other guests and exchange business cards with those who could potentially become Harper MacLaine clients, if they were not already. During the evening Senator Wade gave a short welcome speech referencing his visit to the UK as a fact finding mission with a couple of US arms manufacturers, to look at some of the more advanced thinking from UK manufacturers with the possibility of collaborative working.

"I believe you're the young man who saved my husband's life the other day," a cultured English female voice sounded from behind Rob.

Rob turned to face a silver haired, attractive, middle aged lady, of average height and build ,who was smiling up at Rob. She extended her right hand, offering Rob a firm handshake.

"Helen Wade, George's wife," she smiled, "we met while he was on NATO manoeuvres near my home in Norfolk, hence the accent. It catches most people out," she laughed at the puzzled look on Rob's face.

"Mrs Wade, how nice to meet you. I didn't know you were with the Senator and yes, I must admit your accent did throw me a bit."

"A lady would be very foolish to pass up a shopping trip to London, Mr MacLaine. George does his Senator piece and I spend our children's inheritance in the excellent department stores of London. The arrangement works very well." Helen Wade laughed again. "Don't look so horrified Rob, I'm pulling your leg just a little."

"Sorry, I didn't mean to look horrified, I was just thinking of the damage to our bank account when my wife and my mother hit the shops in London. But I've come to realise that's the norm and I have to say the results of these shopping expeditions are a treat to the eye. I'm sure the Senator would agree." Rob gestured towards the purple dress Helen Brodie was wearing.

"Do I detect a compliment hidden in there somewhere?"

"Absolutely ma'am!" Rob laughed.

"Is your wife with you?"

"Yes, she is."

"May I meet this lucky lady?"

"Yes, if I can find her"

"Let's go look, shall we," Helen Wade took Rob's arm.

The pair walked across the room heading for the alcove in which Rob had last seen Justine.

Just short of the alcove where the women were still in conversation, Mrs Wade stopped.

Let me guess, she said, "The beautiful young blonde lady in the red dress is Mrs MacLaine. Am I right?"

"Yes, how did you know?"

"Woman's intuition, young man, woman's intuition," she patted Robs arm as Justine turned and looked in their direction.

Justine smiled at Rob, excused herself from the others and walked towards him.

"Justine, can I introduce Mrs Wade, Senator Wade's wife. Mrs Wade this is my wife, Justine"

"Justine, I'm pleased to meet you. My husband described you perfectly to me. He said I should look for the most beautiful woman in the room with blond hair and a stunning red dress," Mrs Wade looked up at Rob with a mischievous grin.

"The Senator obviously has impeccable taste in women," Rob said as he slipped his arm around Justin's waist.

"Woman's intuition!" she laughed.

"Ah Helen, I see you've found my Good Samaritan and his lovely wife" Senator Wade approached the group. He laid his hand on his wife's shoulder

"How are you both enjoying the evening, do you have drinks?" Senator Wade called the nearest waiter over to ensure that both Rob and his wife had their glasses recharged, before having his own glass topped up.

"I really don't want to get into deep conversation about work tonight but I will be back in London in September for a week to ten days. After the other day I would like to ask you if you would provide my security for that trip. There will probably be three of us, sometimes together and sometimes on individual visits. That was a close call the other day Rob, way beyond the capabilities of US Army MPs. If you are willing to provide that security, my office will provide you with an itinerary for the group nearer the time and I would ask you please to put a proposal to them".

"Yes, of course I will Senator, just send me the details."

"Good, now would you start our business relationship by calling me George?"

"Yes, with pleasure, George"

"And Helen," his wife added.

"We need to talk to some people Rob, so can we leave you and Justine to your own devices. Make sure you have plenty to drink and help yourself to some food from the buffet."

"Of course George, we are going for dinner with Andy and Sharon later, but we'll catch up with you again and I'll look out for the details of your trip in the summer."

The men shook hands and kissed the ladies before the Wade's made their way across the room to meet their other guests.

"What's this about George's trip in the summer?" Sir Andrew enquired as he approached with his wife.

Rob outlined the gist of his conversation with the Senator and explained his needs for security in the wake of recent events.

"Excellent. I was hoping George might have that conversation with you. I know Harper MacLaine has looked after some pretty high profile clients but a US Senator takes it to a whole new level, particularly if George decides to use you internationally. That's worth a small celebration folks."

"Andy, you think anything other than funerals and tax demands are worth a celebration" Sharon laughed. "Let's eat I'm starving."

"OK let's go, there's a little Brazilian Churrascaria, just off Holland Park Road. They have a great salad bar if you don't want mountains of meat. I've taken the liberty of booking us a table, hope that's OK."

They waved good night to the Wades, collected their coats from their rooms and headed for Holland Park Road, just a few minutes' walk away.

Brazilian Churrascarias are usually a meat eater's paradise as well as a vegetarian's delight due to their extensive salad bars. This one was no exception and the four diners ate their fill and washed it down with two bottles of delicious wine, finishing off with a round of mind blowing but delicious Caipirinhas followed by a brisk walk back to the hotel.

18

The rest of the weekend came and went. Justine and Sharon hit the shops late on Saturday morning, accompanied by an ever willing Helen Wade. They had an indulgent lunch in an out-of-the-way basement bistro that Justine had enjoyed in the past, returning to the hotel late in the afternoon in a taxi weighed down with designer carrier bags.

Rob and Sir Andrew had discussed business during the morning then met up with George Wade for lunch. He was able to flesh out his plans for his summer visit to the UK with a small party of defence orientated businesses. Having endured the attempted kidnap when leaving Salisbury, he asked Rob to put together a proposal for close security for himself and four others, plus a female operative to look after his wife, who was insisting on joining him. Having met up with the shoppers, it was convivial goodbyes all round and home. To Rob's relief, his Maserati, had just enough boot space to hold their overnight bags and Justine's morning shopping.

Sunday passed quickly, a light breakfast of fruit juice, toast and coffee and later a relaxed stroll into the village and a Sunday roast in the Dark Horse Inn, overlooking the river, close to Rob and Justine's house. In the afternoon the couple went over some of the figures Lorna Cameron had sent down from Achravie, made a few decisions based on these figures and emailed back to Lorna. Rob was slightly jealous that Justine had planned a visit up to the estate. She said that she was already putting together an agenda with Lorna for a visit, primarily to go over progress and see first-hand how the second cabin site was looking after she and Rob had agreed some alterations based on the contractors recommendations.

Monday morning was bright and sunny, if a little cold, so Rob decided to drive into London for his early afternoon meeting with Tony Urquhart. The National Crime Agency (NCA) building was a ten minute walk along the Albert Embankment from Rob's Riverside apartment. Rob still had access to the underground car park, where he left his car and walked the rest of the way.

He walked briskly across Vauxhall Bridge, enjoying the early afternoon sunshine, crossed the busy junction to grab a quick sandwich and a drink in the bar where he and Justine had first met. Using his phone, he took a quick photograph and attached it to a WhatsApp message asking, "Where am I now?" which he sent to Justine, getting an almost instant reply suggesting he should avoid spilling any drinks on strange women. Rob smiled as he ate his sandwich, washed down with with a glass of Malbec whilst checking and answering a number of emails.

Rob lefl the bar at twenty past one and walked along Albert Enbankment to Citadel Place where Tony Urquhart's office was situated.

19

THE OFFICE, A LARGE BRIGHT AREA WHICH BENEFITED FROM windows on two sides as it was situated in one corner of the building. It was traditionally furnished, with Tony's large dark wood desk and padded high-back chair situated away from the windows to prevent glare on the large computer monitors which dominated the desk top. Tony rose from behind his desk as his PA showed Rob into the office. He smiled warmly and held out a hand in greeting

"Grab a seat Rob," he invited, gesturing toward a matching padded chair positioned on the other side of his desk.

"Would you like some tea or coffee, Tony?" the woman asked.

"Tea for me please, Lucy. Rob, what can we get you?"

"Tea's fine for me, thanks" Rob replied

"And maybe a few biscuits Lucy, this man doesn't come round often so we can afford to spoil him a bit when he does."

Both men sat in the comfortable chairs by Tony's desk.

"So, how did you enjoy Friday night? It was quite a bash the Senator laid on considering his little adventure earlier in the week."

"Friday night was good, we both enjoyed the reception and we headed out for dinner afterwards with Andy and Sharon Savage,"

"Ah, yes, I hadn't realised till someone told me on Friday that Justine was Andy's niece, I take it that's how you met,"

"Oh no, we literally bumped into each other by accident one night, long story!" Rob laughed as Tony's PA slid a tray of tea and biscuits on to his desk.

"Thanks Lucy," Tony acknowledged as she left the room closing the door behind her.

Tony Urquhart poured and as the two men sipped their tea and ate most of the biscuits, chatted about Senator Wade's intended visit to the UK in the summer and his request to Rob to provide protection for his group.

"I assume you didn't suggest this meeting for a general catch-up, Tony," Rob said, returning his cup to the tray.

"No I didn't, Rob, I wanted to talk to you about your visit to Hamburg last week"

"How did you know I was in Hamburg and why does the interest? Rob asked guardedly.

Tony made a few keystrokes, concentrating on one of the large monitors on his desk "Let me show you something." He swung the screen round and moved his chair to the side of his desk so that both he and Rob were able to watch a video which had appeared on the screen.

It showed a wide dark street, in which a tall man was walking away from the camera. Rob recognised the street as Spielbudenstrasse and the man as himself. As they watched, the Silver Audi pulled up and the two men got out. Rob saw the scenario unfold as it had done previously and the Audi power off down the street leaving the two men lying on the pavement with Rob walking out of shot. Tony stopped the video and turned to Rob.

"Want to tell me what that was all about?" Tony asked.

"That wasn't a chance encounter, these guys were looking for you."

"I'd still like to know what your interest is in my being in Hamburg and why you were filming me in Spielbudenstrasse. If you weren't my friend Tony, I would be walking out of here right now"

Tony thought for a moment. "OK, this isn't about you, we weren't filming you, we were watching Luftballon. You just happened along and gave my guys a masterclass in self-defence. As we were on Achravie, we are working with Europol in a large scale effort to break an international people trafficking operation and catch the people at the top and Bingo! once again, you turn up out of the blue. I wonder if you are looking to exact some sort of revenge on these guys. If you are, I would have to advise against it, Rob."

"Are these the same people, Tony?" Rob was completely taken aback.

"Yes, you know that of course!"

"No, absolutely not! I had no idea, honestly."

"I was in Hamburg trying to trace a girl by the name of Magdalena Petric. Her sister is Andy Savage's new PA, she replaced Justine. She broke down in tears one day when she was talking to Justine and it transpires that her sister, Magdalena, appears to have gone missing. Andy and Justine kind of ganged up on me to see if I would have a look for her, find out what has happened to her. She lived in a flat in Hamburg and worked in Luftballon and was last in contact over a month ago, she phoned her sister to tell her she was coming to the UK, then nothing.

I went to the flat but it's empty and has been for about a month, so I went to Luftballon, asked a few questions, got nowhere and I left. A hundred yards down the road, all of a sudden I have these guys wanting to know why I was asking about Magda. I told them she was the sister of a friend and made to go but they had other ideas, hence difference of opinion, that's the truth. I had no idea NCA or Europol were investigating Luftballon. If I'd known that, I'd have been on your doorstep for intel rather than just flying to Hamburg cold and hoping to get lucky. "

"Call Andy Savage, he'll verify that," Rob insisted, handing Tony Urquhart the handset of his desktop phone.

Tony replaced the handset.

"I don't need to do that Rob. I've known you long enough to know that you are nothing if not honest and I'm sorry, I should have known better than accuse you like that, I apologise."

"So, tell me more about this girl," Tony asked, picking up another biscuit from the tray

Rob related the scenario from the meeting with Andy Savage and the discussion that ensued with him, Rob, Justine and Kasia to his trip to Hamburg and his findings there, all of which led Rob to believe that Magda's apparent disappearance was a cause for concern and worth investigation.

Tony leaned back in his chair and looked hard at the monitor on his desk. "Do you still have her photograph on your phone?" he asked eventually

"Yeah, I will have, why?"

"Can you email it to me now?"

"Sure," Rob replied, taking out his phone he found the photograph and forwarded it to Tony.

A few seconds later Tony's laptop pinged and the photograph arrived on Tony's screen. He studied it for a while then with a flurry of keystrokes and a few clicks of his mouse, he once again swung one of the monitors round for Rob to see the screen.

"Recognise her?" Tony asked.

Rob looked at the image on the screen which was a Europol profile of a young woman, who despite having short almost white hair was still Magdalena Petric.

"Europol, I don't understand, Tony, what's this?"

"Your Magdalena Petric has been working undercover for Europol for over a year, trying to work her way into the trust of these people and doing so very successfully until, about a month ago. Then they lost contact with her. It's as if she never existed. She'd left her job about three maybe four months ago and was working at Luftballon full time as opposed to the part time work she did before. Her flat is empty, as you know, her phone says it is no longer in service and she has not made contact for over a month. Frankly, we're worried about her. She either thinks it's too dangerous to make contact or they've rumbled her and if the latter is the case, well, you know what these people are capable of. So that's why we were watching Luftballon, on the off chance of getting some sort of sighting or clue as to where she might be."

"But Magda isn't police," Rob exclaimed

"No she isn't, officially. About six months ago she approached a Europol officer she had clocked in the club. She told her that since she started working in the club some of the girls had disappeared with no real explanation given other than a hint that they were all Eastern European and had wanted to get to the UK for work and the club managers had contacts that could make that happen. She arranged to meet the officer away from the club as she said it was too dangerous to be seen talking together in the bar. She said that one of the girls was a friend of hers and she knew that this girl had no desire to go anywhere and enjoyed life in Hamburg. She suggested that these girls were being taken to the UK against their will so she eventually agreed to help Europol, who already had their suspicions by the way, to find some evidence"

"And that's what she was doing when she fell off the radar?" Rob suggested

"Yes."

"Do Europol have any idea where she might be, where they

could have taken her if they have rumbled her as an informant. Do they think she is still alive?"

"They don't believe they would have killed her, she is a very attractive young lady, Rob and attractive young ladies generate a good source of high income for them and they are business people so they would probably prioritise the revenue she would earn over anything else. Couple of possibilities then. We think they have a safe house just outside the harbour area or she could already be in the UK somewhere

"We can't get access to either the house or the club without a warrant otherwise we would go in and search the premises, but we have no evidence of wrong doing to warrant a warrant, if you'll excuse the pun."

"OK, so what if I said that I didn't need a warrant and was up for a bit of detective work, totally off the record of course," Rob suggested

"Eh, you know I couldn't accept that offer Rob, but on the other hand, I couldn't really stop you if you made that decision off your own bat. Especially if you were able to have sight of some of the case notes we have here."

"Without your knowledge or permission of course."

"Absolutely. If you took some screen shots of the file while I was in the gents for instance, how would I know."

"How indeed!" Rob feigned disbelief at the mere suggestion.

Tony Urquhart again hit the keyboard and clicked his mouse and a document relating to the operation appeared on his screen. The text at the bottom said it was one of nine pages.

"You will have to excuse me Rob, I need to pay a visit. I'm terribly constipated just now so I could be about five minutes or so." Tony wore a pained expression as he rose from his chair and made for the door. Help yourself to some more tea," he called over his shoulder as he left the room.

Rob pulled his smartphone out of his pocket, scrolled down

the document, photographing each of the nine pages as he went. It took only a few minutes and he was sitting back relaxing in his chair with a fresh cup of tea when Tony Urquhart returned.

"Sorry to take so long, hope you managed to help yourself. Ah you've poured me a cup as well, thanks Rob, very kind" Tony eased himself back into his leather chair and with a knowing smile. sipped his fresh cup of tea, "Everything else OK?"

"Yes, fine. Helped myself to a biscuit as well, didn't think you'd mind."

"Not at all, now where were we? Ah yes, Hamburg. What are your plans in that area now that you know we are watching the club?"

Rob thought for a minute before answering.

"I promised Kasia I would try to find her sister and I intend to do just that. Knowing your involvement I might do things a bit differently but I still need to find her if I can and from what we've just discussed, I think the sooner the better."

"I thought you might say something like that. I would prefer that you didn't carry on looking for this girl on your own, as Europol has put a lot of time and resource into gathering evidence on these traffickers and wouldn't take kindly to any activity that would jeopardise their operation. On that basis, I would like you to liaise with Chris Hall and his team. I can't insist that you do this, Rob, but we go back a long way and I would appreciate your cooperation on this one. I can't put you on the books as such but if we get a result I'll put through some "consultancy" work for you." Tony Urquhart sat back in his chair and looked at Rob over his glasses.

"I wouldn't have a problem with that. I got to know Chris pretty well in a short period of time up on Achravie. He's a good guy and so is Tom Parker. I would need to know that we were sharing everything as we go forward though."

"Unofficially, of course. I've already primed Chris as to the possibility, depending on the outcome of this meeting and he was actually quite delighted by the possibility of "working" with you on this." Tony replied

He leaned across his desk and pressed the intercom button on his phone, "Lucy, can you ask Chris to come in now, please?"

Both men stood up as Chris Hall opened the door and walked across the room, his hand outstretched to shake first Rob's and then Tony Urquhart's.

"Good to see you again Chris," Rob smiled as Tony invited them both to take a seat.

"Guys, I have another meeting in five minutes so I'm going to leave you to discuss the way forward on this. Chris, treat Rob as one of our own, share everything you think is relevant, any intel, theories, plans, ideas, anything you think is going to help to move things forward. Rob if you don't mind sharing likewise. Put together a plan of action and let's get these scum off the streets once and for all." Tony rounded his desk and put his hands on the shoulders of both men, "Good luck, must go." he announced and left the room.

Two and a half hours later Rob and Chris Hall followed him with a plan to return to Hamburg, meet up with the German Europol team and resume their watch on Luftballon and the suspect warehouse by the docks.

20

"GOD, I GOT ABSOLUTELY LEGLESS THE LAST TIME I WAS IN Hamburg" Ryan Hughes proclaimed from his wheelchair, sitting in the Harper MacLaine office. Joe Harper's jaw dropped and Rob almost choked on his coffee. "Did the same the last time I was in Helmand, didn't quite get over that the same." he reflected, "Do you think its places that start with an H?"

"What?" Ryan exclaimed seeing the other two disintegrate into fits of laughter, "Only saying."

Ryan Hughes was of average height and build, with unfashionably long, naturally curly brown hair. He had a short, goatee beard and bright, sparkly brown eyes which gave the suggestion of someone with a lively, ready sense of humour, despite his obvious disability.

As the laughter died down Joe brought the meeting back into order.

"OK, so can you be ready to fly to Hamburg on Thursday morning, Ryan?"

"Yes, no problem. You guys will organise tickets etc.?"

"No need, I've arranged for us to take the Agusta. We have you and me, Chris Hall, Tom Parker and a load of surveillance gear, so best we don't use public transport or normal customs channels. Europol will meet us in Hamburg and take us through." Rob explained

"What sort of surveillance gear?" Ryan enquired.

"NCA's kit for keeping watch on premises"

"Inside or outside?"

"Outside. We probably wouldn't be able to get inside, sadly" Rob replied

"I can get us inside. Well, eyes and ears inside, not bums on seats."

"How you gonna' do that," Joe asked.

"Technology, MAVs, Micro Aerial Vehicles, in US military speak. Little miniature drones to the uneducated. They look like little bugs and we can fly them in through doors or windows, whatever. We can record sound, take pictures even inject people with stuff."

"Stuff?"

"Yeah, stuff. Chemicals, tags, you name it" Ryan added

"Where'd you get that kind of kit," Rob enquired

"US military are having them developed and we'd be helping to test them"

"We", who's this "we" you speak of," asked Joe with a worried look on his face.

"Us, you and me. There's no point in developing technology that doesn't work in the field, Senator Wade asked if I could help get them field tested, he might even pay us some nice American dollars for using them," Ryan beamed.

"You're serious, aren't you? Miniature drones, injecting people with stuff!" Rob laughed

"Oh, deadly serious."

Rob and Joe looked at each other and said nothing.

21

With Pete Hall piloting the Agusta 109S Grand helicopter, it was a short, uneventful trip from the helipad on the Savage Building to Hamburg. With the help of two Europol officers who had been briefed on the arrival of the team and its equipment they soon cleared the airport formalities. The rain fell steadily as they were met in a quiet corner of the airport by a Mercedes SUV. With their equipment stowed on board they were driven directly to a small, modern industrial unit close to the docks area of the city, closely followed by the two Europol operatives in a dark blue Audi. The front of the building contained an office window and a pedestrian door, both of which were covered by roller shutters for security, as were all of the other units in the block. Some of these were unused and still had "To Let" signs displayed on the front of the buildings.

The rear of the unit was approached via a fenced yard area and the SUV was faced with a large, vehicle sized roller shutter door. The driver retrieved a handheld remote from the door pocket of the vehicle and used it to open the door. They drove into a warehouse which could have housed four or five cars or light vans. There was already a black Ford Galaxy and a silver

BMW estate parked in the area. The Europol driver parked the seven seater beside these and switched off the engine. He waited until the blue Audi was parked in the yard and the two officers walked into the building then closed the roller shutter with the remote, which he tossed into the driver's door pocket.

"Welcome to Hamburg," the taller of the two Europol officers said as he entered the warehouse, hand outstretched to greet the new arrivals.

"I'm Karl Shafer, this is Harald Meyer. We are both based in the Europol office in Hamburg, working with Chris and Tom on this human trafficking problem.

Shafer was a man of medium build and height, in his early to mid-forties with slightly receding sand coloured hair. Meyer had Shafer's build although younger by ten years with dark hair and a nose which had obviously been broken at some time. He looked nervous and didn't have the easy manner of Shafer.

"Good to meet you guys," Rob responded. "I'm Rob MacLaine, this is Joe Harper and Ryan Hughes. I assume you've been briefed on our, shall we say, unofficial support roles."

"Yes, we have, sounds interesting. It maybe what we need to crack this case and put these animals behind bars," Shafer stated. "Follow me, let's get some coffee and we can talk." He led the way through to the office at the front of the unit.

The men spent the next two hours bringing each other up to speed with the operation and began to plan the way forward as they saw it. They were amazed by the advanced drone technology that Ryan was able to introduce to the discussions and the potential benefits they could derive in particular from the intrusive nature of the mini drones.

While the discussion went on, the driver of the SUV had offloaded all the equipment, stacked it on racking in the warehouse before leaving.

"OK," Shafer said with a smile, "let's get you guys to your

apartment. It's a new block with elevators to all the floors, so no access problems for a wheelchair. You've got the BMW that Chris and Tom have been using, and the Galaxy. We've taken a couple of seats out of that to enable you to get the chair and some of your kit in and out quickly, if the need arises," he added as the group made its way back to the warehouse.

They decided that Chris and Tom Parker would continue to use the BMW estate and Rob, Joe and Ryan took the cavernous Ford Galaxy, which as Shafer had suggested gave easy access for Ryan, his chair and some of the surveillance equipment which Ryan was keen to deploy as soon as possible.

The apartment Europol had allocated them in Bernhard-Nocht-Strasse was often used as a safe house by the organisation and was ideally situated for their purpose, being only two streets away from Luftballon. There was an underground carpark with a secure entry system and elevators from there to all floors, which made for secluded access to the apartment for Ryan's wheelchair.

The five men quickly shared some of the bread, cold meats and cheese, with which Europol had stocked the apartment. Ryan then gave Chris Hall and Tom Parker instructions on how to set up some of the surveillance equipment. Chris and Tom took the equipment round to the apartment overlooking Luftballon from where they had witnessed Rob's altercation with the two Eastern Europeans. They began setting up the kit which Ryan would monitor from their new base.

Once the surveillance equipment was in place, Ryan took some test footage of the street outside the club, asked the two NCA operatives to leave the window slightly open so that he could, if required, launch a small drone through the open window, then opened a small aluminium case and took out what looked like a large bee.

"This gentlemen will be our eyes and ears inside the club," he explained. "We launch it from here and fly it round to the back of the club, find an open window, door or vent and in we go."

Rob and Joe stared at the small insect-like device.

"You're kidding me," Rob chuckled, "what does that actually do?"

"It's a drone! It has a miniature camera and microphone so we can see and hear everything that goes on in the room and it'll stick to any surface we want."

"You're joking!"

"No"

"I've seen everything now." Joe chipped in.

"Oh no, you ain't seen nothing yet. We've got insect drones that can inject drugs or poison, even plant a pinhead tracking device. Little bugs that look like cockroaches but see and hear everything and as you know, larger drones that shoot you dead with smart bullets."

"OK, so when can we start to deploy these in the club?" Rob asked picking up what looked alarmingly like a cockroach.

"Well, I want to get an insect into the club to see and hear what's going on in the office and as a backup, I'd like to get your little friend there into the club and hidden under something as a backup"

"How do we do that?"

Ryan looked at Rob, "I fly the insect in and someone takes the cockroach, either to the back of the club or, failing that, to the bar and we try to get it through the front of house and into the office area without being noticed and stamped on."

"OK, I'll take the cockroach," Rob replied.

"That's good. If you can find an opening to fly the insect into the club while you are there, that would help at this end."

"Right let's do it. Its dark now and the club will be starting to get busy." Rob stood putting on his jacket.

22

IT TOOK ROB A FEW MINUTES TO WALK THE SHORT DISTANCE TO Spielbudenstrasse. He stood in a dark alleyway for another few minutes watching the people walking up and down the street past Luftballon. There was an alley at the side of the club which looked as if it would give access to the back of the building and having assured himself that he would not be noticed, Rob crossed the road and slipped into the alley. He crept carefully towards what looked like the rear entrance to the club, taking care not to disturb any rubbish lying on the ground as he went.

The side entrance was opposite a recess which gave access to an outhouse and just beyond the door was a small window situated high up on the wall. It had clear glass, so was unlikely to be a toilet, but Rob could not see in from ground level and with a coating of broken glass on the window sill he could not easily pull himself up.

His main priority was to get the cockroach into the club so he took a small Maglite torch from his pocket to guide him. The door was old and down in the left hand corner on the hinged side was a small gap between the door and the doorstep. Rob pushed the small device into the space, as he did this the cock-roach suddenly moved forward into the club.

Rob wanted to see what was on the other side of the window, so he stepped into the dark area leading to the outhouse to look for something to act as protection from the glass on the windowsill so that he could pull himself up to see through the window. Using his Maglite he soon found an old sack which was thick enough for his purpose.

As he turned to make his way to the window, Rob was suddenly aware of voices in the alleyway coming from the street. He stepped back and crouched down in the darkest corner of the recess in the hope that he would not be seen. The two men laughed at some remark in which Rob recognised as being an Eastern European dialect. They stopped outside the door of the club, while one unlocked it the other finished his cigarette. Rob was looking straight at them, they had not seen him.

Just then, Rob's phone started playing the intro to "Layla", Justine's ringtone. The two men turned and one, a tall slim man pulled a SIG Sauer P220 pistol out of the waistband of his trousers." Who's there" he demanded in heavily accented German.

"Sorry" Rob said standing up. "Sorry, call of nature, needed to pee," he said walking toward the men, hands held high.

"Who are you, what do you want here?" the gunman demanded, pointing the handgun at Rob's head.

"Sorry, I needed to pee and it was dark and off the street here, I know I shouldn't but, when you've got to go, you've got to go."

The shorter of the two men spoke to the gunman in what Rob recognised as a Bosnian dialect from his time in Sarajevo,

"Take him inside Gregor, the boss needs to see this one."

The two stepped back to either side of the door and Gregor waved his gun at Rob, gesturing him into the club.

"Now," he shouted" Or I will blow your face off."

Rob stepped close to them, "No you won't, not so close to a busy street with loads of people wandering up and down. You won't hide the noise of a P220 from them and you would fill this alleyway with curious people in thirty seconds. Don't think your boss would like that Gregor!"

The smaller squatter Bosnian closed up behind Rob and he felt the sharp prod of a knife in his side.

"No, but they won't hear me open your guts with this," he growled "So move, smart mouth," he threatened.

"Excuse me, sorry, can I get to the apartment above the club from here?" a familiar voice sounded from the end of the alleyway. "I'm a bit lost I think," Joe Harper added as he walked towards them.

"Actually, no," Rob answered as he stepped past the knife wielding Bosnian who was completely taken aback by Joe's intrusion and giving the man's genitals a quick and fierce squeeze as he passed. The man reacted understandably grasping his private parts with both hands, gasping in pain.

"Let me show you," Rob added taking Joe's shoulder, turning him around and heading out on to the street. Both men ran across the busy street and disappeared into an alley which led them towards their apartment.

"Where the hell did you spring from?" Rob managed in disbelief.

"Well, I was pretty sure you weren't safe to be out on your own so I decided to act as your wing man and Ryan told me you were in trouble, so I came to the rescue."

"Ryan, how did Ryan know I was in a spot of bother?"

Joe stopped and pointed up and behind them at the little insect hovering overhead, "His little friend told him."

As they stood, Rob's phone started to play "Layla" again.

"I tell you, between Tina checking up on me and Ryan watching my every move, my life's not my own anymore," Rob said as he took his phone out of his back pocket "Not a word," he said pointing at his phone "Or I'll not get out to play."

"Tina, did you call earlier?" Rob spoke lightly.

"Yes, I did but you didn't answer," the reply came

"Sorry, I was in a meeting. How are you, how is Achravie?"

"Both good, Lorna sends her love, so do Hamish and Lizzie. Fraser says hello," Justine replied.

"How did your meeting with Lorna and Fraser go?"

"Fine, yes, they're both pretty comfortable with the new set up and doing a good job on both scores. Fraser has really taken to the extra responsibility, seems to be thriving on it. Lorna and I are just heading down to the Red Lion for a bite to eat and more of Hamish's good natured abuse," Justine laughed. "How's Hamburg, any progress on Magda?"

"No, not yet, we're just getting some surveillance equipment into place and we'll see where that takes us. I'll let you know when we have any news, good or bad,"

"You still fear the worst don't you, Rob?"

"Just trying not to get anyone's hopes up too much without any proof. Better to be a bit glass half empty at this stage, that's all."

"I suppose. Oh, that's Lorna outside with the car, I'd better go, Rob. You be careful, don't do anything that's going to get you hurt. I need you back in one piece."

"No, I won't, anyway I've got Joe and Ryan watching over me like a couple of guardian angels, or is that mother hens? Go and get some food and enjoy your evening. Love you."

"Cluck, cluck!" Joe intoned in the background.

"Love you too, Rob. Talk to you tomorrow." Justine ended the call. Rob swiped playfully at Joe as he put his phone back in his pocket.

23

Ryan Hughes sat looking at Rob with a broad smile on his face as Rob and Joe got back to the apartment.

"Good thinking both of you, wasn't sure how you were going to get out of that one"

Joe sat down on a large grey leather settee, "We were good weren't we, years of practice of getting my big friend here out of trouble. Just comes naturally now," Joe responded.

"You just got out of that alley in time. They followed you out on to the street but they got held up by traffic when they tried to cross the road so they lost you. They kept looking for a while though and came into the alleyway you had been in."

Ryan smiled, "Good thing about that was they didn't take time to shut the back door to the club, so before they got back, I was able to get our little friend into the club via the back door."

"You're kidding, that's brilliant!"

"Yes, I thought so."

"So we can hear and see what's happening in the office?" Joe asked

"Not quite, the office door was closed, so for the time being it's sitting on top of a big cupboard in the hallway outside the office. The cockroach is in the office and that'll hear everything that's going on, but it has limited vision because we need to keep it out of sight. Don't want anyone stamping on it to kill the thing."

"So what's happening?"

"Nothing Joe, there's no one in the office just now, but when there is we'll know what's going down."

"OK, I should let Chris and Tom know that we have managed to get eyes and ears," Rob said taking out his mobile.

"Chris?, Rob, we've got a couple of bugs into the club, one in the office and the other just outside, so we're good to go, the minute someone opens that door"

"Good work, guys. That was quick."

"We were a bit lucky." Rob related the events leading up to the planting of the devices so that the two NCA officers were aware of the whole gambit.

"OK, that explains what we saw. We caught you on camera going into the alley, then Joe and then both coming out a bit sharpish with your two friends following on pretty close behind. You guys got across the road quickly but they got held up by traffic, luckily for you. They're back in the club now."

"By the way, the girl Stella that we arrested on Achravie, she's been doing a bit of talking since we convinced her that it was in her interest to cooperate. She's given us some background into this operation. Told us they used two drop-off points in the UK for the girls and drugs. Got told today that she has given us some addresses of their houses where they keep the girls, in Glasgow and Edinburgh. She's been to both. I'll fill you in with some more detail tomorrow."

"Hang on, Tom's just telling me that a silver Mercedes S Class has just dropped three guys at the club door. They seem to be creating a bit of a stir. Shaking hands with the doormen, all chat and smiles. They've gone inside now." Chris finished his running commentary. "You might get some movement in the back office now," he added.

Ryan put on a set of headphones and listened intently for a couple of minutes, then raised a finger in the air. Looking across to Rob and Joe he flicked a switch and took off the phones as the room was filled with the sound of movement and voices from the equipment. Ryan turned the monitor round so that Rob and Joe could also see what the cockroach was sending back.

As Ryan had eluded to earlier, vision was somewhat limited due to the siting of the electronic bug, however the sound was loud and clear. The voices were Eastern European and Rob and Joe both had a smattering of the language. The voices were also raised and sounded angry. The door opened and closed, the voices quietened and Joe and Rob worked out that someone had been sent out to the club to bring someone to the office. The name Gregor had been mentioned. The door opened and closed for a second time and the voices became raised again. Rob and Joe understood that Gregor and his sidekick from the alley were now in the room. They were being berated for the fact that the two intruders had escaped out of the back alley and had been allowed to get away. A heated argument ensued. Suddenly a loud bang sounded followed quickly by an anguished cry and a second loud bang.

The trio jumped as Gregor's face filled the screen, his lifeless eyes staring at the cockroach, his forehead with a large hole in the middle of it.

"Shit! They've killed them. They've killed both of them!" Joe stammered.

"What? What's going on, Rob" Chris Hall's voice suddenly reminded Rob that he had not ended the call.

"Those two guys we had the run in with, they've just killed them, Chris. You need to tell Shafer and his team, get them in there now, before they have a chance to get rid of the bodies.

They won't be expecting a fast response from the police. Let's catch them on the back foot. We need to get down there too, make sure they can't react."

Rob was grabbing his gun and his jacket as he finished the conversation, Joe likewise, as they ran down the stairs of the apartment block, turning towards Spielbudenstrasse.

They ran back through the alley they had used before, careened off the wall at the far side of the next alley as they turned right to head down on towards Luftballon.

Rob phoned Ryan Hughes back in the apartment, they had left in such a hurry they had not had time to take the radios. Rob plugged in his earpiece and microphone.

"Ryan can you see anything?"

"Got a bird watching Spielbudenstrasse, but nothing happening," Ryan sounded distracted. "Hang on I've got the Bee into the office, someone left the door open for a minute, they've just closed it again. There are two bodies on the floor. The big guy we saw going in to the club from the silver Merc, he's just put a handgun into a safe behind the desk. He's putting his coat on, looks like he's for the off."

"Have you got Chris in on this, Ryan?"

"Yeah, on the radio."

"OK, ask him to cover the front door, we'll cover the back. Ryan, can you follow this guy if we let him leave?"

"I'll follow him for a while and drop a transmitter on to the Merc if he looks like going out of range."

"Tell Rob, we can't lose this man, Ryan" Chris came back over the radio.

"We won't lose him, Chris" Ryan retorted "He's mine, I'll know where he goes, don't worry."

"OK, we let this bird fly, see where he takes us, but keep the others here for the police

Just then, the silver Mercedes reappeared and was driven quickly to the front door of Luftballon, pulling up sharply, as the big man who had been seen placing the gun in the safe appeared in the doorway. The two doormen did a quick check of the pavements then ushered the gunman across to the Mercedes, one of them holding the door open for him. He sat in the back seat of the car and the driver immediately accelerated away from the kerb, causing other traffic to swerve or brake to avoid a collision.

"Ryan, keep on that Merc, don't lose it fella!"

"He stopped at traffic lights and I've attached a tiny transmitter from the drone while it was stationary. I can follow that from one of the tablets we brought, it's got about a ten kilometre range. Might be an idea to get mobile and start to follow in case he likes driving."

"You're right," Rob thought for a second, "OK, Joe, can you go get the tablet, Ryan can you ask Tom to bring their car to the front door of our apartment and meet Joe there. I'll go meet Chris at the entrance to his apartment and we'll take Luftballon till the police get here."

Rob was already on the move, striding up Spielbudenstrasse to the entrance foyer of the NCA team's apartment opposite Luftballon. As he got there, he saw Chris Hall standing in the shadows under the emergency stairs, watching the club entrances both back and front. He was talking into his radio.

"Rob's just arrived, we're watching the club. If anything moves before your guys get here, we're on to it, Karl. OK, two minutes, cheers"

"Karl and Harald will be here in two minutes, but police should be arriving any time now" Chris raised his right forefinger in the air as both he and Rob became aware of approaching sirens in the distance.

"Oh great, nothing like telling the bad guys you're on your way," Rob moaned as he headed for the door and out on to the pavement, closely followed by Chris.

The two men ran across the road, dodging the traffic as they went, just managing to get out of the way of a dark blue Mercedes Sprinter van which mounted the pavement with two wheels and slid to a halt outside the club, adjacent to the rear access.

"Take these two guys, put them in the back of the van," Rob shouted to Chris as two men jumped out of the van and headed for the alley. They stopped as they saw two men pointing handguns at their heads.

"Move, back of the van, open it and get in," Chris shouted in his barely understandable German. But the men got the message and complied without any further persuasion.

Rob heard noise from deep in the alley and signalled Chris to stand where the men in the van could see him, but anyone in the alley couldn't.

The noise got louder, voices sounding anxious, urgent, and suddenly two large men appeared from the alley, carrying over their shoulders what looked suspiciously like two equally large bodies wrapped in black plastic. They made directly for the open rear doors of the vehicle and threw their loads into it, stopping when they saw their compatriots standing in the van and making no effort to help. Too late they sensed rather than saw Rob and Chris standing behind them. They gave the aura of being violent men, unlike the two who had arrived with the van. Rob sensed this and gave them the respect they deserved.

"Chris, let's have their weapons."

Chris found that both were armed with Heckler & Koch handguns. "OK, clear Rob."

"Tell them to get in the van," Rob demanded, Chris again made good use of his smattering of German to pass on Rob's command and then shut the doors.

They both stood back from the van as the first of the police vehicles arrived, sirens blaring, blue and red lights flashing.

"Hide your weapon Chris, don't want to attract friendly

fire," Rob shouted as he stuck his handgun in the waistband of his jeans and watched Chris do likewise.

Armed police surrounded the van and covered Rob and Chris as others held back the traffic on Spielbudenstrasse.

"Auf dem Boden!" one of the police officers shouted to both men, "Auf dem Boden!"

"English, Europol," Chris shouted back.

"On the ground, now!" the German officer shouted again.

"OK," Rob shouted back and he dropped to his knees on the ground with his hands behind his head, with Chris doing likewise.

Four German police officers surrounded them pointing their weapons at the pair, shouting words at them that Rob did not understand.

"Police officer, British police officer, get Karl Shafer, Europol. He made the call to get you here." Chris pleaded, realising that the situation was starting to spiral out of control.

"No need, I'm here now." Shafer's voice came from behind them. Offering his Europol credentials to the police officer in charge. "These men are with us, they're the good guys, sergeant. Tell your men to stand by."

"Well timed Karl" Rob smiled. "The guys you want are in the van, we thought we'd wrap them up safely for you." Shafer was dressed in plain clothes but both he and his colleague Harald Meyer were wearing Hi-Viz Police Kevlar vests.

"The guys who killed the two men?" Meyer asked.

"No, these are just the messager boys. They were charged with cleaning up the office and getting rid of the two bodies. Two of them brought the van, the other two brought the bodies out. They're in the van as well. The guy who did the shooting left about five minutes ago."

"You let the shooter get away?" Meyer sounded incredulous

"Didn't say that, pal. I said he left. We have a tracker device on his car and two guys following his signal. We decided to let him run and see where he takes us, so we know exactly where he is." Rob retorted, an edge in his voice.

"But he doesn't know that we know where he is, does he Rob," Chris chimed with a smile.

"No he doesn't, Chris, and neither do you Herr Meyer, but if you're a good boy we might just share that with you," Rob smiled draping his arm around Meyer's shoulders and ruffling his hair."Meyer looked confused then realised that Rob was joking with him and dug his elbow into Rob's ribs, with a wide grin and a shake of his head."

"So, the four in the van?" Shafer interrupted.

"Yeah, Ryan got drones into the club and we have a sound recording of the shooting and both sound and visual, of the shooter putting the gun into a safe in the office then two of the guys in the van cleaning up the office and wrapping the bodies in black bin bags." Chris explained.

"We wanted these guys here to arrest them, we've got all the evidence and we wanted them on their back foot, they wouldn't be expecting such a quick response. They're going to wonder how we were able to react so quickly and if their minds are taken with that, it might distract them from the main agenda, so they can't know about the drones." Rob added.

Shafer nodded and spoke to the police sergeant, he in turn shouted to his men who fanned out round the rear of the van.

The sergeant approached the van, hammered on the back doors and shouted in German.

"OK, you in the van, we are going to open the doors. You are surrounded by armed police officers, who will shoot to kill if you do anything other than stay still with your hands in the air. Now, all of you sit on the floor of the van."

He motioned to one of his officers to open the van doors.

The four men were sitting. The sergeant pointed at the men, one by one and instructed them to shuffle forwards till they were able to step onto the road, at which time they were handcuffed and led away to a police van.

Rob stepped forward to the two bodies and lifted the plastic bags away from their faces.

"These are the guys I had a run in with in the back alley. I think they were killed because they let us get away." He replaced the bags and turned to the two Europol officers. "Please reinforce how important it is that these guys aren't told about our spy drones. They give us the advantage of a technology they won't be expecting, so they won't be looking for it."

"No, I understand. We keep these bugs under our hats, eh Harald" Karl Shafer winked at Meyer who nodded.

"Speaking of bugs, Ryan used one of them to watch the big guy opening the safe so we have the combination. Ryan can you text that to Karl? Ryan also said that the shooter didn't wear gloves, so we should get some positive DNA from the gun."

"Excellent, well done guys" Shafer replied.

24

Rob picked up his radio from the table in their apartment, plugged the earpiece into his left ear and pressed the transmit button. "E5 to E6," he spoke into the small microphone as he tucked the device into his waistband.

"E6 receiving," Joe's voice replied "You guys OK?"

"All good. You?"

"Right with targets, but keeping well back"

"OK. We're going to come to you now, Chris has got the Galaxy keys and I'm with Ryan. We can see you so will let you know when we are close, out".

Joe responded with two clicks.

Rob looked at Ryan who was fiddling with Rob's phone. Becoming aware of the attention Ryan looked up.

"Almost there, that's it. I've downloaded the App onto your phone so you can monitor the tracker from there. Just keep it plugged into a charger as much as possible 'cause it'll eat battery," Ryan advised, handing the phone back to Rob.

"Cheers mate. You OK?" Rob queried, looking across at Ryan as he slipped on his black padded jacket.

"Yeah, I'm doin' what I'm good at and getting better at,

letting you guys do what you're good at, without wanting to be part of it." Ryan smiled slightly at Rob and shrugged his shoulders.

"You're *very* good at what you're doin' right now. We made real progress tonight, something these guys from NCA and Europol were struggling to do. We made that progress because we had eyes and ears in places they didn't have. With the help of your mini drones we have four guys arrested on murder related charges and we are chasing down the guy who did the shooting. He's going to take us to the next level, hopefully and if he does, it's going to be down to you and your little friends, so in fairness you are very much part of it."

Rob's earpiece buzzed "E3 to E5, at your front door" Chris's voice came over the radio.

"On my way E3," Rob responded.

"Must go, see you later, Ryan," he nodded to Ryan and ran down the stairs to meet Chris.

"Right, let's go get 'em," Rob encouraged, as Chris pulled quickly away from the kerb.

Rob brought his phone back to life pressing a button on the side of the instrument and focused, as the App Ryan had installed brought up a map of the area which showed the transmitter the young man had dropped onto the silver Mercedes. The signal was very weak because of the distance but still gave Chris and Rob a target to aim for. Chris knew his way around much of the area, having been involved with this operation for some time so was able to work out the most time efficient route to get to the still moving transmitter.

"E6 to E5," Joe's voice sounded in Rob's ear.

Rob double clicked the send button on his radio in response.

"Rob, our target is stationary. He appears to have stopped outside a factory unit on the edge of the docks area. We have visual from a distance, don't want to get too close, the car is empty. Occupants seem to have gone into the building."

"OK, I have you on screen. Be with you in two"

Joe double clicked.

Two minutes later Chris spotted the BMW estate he and Tom had been using, parked at the side of the road, he pulled the Galaxy into the shadows behind it.

Joe and Tom left the BMW and climbed into the back of the Galaxy.

"They're just round the corner, it's like a little cul-de-sac, main gate going into a yard in front of the building. No way out without us seeing them from here. We checked the back of the building, just a brick wall, no windows or doors. The Merc is sitting out front." Tom observed.

"Any chance we can get to the building without being seen, if they've got a lookout?"

"No, the yard's empty. Anyone at one of the windows would have a clear view of the whole area." Joe replied.

"OK, if we can't find out what's going on in there by stealth, maybe we just call in the cavalry and go straight through the front door."

"How'd you mean?" Tom Parker asked.

"Call the police, tell them we need backup for a raid on the building. Take them by surprise and keep them on the back foot"

"Call Shafer?"

"Yeah, tell him we've got his shooter for him."

Chris did as requested, explaining the situation and giving Shafer the address.

"OK, there're on their way, be here in ten or fifteen minutes, he reckons"

"Great, we just sit tight for now. If anyone leaves, particularly the Merc we follow at a distance"

"Don't suppose there's a kebab shop handy," Tom quipped and got a communal groan in reply.

Ten minutes passed in what seemed like half an hour.

"Listen up guys," Rob said quietly, Chris and Tom do you want to go back to the Beamer and Joe and I will stay here. If anyone does leave before the cavalry get here, you guys sit tight and Joe and I'll follow any escapees at a distance. I've got a bad feeling."

"Sure, what's wrong?"

"Don't know, maybe nothing, just a gut feeling, but let's be ready for all outcomes"

"OK, Tom, let's go."

The two NCA men stepped out of the Galaxy and went back to the BMW and as Rob slid over to the driver's seat of the big Ford, Joe climbed into the front passenger seat.

Another five minutes passed, suddenly the yard lit up with headlight beams and a white Mercedes Sprinter van appeared at the road junction and turned left before heading in the direction of the harbour area. Rob started the Galaxy's engine but let it idle at the kerbside. The yard filled with light again and the Mercedes saloon sped into view, turning right and speeding off in the opposite direction to the van.

Rob thought quickly, "Chris, take the Merc, don't lose it whatever you do. Joe, stay until Shafer gets here. I'll follow the Sprinter."

Joe jumped out of the Galaxy and Rob powered away in pursuit of the white van. Chris and Tom spun the BMW round in the entrance to the yard and with a squeal of tyres, sped after the big Mercedes.

The van turned right into the docks area and continued along the main road between the river and the warehouses and industrial units which faced onto the water. Rob followed at a discrete distance with the lights of the Ford switched off and the vehicle's Sat-Nav showing that the road they were on was a dead end with no other roads feeding on or off it, so Rob felt reasonably safe in holding back. The van had nowhere to go. As he approached the end of the cul-de-sac, Rob could see lights as the doors of the end warehouse opened and the Sprinter drove in. Rob watched the warehouse door close behind the van, waited for a minute or two then stepped out of the Galaxy, keeping close to the buildings, he made his way toward the warehouse. There were no windows to the front of the building so Rob scoured the frontage for cameras. As he got closer and his night vision improved, he picked out one camera swivelling to and fro across the front of the building, obviously set to monitor the large roller shutter door and the smaller personnel door to its left. The warehouse was built right to the edge of the harbour wall so there was no access to the rear of the building from there, but it looked as if there was a narrow alleyway between the warehouse and the adjacent building, which might prove useful.

Rob watched the swing of the camera and timed a run from the dark cover where he stood and the entrance to the alleyway which gave access between the two buildings. As the camera started to swing away from that side he sprinted across the open space into the dark shadows.

25

CAREFULLY PICKING HIS WAY ALONG THE SIDE OF THE WAREHOUSE he reached the rear of the building. The area behind was also in darkness as Rob peered round the corner. Taking a moment to let his vision adjust once again to the change of light Rob could see what looked like a canvas tunnel running from the rear of the building to a boat moored at the quayside. It was similar in size to the trawler he had seen his brother alight from in Achravie, a substantial ocean going vessel for someone who didn't want the world at large to identify what cargo was being loaded, transported or discharged.

Rob double clicked his radio receiving a double click in return. He lifted the small microphone closer to his mouth. "E5 to E6"

"E6, go ahead," Joe's response came back.

"Joe I'm down at ...."

He felt something cold and metallic against his head, just behind his right ear.

"On your knees" a woman's voice told him quietly. "Now! On your knees!"

Rob raised his hands and slowly complied. "OK, let's not do anything we would both regret," he suggested calmly.

"Who are you? What are you doing here?"

"I'm not someone you would know and I'm just out for an evening stroll, I do like boats. Next question?"

"You won't be so smart if I put a bullet in your knee."

"What, and waken up the whole neighbourhood?"

The woman stepped in front of Rob and patted the bulbous suppressor on the barrel of her pistol.

"Not with this on my gun, I won't," she half smiled down at him.

Rob looked up at her as she spoke. "Hello Magda," he smiled up at her, "You look so like Kasia when you smile."

Magdalena Petric stepped back but kept the gun pointing directly at Rob's head. "Who the hell are you, how do you know my name?"

"I'm a friend of Kasia's and she asked me to try to find you."

The woman shook her head emphatically, "You can't, you don't know what you're getting into. You need to leave."

"I know exactly what I'm getting into, Magda, and I want to help you, trust me, we're on the same side here."

"What do you mean? You..."

"I know you're working with Europol, I've seen your file. I want to see these guys brought down just the same as you."

"You've seen.."

"Magda, there's no time to explain now, you need to trust me. I'm here to help you and I won't do anything to put you or the Europol operation at risk. I do this for a living, I know what I'm doing," Rob eased the gun away from his head and Magda let it fall to her side.

"You need to go, if they find you they'll kill you."

"I'm not that easy to kill and trust me, quite a few have tried."

"I told Kasia I would find you and bring you to her."

"I can't leave this now. These people must be made to pay."

"Where are you going from here?"

"I'm going to the UK with six girls on that boat."

"Where to in the UK?"

"Lyndhurst? I've not been there before but they are spooked by what happened at the club."

"OK, take this," Rob held out his hand with a button shaped micro transmitter. "We can follow you with that."

"What?" Magda looked at the device.

"It's a transmitter, just put it in your pocket, nobody will suspect that it's anything other than a button from a shirt or a blouse"

"OK", she took the button and put it in her pocket. "I need to go. You should wait here till we leave. I'll tell them I've checked this area and it's clear. I need to go now"

Magda ran round the front of the building and disappeared from Rob's view.

As he waited in the shadows, he heard voices in the canvas tunnel. A couple of minutes later, the boat slowly slipped its berth and headed out into the river making for the open sea.

Rob sprinted down the alleyway, then, making sure the coast was clear, ran quickly and quietly over to where the Galaxy was parked, thumbing the radio as he went." Joe, how much of that did you hear," he gasped, as he started the engine.

"Pretty much all of it. Magda's on her way to Lyndhurst on a boat with six girls. Where the Hell is Lyndhurst?"

"South coast, near the Isle of Wight. We need to get over there soon as. I'll get the Agusta ready for us, can you have a couple of our guys meet us with two vehicles at Southampton Airport. Will you pick up Ryan and meet me at the airport."

"Will do."

Rob powered the big Galaxy out of the docks, set the Sat-Nav for the Airport and Pete Hall with the Agusta helicopter, calling Chris on the way to have him meet with the others there.

"E5 to E3." Two clicks came back from Chris.

"Chris, where are you with the Merc?"

"He's just parked up and is heading for the front door of a house."

"Right, deflate a couple of his tyres to slow him down then tell Karl where he is and head for the airport, sharpish. We need to get back to England, now. I'll explain when I see you"

"OK"

"E5 to Base, are you receiving"

"Loud and clear."

"Ryan, so you need to get all your kit together, Joe is on his way to pick you up. We're heading back to the UK. Magdalena Petric has your shirt button transmitter and she's on a fishing boat heading to Lymington on the Solent, we need to monitor its output, Ryan. Can you do that on the move?"

"Sure, I've got it on my tablet, it's on its way down the river at the moment. Joe called a minute ago, I've gathered our kit together and I'm ready to go."

"Good, see you at the airport."

All five arrived at the Agusta within a five minute window and the aircraft was quickly airbourne and heading for Southampton with Peter Hall at the controls.

"Chris, can you clear us fast at Southampton?"

"Done, I spoke to Tony on the way here and he will do the needful."

"Ryan, are you still picking up the transmitter?"

"Yes, it's right, there," Ryan pointed at the floor of the Agusta, "We're passing overhead at the moment."

"Good. Joe, did you get our guys to meet us at Southampton?"

"Yeah, two guys, two vehicles."

"Great, looks like we're all organised. Who's meeting us?"

"Tom Johnson and your old buddy Alan Brodie."

"Big Al! How did you manage that?"

"He just happened to be in the country and answered the call. Thought that would please you."

"Tell you what guys" Rob spoke to Chris and Tom, "If you ever needed someone to cover your back, Big Al's the man you'd want. We worked with him a couple of times in Afghanistan. A force of nature is Captain Brodie. He's my size, hence the Big Al. Might have been a Captain but if ever there was a fight he was first one into battle, all guns blazing. He's done some work for us in the past, clients love him, especially the ladies."

26

PETE HALL BROUGHT THE AGUSTA DOWN AS INSTRUCTED BY Southampton Airport and they were met on the apron by two BMWs belonging to Harper MacLaine Security. Pete killed the engines and the rotors slowly lost their momentum. As the party began to disembark the drivers of the BMWs opened the tailgates in readiness and moved to help with the equipment.

One of the Harper MacLaine men was six foot four inches and had the same broad, muscular build as Rob, at first glance the two could have been taken for brothers.

"Hey, Big Al!" Rob greeted the man with a firm handshake and a quick bear hug.

"Rob, good to see you, been a while," Alan Brodie replied with the soft Scottish accent of West Perthshire.

"Yeah, must be all of three years."

"The joys of modern technology and working from home, Rob."

"Speaking of modern technology, Alan, this is Ryan Hughes," Rob explained as Ryan was lifted from the Augusta in his wheelchair. "Ryan is our tech-genius. Master of the Drone and hacker of systems."

"Hi Ryan, good to meet you. That's quite an intro the man's given you."

"I know about Drones but what's hacking?" Ryan looked puzzled and the men laughed.

"This is Tom Johnson," Joe introduced the second Harper MacLaine driver, a short stocky man of Caribbean origin. "Tom, this is Chris Hall and Tom Parker, both with NCA and Ryan Hughes, who's with us."

Johnson quickly shook hands with all three.

"Right, let's get going, we need to be in Lymington, about now."

"Actually, we're about 16 miles from Lymington and we have an estimated twenty mile range on the transmitter. I checked the screen just before we landed and it was still out of range so its looks like they are still not there yet. Last time I had a signal from it they were just east of the Isle of Wight so they appear to be heading in the right direction."

"OK, so we've got a bit of time but let's get going in case we're held up somewhere along the way. Joe, can you, Chris and Tom go in one car and Ryan and I'll go with Alan in the other, that way, Ryan, you can keep me up to date with the transmitter signal"

The party took to the two SUVs as arranged and headed for Lymington.

"So what you been up to since I last saw you, Alan?" Rob asked from the passenger seat of the blue BMW.

"I was looking after a Russian family in Holland Park for a while, the guy was back in Moscow on business, diplomatic stuff and then I looked after these Americans for you guys. I'm just back from Aberfeldy. My dad sold the estate a couple of years before the accident but he kept the house. I've no brothers or sisters so the house is mine now. It's just outside Kenmore, beautiful setting, right on the side of Loch Tay and a wee landing on the Loch. I went up there for a couple of days and ended up staying about three weeks. I talked to an estate agent about selling it, but I'm not sure I want to now."

"Ah, you see, it's the call of home, it's where your roots are Alan. It never leaves you, trust me. Where are you living now?"

"I bought a house in Spain a couple of years ago, wee place called Puerto Ricos in the Almeria Region. It's close to a new development, well reasonably new, pretty up market, built with a wee marina and a few shops. To be fair I've spent more time away from it than living in it but I love it, love the pace of life, really laid back. I bought the place from a Dutch couple when the property prices were rock bottom, I got it for about half what they paid for it. Poor beggers were just desperate to get rid, so I just had to help them out."

"So you were on your way back to Spain?"

"Yeah, believe it or not, when I was finished with the Americans, one of them asked if we could take him up to Edinburgh so I did and Joe had let me hang on to the Beamer while I was in Perthshire. I'd just dropped it off to you at the office. I was chatting to Justine, too good for you by the way, when the call came in from Joe and the rest, as they say, is history. Here I am!"

"Hey, far too good for me old buddie and don't I know it."

"Nah, just kidding, you're well suited the pair of you. You make a great couple, you'll be good for each other."

Rob and Ryan brought Brodie up to speed with the operation as he drove. The three chatted about their military past and laughed as they discussed that they all had parts of their careers they were not allowed to go into any detail on.

The short journey to Lymington passed quickly as Brodie drove at speed and easily through the almost deserted New Forest in the early hours of the morning.

As they approached the town, Rob called Joe in the other car.

"Joe, can you guys hold back just a bit. We'll follow the

transmitter and you can follow my phone signal Joe, rather than follow these guys in convoy."

"Sure, that makes sense," Joe replied.

Following the signal being transmitted from Magdalena, Rob, Ryan and Alan Brodie drove along Bath Road toward the Royal Lymington Yacht Club and pulled into a small open area which gave them a view of the harbour entrance. Brodie switched off the engine and killed the lights.

"Ryan?" Rob looked at the rear seat passenger.

"They're still in the Solent but approaching the harbour mouth, should be here in about 20 minutes."

"OK, I'm going to have a look and listen," Rob said as he stepped out of the vehicle.

27

It was almost four thirty when Rob became aware of the muted tones of a heavy marine diesel engine. Ten minutes later he caught sight of the large trawler he had last seen in the river in Stade and raised his night vision glass to his right eye. It was travelling very slowly to keep the rythmic throb of the engine noise to a minimum, showing no lights as it approached the quayside at the far side of the river. There was a quick flash of light from the quayside, someone obviously had forgotten to disable the courtesy light of a vehicle. He could now see that the offender was a dark coloured Mercedes Sprinter van which was making its way slowly to the side of the trawler. As it stopped it was partly hidden from Rob's sight by the boat so he moved slightly further down the river bank. He could now see a little more but his line of sight was still partially obscured. He watched for about ten minutes, seeing only part of the activity until the van slowly moved away from the boat and made its way to the exit of the quayside area.

As the van moved away, Rob returned to the big BMW, quietly closing the door.

"Right, let's get after that van, see where it's going."

"Wait!" Ryan warned. "The transmitter's not moving. It's not on the van Rob."

"What, are you sure?"

"Absolutely, the transmitter is not on that van. It's still on the boat."

"Shit! I don't like this. Something's wrong."

"Al, get me round to that boat, fast."

Rob called Joe in the other BMW as Alan Brodie accelerated hard down Bath Rd toward the ring road to the other side of the harbour. "Joe, we've got a problem. There's a dark coloured Mercedes Sprinter just left the harbour area, probably with the girls from the trawler in it. Problem is, our transmitter isn't, we think it's still on the trawler. Something's wrong. Either Magda's still on the boat or she's in the van minus the transmitter. Either way, I don't like it"

"Your Sprinter just passed us, we can follow at a distance if you want."

"Go for it Joe, I need to get onto that boat before it disappears and check it out. I need to find that transmitter."

Chris's voice came back to Rob, "Boat's not going anywhere Rob, we spoke to Border Force on the way to Hamburg airport, told them what was going down. They've been shadowing the trawler for the last two hours and their Cutter is sitting just off the harbour entrance, as we speak, so like I say, it's going nowhere."

"That's brilliant Chris, but I'd still like to get on board her as soon as I can. I let a young woman get on that boat when I could have stopped her. I'd never forgive myself if anything happens to her"

"Understood, Rob."

As the two men finished speaking the big BMW powered into the quayside area and the occupants could see that the trawler was in the process of leaving, moving slowly away from the quay.

Brodie headed straight for the quay at speed and at the last minute, excecuted a textbook handbrake turn, presenting Rob with the side of the departing trawler. Rob had the door open before the BMW came to rest and sprinted toward the boat, launching himself at it as it moved away from him. He fell just short of his intended landing place, but managed to grab hold of one of the fender tyres which hung over the side of the vessel. Scrambling to get a grip, he hung there, his arms beginning to ache from the strain. Then with a concerted effort heaved himself up and managing a safe foothold on the tyre clambered awkwardly over the side of the trawler and on to the open deck.

Rob stood and turned toward the vessel's wheelhouse. Standing in his way was a tall, burley man dressed in a short, dark coat and denim jeans and most importantly, aiming a SIG Sauer P220 semi-automatic pistol at his head.

"Stay where you are and put your hands on your head."

Rob did as he was told, conscious that the beat of the heavy marine diesel engine had increased as it pushed the trawler towards the harbour entrance. He also became aware of a second man standing to his right and well away from the other. He too had a pistol aimed at Rob.

"Hello, my name's Rob, what's yours?"

" That's not very nice. I drop in to see you and you want to kill me."

"Shut up!" The first man shouted. "Open your jacket, slowly."

"That's very difficult when I need to have my hands above my head."

"Just do it" the man hissed, stepping closer to Rob.

"OK, OK, don't get your knickers in a twist. I'm doing this slowly, no sudden movements".

Rob looked at the second man, also big. He was standing well back and still holding his pistol aimed at Rob.

Suddenly, all hell let loose. The deck was bathed in bright white light, a voice boomed out over the water and the trawler changed course abruptly.

"This is UK Border Force cutter HMC Valiant, please return to harbour, repeat, please return to harbour."

The man facing Rob, turned towards the light and the loud voice, Rob sprang forward catching his gun arm, he twisted it so that the palm of his hand was facing up and swivelled to put his back to the man whilst resting the man's arm on his shoulder. He buried his elbow into the man's solar plexus, driving the air out of his lungs and pulling his arm down hard. The mans elbow joint snapped and he howled in agony, dropping his weapon on the deck. As Rob grabbed the injured arm and hurled the man across the deck he was aware of gunshots and looked across to the other man in time to see him fall to the deck, a large blood stain spreading across the front of his grey sweatshirt. Rob pulled his own pistol from the waistband of his jeans. He hit the injured man hard on the side of his head and watched as he fell to the deck, unconscious.

Rob looked at the second man as he lay perfectly still on the deck. He was undoubtedly dead and had two large holes in his upper chest. Rob stood and looked over at the quayside to see the formidable figure of Alan Brodie blowing theatrically into the barrel of an M27 automatic rifle.

The trawler had now engaged reverse thrust and was moving back towards its original berth, still bathed in the bright light from the spotlights on board the Valiant which was following them into Lymington harbour. Rob needed to find the transmitter and hopefully a healthy Magda.

In search of both, he headed down a steep stairway into the innards of the vessel. The below decks area of the boat had been greatly modified. This was a vessel used by people who clearly made regular use of it but not for catching fish. There were eight small, what could only be described as cells, built into what would once have been the hold. These were littered with blankets and mattresses and each one had a plastic bucket which Rob could only imagine from the stench, were used as toilets. They were all empty. Moving back under the stairway, Rob found two cabins. The first one he tried was empty, the second one likewise, but had what looked like Magda's coat lying on the floor. Rob felt the trawler bump into the quayside. He could hear shouted instructions from above as the Border Force men boarded the vessel. The noise and vibration of the trawler's engine stopped and he could hear the footfalls and shouted instructions of the Border Force team above him. More shouting followed and a gunshot rang out.

Rob picked up Magda's coat frantically searching the pockets for the button transmitter and eventually found it deep in an inside pocket. He threw the coat on to the bunk bed and turned to the cabin door to be met with a young, short, wiry, Border Force officer who did not seem pleased to see him and for the third time that he night was looking at the business end of a firearm.

"Stay where you are. Do you speak English?" he demanded

"Only with a Scottish accent. I'm Rob MacLaine, I'm with Chris Hall from NCA who called you guys."

"What are you doing down here?"

"Looking for this" Rob held up the transmitter.

"What is it?"

"It's a transmitter, here" he said tossing the transmitter up in the air.

The young officer's eyes followed the object as he made to catch it.

Rob stepped forward and quickly pulled the pistol out of the young man's hand. A look of horror appeared on the his face as Rob pointed the gun at his head.

"Rule number two, never get too close to someone you might want to shoot."

The young man's expression changed to one of disbelief when Rob reversed the gun and handed it back to him, bending down to pick up the tiny transmitter.

"Let's get back up topside and see what's happening. I've checked down here, there's nobody here, fella."

"You said rule number two. What's rule number one?"

Rob smiled, "Never point a gun at anyone unless you're prepared to shoot them. Your eyes told me you weren't."

"I need to check, that's what I was sent down here to do " the officer replied and turned to the main cargo area and the other cabin.

Rob climbed the ladder to the deck and saw Alan Brodie, still holding an M27 automatic rifle, standing on the quayside talking to what appeared to be the commander in charge of the Valiant and another officer. Two of the trawler crew were on the quayside on their knees with their hands behind their heads, a third was writhing on the ground holding his knee as a dark red stain soaked his trouser leg.

As Rob appeared, Brodie pointed over to him and the others looked in his direction.

"Rob, over here," he shouted.

Climbing over from the trawler to the quay, Rob strode across to join them.

The senior officer held a hand out in greeting, "Anthony James, I'm in command of the Valiant, good to meet you Mr MacLaine. Mr Brodie has been filling me in regarding your presence here and NCA has confirmed your role."

"Rob, please. Mr MacLaine was my father and I didn't like him much. What happened to him?" Rob enquired, nodding over to the prone figure, who was still in obvious pain

"He didn't believe I'd shoot if these three tried to do a runner, so I proved him wrong," Brodie explained.

Rob shook his head with a wry smile , "Somethings never change do they, Al?"

"Anthony we need to go. We had a transmitter planted on someone on the boat but it got left in one of the cabins. Our other car is following their van but we need to be with them"

"Sure. I will need to get a statement from you guys at some stage"

"Not a problem," Rob said shaking hands with James.

28

BRODIE POWERED THE BIG SUV OUT OF THE DOCKSIDE AREA while Rob spoke with Joe and Chris in the other Harper MacLaine car.

Rob explained to the others what had happened at Lymington and what they had found on the trawler, including the transmitter Rob had given Magdalena Petric.

"OK, we still have eyes on the Sprinter, we're heading up the M27 eastbound. It splits in about three miles then we head either north for Winchester or to Southampton, I'll let you know which way we go when we get there," Joe explained.

"Tell Joe it's fine, he's got a tracker on his phone. I know exactly where he is and we'll just follow his signal," Ryan interrupted.

"There you go, mate. Better keep that away from Suzy," Rob laughed

"Well, we better not let Justine know about yours Rob."

"What, you've got a tracker on my phone?"

"Yeah, well CEO and all that, can't lose an important guy like you, boss."

Rob could hear the howls of laughter from the other car which was joined by Alan Brodie and Ryan.

"Cheeky sod."

"Rob, on a slightly more serious note, we have an NCA car waiting at Nursling, this side of Southampton and a motorcycle sitting just off the M3 at Eastleigh. That way we can alternate the tail whatever way they go. We don't want to be too obvious, if we can see them, they can see us. Shafer says the guys they arrested are keeping pretty tight lipped in the main but one of them is singing his heart out. He says if he goes to prison, he'll be killed. Says they only use two UK points of entry, Lowestoft and Achravie. We know they're not heading to Achravie and Lowestoft is a fair drive, a bit risky when you've got a van load of illegal imigrants."

"Yeah, I wouldn't risk that either. Let's see where they go. That's good we've got two other vehicles."

Joe's voice came through, "Guys, we've just pulled onto the M3 heading north"

"OK"

As the silver BMW X5 headed north, keeping the Sprinter van in sight but at a distance, Brodie quickly cut the gap between the two cars to less than half a mile and sat there, just able to see the lead SUV in the early morning light.

Chris Hall confirmed that the two NCA vehicles, a blue Skoda Octavia and a Kawasaki ZR motorcycle had joind them and that Tom Johnson had pulled back to let the Skoda take lead position.

As the vehicles neared Winchester, large heavy drops of rain started to bounce noisily off the windscreen, clattering overhead as they grew in intensity on the BMW's glass roof panel.

The windscreen automatic wipers had sensed the rain and now switched to fast as they struggled to cope with the volume of the deluge. Traffic, such as it was, had started to slow due to the sudden loss of visability as the rain hammered down on the motorway in thick, dense sheets.

Chris Hall's voice came across the radio, "Van has now turned off the motorway and is approaching a roundabout, taking the second exit for A34/A33."

Alan Brodie followed, just making the traffic lights by accelerating quickly as an amber light replaced the green.

"Taking left fork, repeat, left fork A34 North."

Brodie did likewise. There was silence in the BMW, everyone peering in vain through the heavy downpour for a sight of the vehicles ahead.

The torrential rain began to ease as they progressed along the A34, still at a much reduced pace. As the traffic began to pick up speed, Chris's voice could again be heard over the radio.

"Turning off the A33 signposted Worthy Down, South Wonston." There was a short silence, then "Taking A272 Salisbury, Stockbridge".

Brodie followed the signposts.

Ryan was working at something in the back of the car while the others were concentrating on the Mercedes van's route and as they followed it according to Chris Hall's instructions.

"Guys, do we think we are getting close to where these guys are heading?" he enquired.

"I would think so," Rob replied. "This isn't a major road and the more minor the road the closer we could be getting to their destination. Why do you ask?"

"If we were thinking that we should launch a drone to find them before we lose them, this might be a good time. I've got one ready to fly but you would need to stop for a minute to make sure we don't do any damage when we launch."

"Good thinking Ryan. Pull over, Al."

Brodie glanced in his mirrors and quickly pulled in to the side of the road.

Ryan buzzed his window down and held the drone at arms length with his left hand as he pulled back the joystick controller to launch the drone with his right hand. They watched as the device gained height and disappeared into the rain which was once again beginning to fall relentlessly.

"OK, we're good to go, Al."

Brodie accelerated away and began to follow the others along the rain-soaked road, splashing through large pools of surface water as they went.

"Just passing over Joe and Chris in the other car. OK, I can see the Sprinter ahead. They're slowing down, I think they're looking for a turmoff."

"Chris, we've got eyes on the Sprinter with a drone, ask your guys in the Skoda to pull up closer and if they turn off, get them to carry on past then stop a fair distance up the road, out of sight," Rob instructed.

"Pull up closer and overtake if they turn off," Chris repeated for clarity, "I'll let them know."

A couple of minutes later, Ryan spoke, updating everyone, "They're slowing down again. Yeah, they've turned left into a farm road."

"The Skoda just passed and went straight on. It looks a bit bumpy down there, lots of potholes full of water judging by the way the Merc's bouncing around and throwing up spray."

"Whoops, big trees down there, almost flew into that one. Can we pull over guys, we must be approaching their turn-off."

"Sure," Brodie pulled the BMW on to the grass verge and stopped, switching off the lights.

" OK, we're there. There's a house just beyond these trees, two storey, brick built plus a few outhouses, looks like an old farmhouse, with a car sitting round the side of the house. Dark colour, can't make out what it is. House looks to be in darkness, either there's no lights on or all the curtains or shutters have been closed. Target has just pulled up to the front door, stopped, lights out. Someone's just got out. Still haven't switched off their door courtesy light. The front door of the house is being opened from the inside, the driver's gone in, door closed again."

All was quiet for a few minutes, then,"farmhouse door opening again, three males coming out, the driver and two other guys. Big fellow from the front passenger seat of the van is getting out. Thay're all making for the rear doors of the van. Big guy just high fived the other two guys from the house. They look comfortable together, like they know each other. Two guys from the house have just produced handguns and are waving them at someone inside the van. Moving round a bit so that I can see the van better. There are girls, young women, coming out of the van and being ushered into the house. I'm counting six, no, wait, seven. The last one doesn't look to be in good shape."

"What colour hair does the last girl have?"

"Hard to tell in the light, but looks to be light blonde, almost white I think."

"Magda, that's Magda, they must have sussed her. We need to get her out of there as soon as possible, her life is in danger."

Rob thought for a moment. "Joe, can you and a couple of guys make your way down to the house and keep a watch on the door. Once you are in position let us know and Ryan, I want you to find a safe place near here where we can hide our vehicles, we don't want to alert anyone who comes to the house by showing them all this lot."

"OK," from both Joe and Ryan

A few minutes later, Joe confirmed that he, Chris Hall and Tom Parker were in position by the house. He and Parker were watching the front while Chris Hall was making his way round to watch the back of the building.

"OK guys, just about one hundred yards past their turn off, there's an entry into a field, the gate's broken and we could get in there easily," Ryan suggested.

"Right, go for it everyone, nice and steady, keep the noise down and park for a quick exit, just in case," Rob instructed.

29

THE DRIVERS MOVED INTO THE FIELD SLOWLY. THE SKODA struggled up a gentle but muddy and deeply rutted entrance to the field. The motorcyclist had to fight to keep his machine upright but the two big four wheel drive SUVs made light work of the terrain and all vehicles were quietly parked facing the exit back on to the road.

Rob turned to Ryan who was sitting in the back seat of the car, bathed in the vivid green glare from the screen showing the view from the hovering drone.

"Can you do me a recce of the outside of the house Ryan, back and front?"

"Sure, here we go."

Ryan piloted the drone back to the house, carefully avoiding the branches of the large trees as they dipped and swung in the wind. He showed Rob the front of the house where a black Range Rover Sport and the Mercedes Sprinter were both parked. The sun had not fully risen above the horizon and the morning light was still sparse and watery, not helped by the heavy dark clouds and squally rain showers that diminished the visibility further. The house, which was still shaded by the tall, mature, surrounding trees appeared to be a typical red brick farmhouse with a central front door and five windows on the front facing wall. The door was shielded from the elements by a shallow brick built porch. The internal wooden shutters on all of the windows were closed. Moving round to the side of the house there were no doors, only a small upper floor window glazed with a ripple effect glass, probably a bathroom. A high hedge marked the perimeter of the garden and this continued round to the rear of the property. The back wall of the house had a door to the garden and four windows overlooking it. There was a large area of grass which was too unkempt to be called a lawn and in the far corner of the garden sat a large outhouse with two wooden doors. Ryan moved the drone to the other side of the house which was bereft of both windows and doors. The whole property was surrounded by a wide ring of deep gravel, which reminded Rob very much of "Uncle Charlie's" cottage on Achravie.

"We could do with one of your bugs inside that house, Ryan", Rob mused.

"Mm, let me bring that one back and I'll try to get a little one up close to the windows to have a look. Quite often these wooden shutters don't close one hundred percent, so we might get lucky," Ryan replied.

The tiny drone was much less stable in the wind than the larger one and took tighter controlling, but Ryan got it to the front of the house and homed in on the ground floor window to the right of the front door. The shutters, however, were fully closed and there was nothing to see so Ryan moved to the other ground floor window, the little drone being buffeted by the strong, gusting wind. There was a sliver of light showing between the shutters on this window, so Ryan struggled to get the drone positioned to see a group of men and hear raised voices, although not close enough to make out what was being said. The men were obviously agitated and tempers were flaring, judging by the body language and hand gestures.

"See if you can find the girls, Ryan," Rob sounded impatient. Ryan took the drone up the wall of the house and tried to look into the room immediately above where the men were arguing. Again, the shutters were not quite closed and a gap allowed Ryan to look into the room.

"Three, five, six girls Rob, all sitting or lying on mattresses on the floor, no girl with white hair, but I can't see into the corners of the room at the front wall, she might be there but I'm not seeing her."

"OK, try the back of the house."

Ryan took some time to guide the drone to one of the back windows. The gusting, squally wind now being accompanied by sheets of heavy rain, both making guiding the small, light drone very difficult. The back of the house was more sheltered from the elements by the trees and having reached one of the windows it became easier for Ryan to manoeuvre the small, drone into position to try to see into the room.

"Nothing Rob, room is in darkness, can't see a thing, let me try the last window. Wait, I think I heard a noise. Hang on," Ryan kept the drone in position at the third window. "I'm pretty sure something moved in there but the room is too dark, it's hard to see anything."

Ryan strained to see, "Yeah, pretty sure there's someone in there, but can't be one hundred percent sure."

"Try the last window."

"OK."

"Door's slightly open and there's a little light in the room. Looks empty, Rob."

"Try the last room again, the dark one."

Ryan moved the drone back to the previous window.

"Jesus!" Ryan's head snapped back in surprise as he stared at the screen. "It's Magda, she's at the window, the girl with white hair. She's opened one of the shutters. She hasn't seen us but I can see her now."

"OK, we need to figure a way to get to her." Rob ran his fingers through his hair, thinking out loud.

Alan Brodie looked across at Rob. "Easier said than done. We need to get into the house and either take out the guys who're guarding them or try to get upstairs to Magda without being seen and then get her out. Either way there are at least five guys in the house and we have to assume they're all armed. If any of them see us, we might just end up in the middle of a firefight and that puts all the girls in danger."

Chris Hall's voice filled the car, "Alan's right, we can't just go storming in there, it would end in a bloodbath."

"Point taken, but we can't just sit here. It's going to be daylight in the next half hour."

"Rob, the front door has just opened," Ryan warned.

"Maybe they're going to be on the move," Brodie suggested.

"Could be. Can we get a transmitter on that van, Ryan?" Rob asked.

"Sure, I've got a magnetic bug, but I need someone to fly it there."

"I can do that, I've used these things a couple of times," Brodie replied.

"What! when, where have you used these things," Rob looked surprised.

"Secret squirrel stuff Rob, if I told you that I'd need to kill you after," Brodie joked, winking at Ryan.

"Kill me, you'd not get paid. Secret squirrel my arse, more like Basil Brush with you, Boom! Boom!"

Ryan explained quickly to Brodie how to navigate the small bug shaped drone and watched as he piloted the device, using the built-in camera, over the trees and placed it on the roof of the van.

While he tutored Brodie, Ryan kept an eye on the front door of the house watching for any movement.

First, the two men who had brought the van to the farm came out of the front door. One of them opened the rear doors while the other retrieved something from under the seat in the cab. He took the canvas wrap off an M27 assault rifle and walked back to the rear of the van. He shouted something inaudible to those still in the house.

A third man appeared at the door and began to usher the girls out of the house. The two men at the back of the van herded them into the the rear of the vehicle, offering rough encouragement, pushing and shoving them all, shouting at them and brandishing their weaponry. The girls, obviously frightened and disorientated, were almost tripping over each other to get into the vehicle and out of the direct line of fire of the guns. Six girls were herded, crying and almost hysterical into the Mercedes van. There was no sign of the girl with the white hair, the girl who Rob and Ryan were assuming was Magdalena Petric. As the last of the terrified girls scrambled into the van, the rear doors were slammed shut.

The third man to appear from the house, small and burly with short dark hair, disappeared back inside while the other two, who had driven the van previously, made their way to the front of the vehicle. The taller of the two, who had retrieved the M27 from under the seat wrapped it up again and slid the weapon back under the seats. The two men climbed into the cab and sat talking animatedly to each other as the rain started to hammer down on the roof of the vehicle. The front door of the house reopened, two men appeared in the small porch, they high fived each other and the smaller man strode out into the wind and rain, pulling the large collar of a leather jacket up to shield his face from the elements as he ran to the front of the van and climbed in beside the other two. The driver started the engine, all three fastened their seatbelts and the van started to reverse along the front of the house and turned with a three point manoeuvre to start back down the drive.

"Tom, Chris, get ready to follow that van. Chris, can you see the transmitter on the van with the app on your phone? If not take my phone, it's got the app downloaded to let you follow the transmitter," Rob shouted to Tom Johnson in the other Harper MacLaine car.

"It's OK, Chris, can see it," came the reply.

"OK, great! Keep us updated, guys"

"Joe, can you stay with us, we need to get Magda out of there and there's only two guys with her now,"

The Mercedes van reached the end of the track and turned right, heading back towards Winchester. Johnson gave it a couple of minutes and pulled on to the road to follow the van at a safe distance and to watch it's progress, courtesy of the tiny transmitter attached to its roof.

As Rob, Ryan and Alan Brodie watched the BMW pull out on to the main road, Joe Harper slipped into the back seat.

"What now?" he asked.

"We get Magda out of there, that's what now."

"Still not easy though," Joe warned.

"No, but I don't want us to be sitting out here ruminating while these guys kill Magda, we need to do something quickly and I've got have a plan."

30

JOE HARPER SAT IN THE DRIVER'S SEAT OF THE BMW WITH THE engine running. It was now almost daylight, although the heavy, rain-filled, low cloud and squally sheets of, intermittantly, torrential rain gave the impression of dusk.

Rob and Alan Brodie advanced down either side of the narrow, uneven track leading to the house. Both kept to the bushes, moving slowly and stealthily towards their target. Neither was particularly dressed for the adverse weather conditions and the combination of heavy falling rain and the already wet undergrowth which provided their cover, meant that both men were soaked to the skin as they approached the house.

As the two studied the immediate surrounds of the building, the six indicator lights on the Range Rover flashed and blipped. The front door to the house opened and a tall figure wearing a hooded waterproof jacket appeared and ran to the car, leaving the house door open and swinging slightly in the wind.

The Range Rover's engine started, the reversing lights came on and the big vehicle began to reverse and turn moving towards the door of the house. The driver had obviously pushed the button to release the tailgate as it slowly opened during the manoeuvre.

"Joe, stand by, we have movement here. Get ready to join us." Rob spoke quietly into his microphone and received two clicks in response.

Two minutes later, both remaining men appeared in the doorway carrying a body sized object wrapped in a blanket and unceremoniously dumped it in the back of the Range Rover. As the shorter of the two men went back to close and lock the front door of the house the other closed the tailgate, then both ran round to the front of the car, stepped in and shut the doors. The engine started and the headlights bathed the area in front of the house in harsh, white light.

"Joe! Now! Al, done this before."

The Range Rover accelerated forward spitting gravel from all four of the massive tyres as the vehicle scrambled for grip on the loose surface.

The vehicle started to bounce down the heavily rutted track, spraying muddy, brown water as it went, suddenly it was confronted with an oncoming BMW X5. Both slithered to a halt, their bumpers inches apart.

As the occupants of the Range Rover struggled to comprehend, both doors were ripped open and they were suddenly confronted by two large rainsoaked figures, pointing handguns at their heads.

"Out of the car! Out of the car, now!" Both intruders shouted loudly at the occupants,. "Out, now!"

The two wet figures stood back to allow the driver and passenger to undo the seatbelts, get out of the vehicle and stand in the pouring rain with their hands held aloft.

"Hands behind your backs!" Rob shouted while moving behind the driver, pulling his right arm behind him. He stood back as Joe Harper grabbed the other wrist and secured the man's hands with strong cable ties then repeated the procedure with the still surprised passenger, finally pulling a Sig Sauer P220 handgun from the waistband of his jeans.

"Take them back to the house," Rob shouted, stepping into the Range Rover, he racked the seat back, engaging reverse and shot back onto the gravel parking area. Joe and Brodie walked the two prisoners back to the front door of the farmhouse,. Brodie quickly found the keys to the house and opened the door, pushing the two men ahead of him. Rob followed watching the two men while Joe and Brodie cleared the other rooms to make sure there were no other hostiles hiding in the house.

"OK, immobilise these two, I'll check on Magda." Rob turned back to head for the Range Rover, dreading what he was going to find and praying he was not going to be forced to tell Kasia of her sister's demise.

He opened the tailgate and started to unwrap the blanket and there was Magda Petric. Her body was still and cold and Rob felt her neck for a pulse but found nothing. He turned her head to look at her face, dirty and bruised but still beautiful.

"Magda," he said softly. Suddenly, Rob thought he saw a flicker of her eyelids and felt again for a pulse. After a few seconds he found one, faint and very weak but still there. Magda was still alive but only just.

"Joe, she's just about alive, we need to get her to a hospital. Can you move the Beemer and come with me"

"OK"

While Joe retrieved the BMW, Rob carefully laid Magda across the rear seat of the Range Rover.

"Al, will you stay with these scumbags. Call Chris and ask him to come get them"

"Sure."

Joe and Rob climbed into the Range Rover and taking as much care as possible with the uneven surface of the farm track made for the main road.

Rob turned right at the end of the track and accelerated in the direction of Winchester. "There must be a hospital in Winchester, Joe."

"You'd think, place that size. I'll check," Joe took his smartphone out of his hip pocket and searched.

"Royal Winchester Hospital, Romsey Road. Follow the signs for Winchester at the roundabout down here and I'll stick it in the Sat-Nav. My old man's got one of these so I know my way round it"

For the next ten minutes a cultured female voice gave Rob instructions, finally telling him,"Your destination is on the left."

While Rob powered the Range Rover along the route, giving little consideration to any other vehicles he encountered, Joe found the telephone number for the hospital and having finally been put through to A&E alerted them to their imminent arrival and the circumstances. As they drove under the canopy which covered the Ambulances only area, they were met by a crash team from the department. The doctor did a quick check for signs of life and having announced that Magda was still alive but only just, the team eased her out of the car, on to a trolley and disappeared inside.

"Can you park this up" Rob asked Joe, tossing the keys to him, "I'll go with them and explain the background."

Without waiting for a response, Rob ran into A&E to find Magda and explain more of the circumstances. Clarifying that she had not overdosed herself but had been given what had probably been intended as a fatal dose of, probably heroin, by a gang of people traffickers.

Having got his message across to the medical team, Rob was asked to wait in the waiting area of the department while Magda was taken to a cubical for treatment.

Joe came in, grabbed a couple of almost coffees from a vending machine and sat with Rob. Ten minutes later two uniformed police officers approached.

"Are you the two who brought in the young lady with the drugs overdose?" one of them challenged. He was standing arms folded, legs apart directly in front of Rob as he spoke. Underneath his uniform and Hi-Viz body protection he looked painfully thin. This appearance was exaggerated by the fact that he was about six foot tall. His colleague was a petite young woman with her blond hair cut in a tidy bob.

"Yes" Rob replied, without looking up.

"Yes, we were," Joe added, sensing that Rob in his concern for Magda was not in a very communicative mood. Joe stood up and moved to the side hoping to divert the police officer's attention away from Rob.

"Want to tell me more?"

"Not really. I don't mean to be obtuse but this is very complicated and involves the National Crime Agency, so I would rather they decided how much of this they want to become public knowledge," Rob said looking up at the policeman. "Give me a moment."

Rob took his phone out and having scrolled down his contact list, hit the call button on. The call was answered immediately.

"Rob, where are you?" Tony Urquhart asked.

"Hospital in Winchester with Magda Petric and two police officers who want to know what's going on, hence the call."

Rob listened for a few seconds then held out his phone to the constable, "Speak to the Deputy Director, Organised Crime Command, his name is Tony Urquhart"

The man took the phone and listened for a few moments before offering "That would be Inspector Prior, Robert Prior. Yes sir, no sir, she looks to be OK. Thank you sir."

He stood for a minute looking at the phone, before handing it back to Rob.

"Wait here" he added, gesturing his colleague to the other side of the room and speaking to her quietly and intently, both of them occasionally glancing across to Joe and Rob, before approaching them again.

"Mr. Urquhart is going to contact my gaffer Inspector Prior. I need to wait with you till I get clearance from him, if that's OK."

"Sure, sorry, you've got a job to do," Rob replied

"Can we get you anything in the meantime, gentlemen" the WPC asked.

Rob looked up at her, "How are you with miracles?"

"We occasionally manage the impossible but miracles take a bit longer, sir"

Rob looked in the direction of the cubicles, "Not sure she's got that long"

"Someone close to you, sir?" the tall skinny constable asked

"Friend of a friend, but still important to me."

Just at that moment, the man's radio came to life and he turned away to answer it. After a brief exchange, he turned and walked back over to Rob.

"That was my gaffer, he said to offer you any assistance you require, sir, otherwise just to leave you to it."

"Thanks, officer but I don't think you're going to be much use to us if you don't do miracles, but thanks anyway," Rob stood and shook their hands.

As he stood, one of the staff appeared from the cubicle area and approached the four. She was a tall slim woman who looked to be in her forties. She was dressed in blue scrubs.

"Everything OK?" she addressed the police officers.

"All good, sister. These gentlemen have friends in some high, law enforcement places and they assured our gaffer that they're good guys. Asked us to offer them any assistance they required. They say they're all good so we were just going to leave them with you, if you don't mind."

"That's fine, off you go" she said, then turned to Rob and Joe, "Sorry gentlemen but when we admit someone in that condition and in these circumstances, our protocols dictate that we call the police, I hope you understand"

"Not a problem, sister. How is Magda?"

"She'll live. You did the right thing and got her here in time, otherwise she would most certainly be dead by now. A large dose of heroin depresses heart rate and breathing to such an extent that a user probably won't survive without medical help. Dependant on the size of the overdose and with what this young lady has had, she would have died within half an hour if you hadn't brought her here when you did. We've given her two injections and we are getting a reaction now, so we are optimistic we got her in time."

"Thanks sister," Rob said quietly.

"Someone did this to her?"

"Yeah, people traffickers, but their days of freedom are numbered, this lot anyway. You're sure she's going to be all right?"

"Yes, she was responsive when I came to see you. She has taken a bit of a beating as well, might have broken a rib or two so we're taking her down for a scan to see what we find. We're going to keep her for an hour or two for tests, so if you have other things to do, now might be a good time."

"OK, that's fine, we do have a few loose ends to tidy up"

"Pop back about midday."

31

———

JOE AND ROB RETRIEVED THE BORROWED RANGE ROVER FROM THE hospital car park and headed back to the farmhouse. Rob called ahead to update Brodie and alert him to their return. By this time the rain had stopped, most of the dark clouds had lifted and although the wind was still gusting fairly strongly, the atmosphere, like the moods, had lightened markedly.

When they got into the farmhouse, the two hostages were still cable-tied and had been taped to chairs with strong gaffer tape, lengths of which had also been stuck over their mouths. Neither of them reacted when Rob and Joe returned, they both sat, heads bowed, staring at the timber floor.

Alan Brodie and Ryan were in the spacious farmhouse kitchen, sitting at a large wooden, table, nursing mugs of tea. Brodie stood, walked over to the worktop, and boiled the kettle to make a pot of tea. He used bread from the kitchen larder to make some toast for them all and Ryan in his light fold-away wheelchair raided the fridge for butter and marmalade,

That done, they sat and discussed the operation as they had always done in previous battlegrounds. Brodie was fascinated by the drones and the possible uses for them by Harper

MacLaine. He and Ryan had spoken at length as they sat in the farmhouse waiting for Rob and Joe to return.

"I've got a couple of calls to make, guys," Rob said, making for the front room. He entered a generously proportioned sitting room, closing the door behind him. He pulled out his phone and sitting down on the well-used red leather Chesterfield settee, scrolled down his contacts again and hit "Call".

"Rob!" Andy Savage's voice sounded at the other end, Rob had called his mobile rather than the office number.

"We've got Magda, Andy. She's a bit the worse for wear but she's being taken care of in the Royal Hampshire County Hospital, Winchester and she's on the mend. Do you want to tell Kasia or shall I?"

"She's in hospital? Winchester?" Concern showed in Andy's voice

"Yeah, it's a long story, Andy, but she was working with the police to catch some people traffickers and they clocked her. They filled her with heroin and we think were about to dump her body somewhere and let her die, as these animals do. But we got to her in time, rushed her to the nearest hospital. They're treating her in A&E and she was responding when we left. I'm going back in to see her this afternoon, so I can update you then."

"That's great Rob, I'll talk to you later. Here's Kasia. I'll let you speak to her."

"Rob, have you found her, is she all right?"

"Hi Kasia, yes and yes. We found her and she's going to be OK. She's in hospital at the moment but is responding to treatment and they say she'll make a full recovery. She was helping the police, Kasia, she got herself into trouble with some nasty people. But we've got them and Magda will be fine."

Rob could hear Kasia's sobs, he stopped to let her cry.

"Rob? It's Andy. I'll bring Kasia down to Winchester, we'll

leave now and be with you in about two hours or so. We'll meet you at the hospital. I'm sure we'll find it OK."

"Royal Hampshire County Hospital, Winchester, it's on Romsey Road. You can't miss it. Let me know when you get there."

Rob cut the call, found Justine's number and called to tell her the news.

She listened to Rob's edited version of the events of the last two days and shed a few tears of relief, happy that Rob was safe and that they had managed to find Magda in time.

"I'm going to head back to Winchester and visit Magda in the hospital, just to make sure she's recovering and that there've been no setbacks or complications. I'll meet up with Andy and Kasia, then head home with Joe and Ryan sometime this afternoon."

By the time Rob got back to the kitchen, Brodie had received a call from Chris Hall to say that they had intercepted the Mercedes van on a stretch of the A31 as it headed towards Guildford where they had taken the two men into custody. The six girls were being transfered for medical examination to an army hospital in the Keogh Barracks near Aldershot, then a debrief to ascertain who they were and what they had endured during their ordeal.

Chris had said that he and Tom Parker were on their way back to the farm to pick up the two Eastern Europeans to take them for interrogation with the men from the van plus the crew of the trawler, who were already in custody.

The four men were sitting at the table in the farmhouse kitchen. Brodie had found the makings of some sandwiches in the surprisingly well stocked fridge, when they heard a vehicle approach. First splashing through water logged potholes of the farm track leading from the main road and then crunching loudly through the deep gravel at the front of the house. They heard two car doors slam shut, a few footfalls later the front door opened and the two NCA officers appeared in the kitchen doorway.

"How's the girl, Rob," Parker asked

"She'll be fine, Tom, we got her in time, but only just from what the A&E Sister told us."

"Good result all round then," Hall added as he helped himself to a mug of tea. "How are our guests?"

"They're next door," Brodie informed them.

Hall went to see for himself and returned with a smile on his face,

"They're not going anywhere in a hurry, are they," he laughed, "You've got them trussed up like a pair of prize Christmas turkeys."

"Better safe than sorry," Brodie said with a smile. "They're all yours now."

"We'll take them to a safe place and find out what they have to say for themselves, but we want our forensics team to have a good root around in here, so you guys are free to leave any time you want"

"Tom Johnson's on his way back to pick up anything that needs picking up, including people, Rob. I thought he could take Ryan and his kit and either Joe or myself back up to the office"

"OK, that sounds like a plan, Al, why don't you go with them, Joe and I are going back to the hospital to meet Andy Savage and Magda's sister, they're coming down from London to see Magda."

"Great, I might be able to get a flight back to Murcia or Almeria tonight"

"Back to your Spanish senorita," Joe teased with an exagerated wink.

"No, no senorita. I live a sad, solitary existence in my beach-side house. I'm never there long enough to have a Spanish senorita to go back to, you guys work me so hard, sending me to all these foreign lands at the drop of a hat," Brodie responded theatrically"

"Aw, get the violin out Rob, I think I'm going to shed a tear"

The men all laughed as Rob stood to go. Brodie threw him the keys to the BMW and the two big men embraced each other in an enthusiastic bear hug, each slapping the other man's back.

"Thanks again for everything Al, you've been a big help as usual, it's always a pleasure to work with you. Let's not wait for years to pass before we get together again."

"No, let's not. Why don't you and Justine come out to Puerto Ricos for a break some time?"

"Now there's a good idea, I might just take you up on that."

"Right, Chris, Tom, we better get a move on if we're going to catch Andy Savage and Kasia at the hospital. Good to work with you both again, seems like we got this serpent by the tail, I hope you can find its head and cut it off before too long."

"We're working on it Rob. Bye for now."

"See you back at the office tomorrow, Ryan, thanks for all your help."

Joe and Rob stepped into their BMW, Rob fired up the powerful engine and they headed back to Winchester.

32

———

THE ROAD IN TO WINCHESTER WAS BUSIER THAN IT HAD BEEN, BUT as there was not the same urgency in the journey the two took time to admire some of the beautiful historic buildings which adorned the city centre as they made their way back to the Winchester hospital. They parked in the car park and made their way round to the main hospital reception at the front of the large, imposing red brick building and enquired as to where they might find Magda.

The receptionist made enquiries and found that, as a precautionary measure, Magda had been taken to a high dependency unit on floor C of the Nightingale Wing. She gave them directions on how to get there.

The two friends waited patiently for the lift, both feeling tired, exhausted by the intensity and physical exertion of the last few days. Magda was safe, if not sound, for the time being and the National Crime Agency were a few steps closer to shutting down a vicious people trafficking ring, which it appeared was now dipping it's toe into the very lucrative drugs market. Job done, time to go home.

The lift arrived taking them to floor C where they found the

High Dependency Unit. As they passed an open door, they heard a conversation being held in a familiar Eastern European language and Joe touched Rob's arm to stop him.

They approached the door and looked into an office. Sir Andrew Savage sat in a chair in the corner with a bemused, glazed expression on his face. He looked round as the two approached.

"Oh, thank goodness, someone who speaks a language I understand!"

Two women who had been having an animated discussion in their native language, stopped mid-sentence and turned to face the door. One of them, tall and slim, was dressed in green scrubs, obviously a member of staff, the other was Kasia Petric.

Kasia almost flew across the office, she threw her arms around Joe who was nearest to her and then Rob. Rob could feel her sob as she hugged him tightly.

She suddenly realised what she was doing and let Rob go, a look of embarrassment on her face. Tears were running down her cheeks as she turned to the woman she had been talking to.

"These are the men who saved my sister's life," she sobbed.

"Kasia told me all about you. I'm Dr Katic, I'm looking after Magda and my family live not far from Kasia and Magda's parents. I apologise if we got a little carried away in our own language," she said, turning to Sir Andrew.

"How is Magda?" Rob enquired.

"She is recovering. She was very heavily drugged with heroin and her organs were starting to fail when you brought her in. She was less than one hour from dying at that point, so you did indeed save Magda's life."

"There were a few others involved as well, but the main thing is that she is on the mend."

"She is still very weak as you can imagine, but she asked to see you when you came in. I'm not sure if she is awake but we can check. I can only take two people to her bed, so Kasia, do you want to come?"

"Yes, please."

The doctor lead them along a short corridor, through a set of swing doors and into the High Dependency Unit. There was a hushed atmosphere compared to hospital wards that Rob had visited in the past, with an underlying, background symphony of clicks and bleeps from the monitors and machines that were the tools of the Unit.

Dr. Katic pulled back the curtains surrounding one of the beds. A nurse looked up from the tablet she was inputting data into and smiled at the newcomers.

"Can you give us a few minutes, Nicky?"

"Sure, although, I'm not sure she'll stay awake or be aware of you."

Kasia moved forward and took Magda's limp hand, "Magda, you've got a visitor."

There was no response from the pale, prone figure lying on the bed, covered by a blue, cellular blanket. She was connected to drips by cannulas in her wrists plus monitors via adhesive pads attached to her chest. Kasia stroked her arm but there was no response from her sister.

"Maybe best we leave her for now Kasia," Dr Katic said softly.

Kasia looked up at Rob, "I'm sorry Rob, I tell her you are coming this afternoon and she said she needed to speak with you."

"It's fine, Kasia, there's no rush. Let her get better and then we can talk."

"Talk now," a weak voice whispered

"Magda?" Kasia bent over her sister.

"Is he here? I need to speak with him."

"I'm here Magda."

"You must get to the other girls, if things are going wrong, they kill them."

"It's OK, Magda, the girls are safe, we have them. The girls are all safe and the low lives who had them are all in police custody. You've got to concentrate on getting better."

Magda's eyes opened and a tear trickled down her cheek as she looked at Rob. "You saved my life," she managed and her eyes closed.

"She needs rest now," Dr Katic said with a hint of concern in her voice.

They left the ward and walked back to the office where Joe and Andy Savage were waiting.

"Sounds like you guys had a bit of an adventure to find Magda. Why don't we go down for a coffee and you can fill us in on some of the details," Andy suggested.

"Sounds like a plan," Rob replied, "Kasia, why don't you join us, you look worn out."

33

THE FOUR MADE THEIR WAY DOWN TO THE GROUND FLOOR COFFEE shop which Andy Savage had noticed on the way in. They ordered coffees and teas for all four and blueberry muffins for Joe and Rob.

Over the next half hour or so, Joe and Rob gave Kasia and Sir Andrew a sanitised version, for Kasia's benefit, of the events of the days since Rob's first trip to Hamburg. Kasia was horrified to discover her sister's involvement with Europol and her undercover activities on their behalf. Sir Andrew, on the other hand, while sympathetic to Kasia's feelings, was elated to hear of the role the drones had played in the group's activities. Kasia finished her coffee and stood up to go back to be with her sister.

"When I asked you to help me to find my sister, I did not know it would be dangerous, I just thought. I do not know what I thought, I just wanted to find Magda and make sure she was safe. You did not need to do this, either of you, but without you, Magda would probably be dead now." Tears started once again to trace down her cheeks and she wiped them away with her sleeve. "I don't know how to thank you, how do you thank someone for your sisters life. I do not know what to say."

Rob stood and held his arms out and she moved close to him as he wrapped his arms round her shoulders. "You don't need to say anything Kasia, just go and make sure she gets back on her feet and back to normal life soon. Jobs not done till you and Magda walk into our office with a bottle of Champagne." He looked down at her and kissed the top of her head.

"OK, we need to go. The Police will want to speak to her when she is well enough to talk to them. We've told the local boys about NCA's involvement, so they probably won't come calling. Andy, are you OK to stay with Kasia just now?"

"Yeah, I've booked her into a hotel for a couple of nights and Sharon is coming down tomorrow, so that she's not on her own. We'll pop into the town later and pick up a few overnight things for Kasia then I'll head back up the road."

Andy stood and moved round the small, low table and shook hands with Joe and Rob.

"Rob, Joe, thanks. Thanks for going the extra mile. Even your good Samaritan might have given that a body swerve when he found out what was involved. That's twice I've got you into a scrape lately, Rob, your wife will kill me the next time she sees me," he laughed.

Kasia and Andy Savage waved as the two men left the coffee shop and made their way round to the car park to pick up their car.

Rob fired up the powerful, throaty engine and followed the convoluted, exit route back to Romsey Road and from there, through the centre of the historic, old city on to the M3 Motorway. Joe entered Bourne End into the car's sat-Nav and they were on their way.

Just over an hour later, Rob pulled into the drive leading to "Achravie", as Justine had renamed their recently acquired home. He passed Joe's Audi, which was parked in the drive where he had left it on departure to Hamburg, pulled up in front of the house beside another car he did not recognise.

As he and Joe opened the front door, Rob heard laughter and two voices he recognised immediately, Justine and Alan Brodie. Justine was walking towards Rob and Joe as Brodie rose from one of the settees.

Justine threw her arms around Rob and hugged him tightly, before turning to Joe and kissing him lightly on both cheeks.

"Mm, touch of favouritism there," Joe complained and got a playful slap on the arm.

"Think yourself lucky I let you in the house at all, after you've been leading my husband astray again."

"No, no, no, no, it was Alan Brodie's fault. He led us both astray. Nothing to do with me," Joe pleaded.

"What's he been telling you," Rob asked, frowning over at Brodie.

"He wouldn't tell me anything, that's the problem. That's how I know you lot have been up to something dangerous," Justine said. "Actually, he did tell me about his new house in Spain. It sounds beautiful and we have an open invitation to visit."

"Justine's right, you're welcome, anytime, you and Suzy as well Joe. Even if I'm not there, I can leave a key for you and let you children play."

"Alan couldn't get a flight tonight, Rob. I said he could stay with us, he's flying back to Almeria tomorrow afternoon."

"Yeah, that's fine, of course he can, give us a chance to catch up. You can buy dinner for us all at the Dark Horse, you up for that Joe?"

"Thanks, but I should get back, see Suzy and my Scottish son"

"Scottish son, what're you on about, man," Brodie queried.

"Long story, I'll tell you later?" Rob laughed. "I take it that's your Audi sitting at the door, by the way?"

"Yeah, rental car from the airport."

"Speaking of Audis, I'd best get going. Not sure when I'll see you next Alan, so look after yourself and enjoy Spain," Joe said, shaking hands with Brodie and making for the door " Don't let these two bore you with old war stories, Tina. See you tomorrow."

"Let me grab a quick shower, guys, then we can head out" Rob suggested.

"Actually, I've done a huge Lamb Tagine. It's in the oven and it'll be ready in about twenty minutes." Justine called after him as he climbed the timber staircase to the ensute shower room.

Rob stopped halfway up, "Oh, OK, that sounds brilliant, we should open a couple of bottles of Malbec to go with it. I'll not be too long, Al."

Rob disappeared up the stair to shower and Justine pulled a couple of bottles of Rob's favourite Malbec from the wine rack in the kitchen and handed them to Brodie.

Rob, true to his word, did not take long to shower and change into a pair of denim jeans and a white T-shirt. He joined the others in the spacious, farmhouse style kitchen. Justine had set three places at the table which sat at the back of the kitchen, beside a set of patio doors which opened out on to the large paved terrace. She served up plates of her fragrant lamb tagine, which was accompanied by a home-made lemon cous cous, while Rob poured two glasses of Malbec for Brodie and himself. Rob retrieved a chilled bottle of New Zealand Sauvignon Blanc and poured a generous measure into Justine's glass and all three settled down to enjoy their dinner.

They ate and drank and talked and laughed, the time flying by, finally struggling up to bed in the wee sma' hours, Brodie reminding the other two that he would need to be away reasonably early the same morning.

Sleep came quickly and easily to Rob, a combination of the physical exertions of the past few days and the food and drink he had just consumed. He sank gratefully into the large, welcoming king size bed. Justine snuggled into him and they both almost instantly fell sound asleep.

As Rob and Justine emerged the next morning about seven o'clock they heard Brodie moving around in the guest room. They went downstairs into the kitchen to prepare some breakfast. Rob prepared the food while Justine set three places at the same table they had sat at the previous night. Justine took time, as she often did, to look out over the garden towards the stream which formed the southern boundary to their garden. The rain of yesterday had gone, replaced by part cloud and part blue sky, rewarding the watcher with short flashes of autumn sunshine. The stream was high, flowing quickly over the stones and boulders which formed the riverbed, the water splashing and gurgling as it passed.

"Morning all," Brodie offered as he arrived in the kitchen, swinging a heavy rucksack off his shoulder and dropping it by the door, getting a cheerful "Morning Al," from both Justine and Rob in response.

"Something smells good," Brodie added rubbing his hands in anticipation.

"Oh, just a simple bacon, sausage and eggs with some toast and coffee, Al. Can't have you flying back to Spain on an empty stomach."

"What an employer, Justine, not only pays me big bucks, but feeds me too."

"You stopped being an employee yesterday, this morning you're an old mate in need of a bed and a meal to keep you from homelessness and starvation. I'm sure Joe can cut your day rate next time if you feel overpaid and guilty about it."

"No, no, someone's got to fund the life style I intend to become accustomed to. Might as well be you."

"Sit, eat, don't want you missing your flight back to your life of sandy beaches, cervesas and senoritas."

"No chance of that, Rob."

The three sat at the kitchen table and enjoyed their breakfast and were just starting their second round of coffees when they heard a car pull up outside. Justine got up to see who it was and saw Joe Harper step out of his silver RS4.

She knocked on the window to catch his attention beckoning him in.

Joe opened the outer door and passed through the Harper MacLaine office, letting himself into the house as he had been invited to.

"Morning all," he greeted the others, "just in time for a coffee I see. How are we all this fine morning?"

"All good Joe, all good. Al's just about ready to head for the airport after his coffee," Rob explained.

His mobile rang as he was speaking so he pulled it from his back pocket and looked at the caller ID. He saw the call was from Tony Urquhart.

"Tony, you're at your desk early, wife kick you out this morning?"

"I wish, Rob. I need your help"

"OK, is this as serious as you sound?"

"Perceptive as ever. We've been talking to the people we've arrested from Lymington and Winchester and getting a bit heavier with woman from Achravie. We know who the Mr Big of this whole operation is. His name is Zlatan Kovac, also known as Uncle Charlie and we know where he is right now."

"And you want my help to do what, exactly?" Rob asked hesitantly.

"I've had a directive from above, the powers that be want him taken out. The Agency can't do that Rob, but you can, quietly, if you get my drift. It would be deniable and off the books, but we would pay you a substantial consultancy fee."

"OK, send me the details, Tony. We'll have a look at it and get back to you." Rob ended the call.

"Tony Urquhart?" Joe enquired."

"Yeah, they've identified and located the guy heading up our trafficking ring. Tony wants us to follow it up." Rob rose from the table.

"Al, got to get on with this, it's pretty urgent by the sounds of things. Thanks again for your help mate, I know it was short notice. It was really good to work with you again. Hope you have a good flight back and Tina and I might just take you up on the holiday offer, you could just rue the day you put the idea into Tina's head." Rob shook Brodie's hand, exchanging a quick bearhug with his friend and having lightly kissed Justine, Joe and he strode through to the Harper MacLaine office shutting the door behind them.

34

Rob quickly filled Joe in on the short conversation with Tony Urquhart. A message appeared in Rob's email, opening the folder he found a number of encrypted documents from Urquhart.

"We need to get a team together, soon as. We could do with Ryan and his drones," Rob said as he scan read the documents. I think we need to be a bit clever on this one"

"He'll be here in about ten minutes if he's as good as his word," Joe replied.

Just at that moment, Alan Brodie walked in, closing the door behind him as he smiled at Rob and Joe.

Rob looked quickly at his watch.

"You're going to miss your flight, Al"

"I've just deferred that Rob, your little conversation next door sounded quite intriguing and I thought you might need a little protection out there."

"You'll stay and help?"

"Nothing pressing at home, so why not."

"Brilliant. Ryan, Captain Brodie here, you and I, that's all we need, Joe."

"Tony Urquhart says the men in grey suits want this guy taken out, Al, this is a kill order."

"Not be the first one, Lieutenant MacLaine" Brodie responded with a glint in his eye.

"Trigger happy psychopath!" Rob laughed. "But thanks, I appreciate you staying"

The three heard the crunch of gravel as a car approached the house. They turned to see Ryan's blue, wheelchair accessible car reverse park just outside the door. Minutes later, Ryan swung his wheelchair into the desk space he had been allocated earlier.

"You guys look as if you're up to no good, what's happening?" He looked at Brodie, "Why are you still here?"

Rob explained quickly.

"What'd you need me to do?"

"You sure you want to be involved Ryan. This is a highly illegal gig, NCA won't own us if it all goes to ratshit."

"We could take him out with a drone and a smart bullet, we don't even need to be anywhere near the scene."

"He's right," Joe said, " we could do this at arm's length, make sure we're seen somewhere well away from him."

"OK, let's get hold of Tony," Rob leaned over his desk and connected an encrypted call to Tony Urquhart's office.

The phone rang three times before Urquhart picked up.

"Tony, its Rob. I've got Joe, Alan Brodie and Ryan Hughes here and they'll see this through with me. They know what's involved and are OK with the intended outcome. What can you tell us other than the limited information in the files you sent across? They tell us about Zlatan Kovac, but not much else."

"Morning all, thanks for agreeing to do this. The call from on high said this guy has to be taken out. The National Crime Agency can't be seen to be executing bad guys willy-nilly, so we needed a trusted contractor who won't leave any fingerprints. I immediately thought of your band of merry men and their undoubted talents in these areas, as displayed during years of military black ops that only you, I, and a chosen few know about.

It's one of these situations gents where we actually have no hard and fast evidence against this guy that would stand up in court. We know he's as guilty as sin, there's no doubt about that, too many people have given up his name. We've been distilling evidence, third party statements and circumstances over a long period of time, he was just a shadowy figure in the background, no face, no name, never near the action, nothing to link him with the trafficking or smuggling.

But as of now, we've got a couple of senior guys in his organisation, one on the trawler the other at the farmhouse, both singing like larks. The woman Stella from Achravie doesn't fancy the rest of her natural in Cornton Vale Women's Prison, so she too has joined the dawn chorus. Her real name is Stella Kovac, Zlatan really is her uncle and she was expecting him to come galloping to her rescue when she was arrested. Instead he has totally ignored her plight, so she is one unhappy lady. Every one of these is singing Zlatan Kovac. Once we got his name, we were able to track him down quite easily. He doesn't really hide, he knows that even if we ever arrest him and take him to court, we'd have nothing other than hearsay, we would never be able to convict him, so like a lot of these gang leaders he thinks he's untouchable"

Ryan laughed, "That's the thing, with a drone, we don't need to touch him."

"Sorry, didn't hear that. Here's the rub guys, officially NCA can't be involved or even know what you're doing. We'll support you any way we can, but it needs to be at arms length. We can provide a clean up squad to get rid of the body, quick cremation with no flowers, but if things go wrong for any reason we will deny all knowledge of your actions. You'd be on your own. Harper MacLaine will however, be paid a six figure sum of money for a chunk of protection consultancy."

"Which we will share equally with the team here. We all take the risk, we all get the reward" Rob interjected.

"Where is he anyway, this Zlatan Kovac?"

"Right now, he's in Lymington, believe it or not. We found him on the Isle of Wight, he parked a sodding great Bentley in the car park at the ferry terminal in Yarmouth and came over to Lymington with a couple of minders. We think he didn't know what happened to the trawler and came over to recce, albeit at arms length. The trawler's still there but sadly for him, the Valiant and Border Force are still in attendance, they're tearing the vessel apart having found evidence of class A drugs on board. We don't know how long he will be in Lymington, but he will head back to the Isle of Wight, he has a house there and as I said earlier, a sodding great Bentley."

"By the way, how was Magdalena Petric when you left her yesterday?"

"On the mend, Tony, we got to her just in time."

"Good, a very brave girl doing what she did. Europol is delighted with her efforts in infiltrating Kovac's operation. They'll give her any support she needs, medical help, counselling, whatever."

"Good."

"Listen, Rob, I've sent you photos and video footage of Kovac. Our team is watching him and they'll stay with him till you guys take over surveillance. This needs to happen quickly, while the whole operation is in turmoil and before he sets up other deputies to run things for him"

"Does he live alone on the Isle of Wight?" Rob enquired.

"No, his wife lives with him, why?"

"Because we won't take him out in front of his family, Tony"

"I understand that. OK, I'll let you crack on chaps. Keep in touch with Chris Hall, he's still running the operation at our end. Good luck and thanks, guys." Urquhart ended the call.

The four Harper MacLaine men sat looking at each other for a few moments before Joe thumped his desk and said "Right, let's get an action plan in place, we need to get this right. Ideas, everyone?"

35

Rob, Joe, Alan Brodie and Ryan Hughes studied the photographs and video footage, of varying quality, but sufficient to embed Kovac's face and demeanour into their heads. They would certainly recognise him without a shadow of a doubt. This was a procedure that all four were familiar with. Noticing the details of a targets physical features, sharing them with the group, picking up the person's demeanour, their movements, their little habits and pointing them out to the room, missing nothing and reinforcing them in everyone's minds. Taking out the wrong person was not an option, killing someone could not be undone, nor could the repercussions of such an event.

The files Tony Urquhart had sent across also contained photographs of Kovac's house on the Isle of Wight and gave the team an address which allowed them to look at the house and the surrounding area on mapping software. While the team were aware that their remit from NCA had certain time constraints, none would rush the planning and preparation process. All the "what ifs" had to be teased out and dealt with, How to exfiltrate, then a backup plan had to be put in place.

The four men worked on their strategy. The morning passed, punctuated with numerous cups of coffee and a few phone calls to the NCA personnel. By lunchtime the team were satisfied that they had a successful plan of action with a low risk of them being associated with the killing in any way. Rob went back to the house and explained to Justine that the team were heading to the Isle of Wight to finish off their mission by finding the head of the trafficking ring. Joe had done likewise with Suzy. Justine sensed the unease withn the group and with Rob in particular. He explained that they were going on a clean-up and placated her by saying that they were not going to be in any real danger. Ryan had his drone related equipment in his car and had intended to leave it in the Harper MacLaine office. They had agreed that it made sense to take two cars, as a car with two men in it, would attract less attention than one with four. Joe and Brodie packed Ryan's equipment into Joe's Audi while Rob got updates from Tony Urquhart. Kovac was still in Lymington, having lunch by himself in a harbour side hotel. He seemed relaxed and in no hurry to go anywhere. The NCA team were keeping him in sight at all times but had no knowledge of the whereabouts of the two minders.

Rob left the house with Justine, his arm round her slim waist. She by this time, was dressed in a pair of skinny denim jeans and a blue striped top, her long blonde hair tied back in a ponytail, Joe and Ryan sat in Joe's Audi, Alan Brodie was waiting in the driver's seat of the Harper MacLaine BMW, the SUV's V8 engine burbling quietly.

Justine kissed Rob, her arms tightly wrapped around his neck. "Be careful, all of you. You feel very tense and that usually means trouble." She squeezed his hand.

"We will."

He smiled and walked across to the car. He sat in the front passenger seat, closed the heavy door, snapped the seatbelt into place and looked over at Brodie.

"OK, let's do it Al," was all he said as Brodie slotted the gear-lever indo drive and powered the big vehicle out into the lane, heading for the main road followed closely by Joe's Audi.

Brodie drove quickly and smoothly, utilising its power. Soon the two cars were turning on to the M40 Motorway. A slight drizzle was now falling from a grey, overcast sky. Both cars were eating up the miles easily as they headed for Lymington they quickly reached the junction with the M25 and headed south. As they accelerated from motorway to motorway, Rob's phone rang.

"Rob! Chris Hall. Magda's gone, we think they've taken her."

"What! Gone, how?"

"Sharon Savage went in to visit her about half an hour ago and she wasn't there. She asked the staff if she had been moved and they said no. They'd just started to look for her when a cleaner went into a cupboard opposite her room and found her police minder, dead, his throat had been cut. We're on our way up to Winchester now, we've asked for CCTV of the corridors and carparks. Where are you?"

"Just joined the M25, we're heading to Lymington."

"Right, head to the Hospital in Winchester, Rob, we'll meet you there. Magda's safety and whereabouts are number one priority."

"Does Tony know?"

"Just spoken to him, he's fully in the picture and it was he who asked me to get a hold of you as quick as. We'll be in Winchester in about twenty minutes, see you there." Hall ended the call.

Rob looked over to Brodie as he felt the car drop a gear, surging forward onto the main carriageway of the motorway, pushing its occupants back into their seats, "You got that Al?"

"Yeah."

The big V8 engine growled throatily as the car picked up speed, Brodie's foot, hard on the accelerator, taking the engine revs close to the red line as the automatic box went up through the gears. Rob quickly called Joe and briefed him on the conversation with Chris Hall, which explained the sudden acceleration of the BMW which Joe had just witnessed from the following Audi.

"You two guys head down to Lymington, no sense in all of us clogging up the car park in Winchester Hospital. If we know Kovac is behind this and we know he is going to go back to the Isle of Wight, might be an idea if you two still head there and wait for him."

"Sounds good to me."

Joe tucked the Audi in behind the BMW and the two cars sped round the M25 towards the M3 and then to Winchester and Lymington. The M25 motorway has been described by many unlucky souls as the biggest car park in the country. Thankfully, that morning, traffic was flowing freely and both cars were soon passing Heathrow Airport heading down on to the M3.

A section of the M3 had a fifty miles an hour speed limit with average speed cameras which has a tendancy to cause traffic to bunch, up making fast progress almost imposible and Brodie and Rob were becoming increasingly frustrated at their lack of progress. Thankfully, the motorway reverted to a seventy miles an hour limit within a few miles and as the traffic gathered speed Brodie gunned the big BMW and again started to make fast progress towards Winchester. Rob had messaged Tony Urquhart asking him to alert the motorway police to their speedy progress, giving him the registrations of the two vehicles and requesting that they be allowed to progress at best possible speed.

36

THE SATNAV HAD INDICATED THE JOURNEY TO WINCHESTER would take one hour and ten minutes but just over forty five minutes after leaving Bourne End, Brodie drove off Romsey Road and pulled the car into the hospital car park in Winchester.

"When did you get your pilot's licence, Al?" Rob enquired as the two exited the car and made their way into the hospital to meet up with Chris Hall.

"Cheeky, sod."

Their adrenalin fuelled banter was interrupted by the sight of Tom Parker at the entrance to the hospital Intensive Care Unit. Blue and white Police tape barred the entrance to the unit and two police officers wearing stab-proof vests and black gillets trimmed with Hi-Viz tape stood at the entrance. They lifted the tape to allow the three to pass under.

"This way," Parker beckoned, leading them along a short corridor until he turned into a small office opposite a cupboard which was the centre of attention of two "scene of crime" officers.

Rob and Brodie followed him and found Chris Hall and two

other police officers in the office looking at a large monitor on the desk. The three looked up as Rob and Alan Brodie entered.

"Rob, Al, this is Superintendent Napier," Chris gestured to the tall grey haired, uniformed police officer, " DCI Hope," he nodded toward the other man whose main focus was the computer screen.

The two officers acknowledged Rob and Brodie briefly before turning back to the monitor.

"Gentlemen, Rob MacLaine and Alan Brodie, both of Harper MacLaine Security. They are working with NCA and Europol on this case." Hall explained.

"We have them on CCTV Rob," Chris Hall began.

"Show us," Rob asked Chris Hall.

"May we gentlemen?" Hall asked the two police officers, who totally ignored him.

"Excuse us, please" Rob insisted and reaching across the desk, swivelled the screen round to look at the CCTV footage.

"Hang on a minute. One of our officers was killed here today and we aim to find out who killed him," DCI Hope made to grab the monitor back but was stopped when Rob's right hand gripped his hand in a vicelike grip

"I think you'll find we can tell you who killed your colleague, if we can see the footage DCI Hope," Rob replied with a tone of voice which left the police officer in no doubt that Rob would not be denied the access he wanted. He withdrew his hand quickly as Rob released it.

"OK," Chris Hall started. "We have two men, big guys, in porters uniforms, pushing a wheelchair toward the unit, here. The police officer approaches them and they all three disappear from camera. Now, here, the two guys reappear and enter the ICU. Then, wait for it, here they are with a female patient in the chair, we can't see her face, they disappear down the corridor. Then, we pick them up outside the door you came in and, look, they throw her into the back of that silver Ford

Transit Connect van and drive away." Chris stopped the CCTV feed.

"Can we see that once more, please," Rob asked.

Rob and Brodie watched again as the two large male figures came into view pushing a hospital wheelchair. Aware that they could be seen on CCTV they were deliberately keeping their faces away from view, until they came to the door of Magda's room

They raised their heads as they were approached by the police officer guarding the door to the room. All three men seemed to stagger out of camera shot in a direction which would take them close to the cupboard where the police officer's body was later found. Shortly aftrer, the two men reappeared and entered Magda's room in the ICU.

The corridor was quiet for about two minutes and then the two men reappeared, still pushing the hospital wheelchair but this time with slumped figure of a woman draped in a white cellular blanket. The feed stopped momentarily, flickered slightly and then restarted with footage from the camera adjacent to the door at the end of the corridor. As the feed started, one of the two men reappeared with the wheelchair and seconds later a silver Ford Transit Connect van came into shot and stopped beside the wheelchair. The second kidnapper got out of the van and opened the rear doors. Both men then struggled to lift the motionless woman out of the wheelchair and unceremoniously dumped her into the back of the van, slammed the rear doors shut. They locked the doors, got into the van and drove off, leaving the wheelchair against the wall of the building where it had rolled and come to rest.

"What do you think, Chris."

"Yeah, that's Kovac's heavies who came over on the ferry with him all right, they'll be on their way to Lymington, if not the Isle of Wight by now.

"In which case we'll pick them up." the tall figure of Superintendent Napier said quickly, almost defensively.

"No you won't, please. I know you've lost one of your own and trust me I know how that feels, we both do," Rob looked over at Alan Brodie, who nodded slightly. "NCA have instructions from men in grey suits, way above our pay-grades, on how to deal with this and we've been contracted to carry out these instructions, so please let us do our job gentlemen"

"OK, Chris, Joe and Ryan are probably in Lymington by now. Do we know where Kovac is?"

"Twenty minutes ago he was still in Lymington, there have been no ferry sailings since then, so he must still be there I guess, but I can check, that's not a problem"

"Thanks, do that Chris, we'll head on down there now, if you can keep us up to date with Kovac's movements and any sightings of that Transit"

Rob turned to the two police officers, "Gentlemen" he said shaking hands quickly with them, slapped Brodie's shoulder and the two made for the door, with a nod to Tom Parker, who was standing in the corner of the room by the door. Ever the watcher, Rob thought with an inward smile as he passed the slight, ginger haired NCA officer.

Rob called Joe Harper as they walked back to the car park.

"Joe, this is beginning to look like it's down to Kovac. His two heavies from the Isle of Wight crossing have grabbed Magda from the hospital, bundled her into a silver Transit Connect and hightailed it. They have to be heading for Lymington so I'll text you the registration of the van, we've got the whole thing on CCTV. Kovac obviously wants her back."

"Looks that way, Rob. The NCA guys have got eyes on Kovac, he's sitting in the coffee shop in the ferry terminal, nursing a cup of something and the remains of a sticky bun. He's certainly not hiding, that's for sure. We're caught up in some traffic in Lyndhurst, but we'll be in Lymington in about ten, fifteen minutes, depending on traffic."

"OK, Joe, you should make the next ferry. If Kovac gets on it look out for that van. Let me know if it is on the ferry."

"Will do, that's us clear of Lyndhurst and making good time again. Ryan's booking ferry tickets on the phone as we speak. Too late to buy them online, so bear that in mind. You're looking at about a thirty, thirty five minute journey to get to Lymington, so you're not going to make the same ferry."

"Doesn't matter. As long as we keep tabs on Kovac and the silver Transit with Magda, we're all good. Ask Chris to connect you with the NCA team in Lymington and get them to keep you up to date till you get there"

"OK, will do."

"Best we don't draw attention to ourselves from here on in, Al."

"Yeah, I'm keeping as near as dammit to the speed limit for that reason, Rob. "

Five minutes later, Joe called to let Rob know that he had arrived in Lymington and was waiting to board the ferry.

"Ferry looks busy Rob, no sign of a silver Transit Connect though. I can see right up the queue from here and we're pretty near the back of the queue."

"Oh, hang on. Kovac is on the move. He's just left the coffee shop in the terminal and is walking to the ferry now. He has literally just walked past us and is boarding as a pedestrian passenger. We're on the move and we're just driving on to the ferry now."

"OK, keep an eye open for the Transit, Joe"

"Need to go, talk later" Joe cut the call.

Brodie drove at just above the speed limit all the way down to Lymington, experiencing the same traffic holdup through Lyndhurst as Joe and Ryan had.

On entering the ferry terminal area he parked slightly away

from the terminal and the queueing traffic. The ferry carrying Kovac and the watching Harper MacLaine men well on its way to Yarmouth. Another ferry was just about to tie up at the Lymington terminal, to discharge it's cargo of cars and people into the early evening sunshine of the South Hampshire coast, in readiness to onload a similar cargo for the return trip to Yarmouth.

"We need to find the Transit, before we board, Al. Just pray we were right and they're going to head for the Isle of Wight, if not we're going to look very stupid." Rob said. "You stay with the car and be ready to join the queue when I give you the nod and I'll go look for the van."

Brodie nodded and Rob closed the door heading towards the queue of traffic waiting to board the ferry.

The Lymington ferry terminal consisted of a long, low modern building which housed the ticket office and a café. There was a small rail terminal close to the ferry and ample car parking for those wanting to sail as pedestrian passengers. This crossing was popular with tourists and day trippers who could sail to Yarmouth without a vehicle and pick up an open-top bus tour of the island.

As he walked he watched the cars and light vans begin to shuffle forward to close up the gaps between them, becoming impatient to board the waiting ferry.

He tried to look as relaxed as possible to the casual observer, making good use of the the late afternoon sun being directly behind him. He was little more than a dark sillouette to anyone looking behind from the vehicles waiting to board. As he progressed down the line towards the ferry, he tried to look into the cars and small vans to ascertain whether or not they carried suspect drivers or passangers who could possibly be part of Kovac's operation. Finally he spotted a silver Ford Transit Connect. Rob mentally checked to confirm the registration. He looked at the face he saw reflected in the rear view mirror, which he recognised as belonging to one of Kovac's heavies from the hospital CCTV. The man looked tense but had obviously not seen Rob.

As he passed the van, Rob took his mobile phone out of his pocket, lifted it to his ear and spoke, to nobody. He didn't risk looking towards the van but kept his face partly hidden by the large screen smartphone and kept up his one way conversation till he had passed the van. He kept walking, took the phone from his ear and called Alan Brodie.

"Al, I've got them in the queue for the ferry, they're committed to boarding, so get in the queue and follow. I'm going to board the ferry with the other pasangers, I'd just draw attention to myself if I came back now."

"OK, understood, I'm moving now. Catch you on board"

Rob ended the call and and brought up his boarding ticket online as he shuffled slowly forward with the other passengers waiting to board the ferry.The vehicles had now started to rattle up the sloping metal ramp and onto the car deck. Rob glanced across at the silver van as it passed but the driver was looking straight ahead, concentrating on positioning the vehicle as directed by the deckhand.

The passenger seat was empty, Rob was stunned, he had not expected this. He hit a button on his phone's screen.

"Al, there's only one guy in the cab of the van. The other guy must be either in the back or he's loose somewhere."

Brodie thought for a moment before he replied, "He won't be in the back Rob, they both sat in the front when they left Winchester and they locked the doors then, the're not going to risk opening those doors and someone seeing inside. He must be on the loose, either in Lymington or on the ferry. My guess would be the ferry, they both came over with Kovac, so they'd both go back together. Be careful and be aware Rob, I'll stay clear of you on the ferry and watch your back."

"You're right Al, They must have split up at some stage, but he must be on the ferry, why cut your numbers when you need to handle a hostage, it doesn't make sense."

"Need to go, Al," Rob was now facing the ticket inspector and needed to show the young lady his electronic ticket displayed on his phone's screen.

37

As Rob climbed up to the passenger deck he could see Brodie parking on the car deck. He left the vehicle, locked it and made his way to the passenger deck.

The ferry was not busy, a combination of out of season and time of day. Rob was careful not to inadvertently bump into the driver of the silver van. He had seen him climb the same stairway that Brodie had just used and kept watch on him. The driver went to the kiosk and bought a coffee and a chocolate bar as the ferry moved away from the pier and headed for the open waters of the Solent to start its forty minute crossing to the picturesque little village of Yarmouth on the north west corner of the Isle of Wight. The man drank his coffee, ate his chocolate bar, then went for a slow, casual stroll around the ship. Rob followed him at a distance always trying to keep out of the man's field of vision. Like his companion, he was just over six foot tall. Broadly build, he had developed a noticeable paunch, unlike the other man who looked much fitter and trimmer around the waist. He had short mousey hair, carried a small black rucksack over his left shoulder and still wore the porter's uniform he had been wearing in the hospital CCTV footage.

Rob was watching from beside one of the ferry's lifeboats as the man stopped outside the men's toilets to allow a small boy to leave. He then entered allowing the door to close behind him.

Rob was about to move away when he felt a hand on his left shoulder and a sharp metal object between his right lower ribs.

"Move behind the lifeboat," a deep voice with eastern European tones said quietly.

Rob did as he was told and moved with the man behind the lifeboat, out of sight of the few passengers in that area of the deck.

"Keep your hands where I can see them and no sudden moves my friend or I will kill you and feed you to the fishes. Why are you following my friend?" the man demanded.

Rob turned slightly and saw his attacker was the second kidnapper from Winchester hospital's CCTV. He was a few inches shorter than Rob but more heavily built with a slightly bloated appearance which suggested the use of steroids as well as the gym. He had a face pockmarked by earlier acne, his nose appeared to have been broken at least once, his head was shaved and he had a few days growth of beard. His porter's uniform had been replaced by a black, hooded sweatshirt and a pair of denim jeans.

"I won't ask you again. Why are you following my friend?"

The big eastern European did not live long enough to have his question answered. He had not seen or heard Alan Brodie move in behind him. The last thing he felt was Brodie's sharp knife enter the back of his neck at the base of his skull. His spinal cord was severed, causing all body functions to cease, leaving him completely paralysed, death immediate, silent and merciless

The man folded like a puppet which had just had it's strings cut. Brodie helped his victim to the ground noiselessly, pulling him behind the lifeboat, rolling him on to his side, pushing his legs up into the foetal position.

"Not exactly sleeping beauty, but he looks peacefull enough."

The last part of Brodie's sentence was drowned out as the ferry's PA system announced that all drivers and passengers should return to their vehicles in readiness for disembarking in Yarmouth.

"What kept you?" Rob enquired.

"I was waiting for you to buy me a beer."

"Humph, you'll wait long enough for that pal, but thanks anyway for turning up. We best get on our toes, Al," Rob slapped Brodies shoulder and moved off towards the car deck with Brodie in his wake.

As the two hit the car deck they became aware of the silver Transit's engine starting and both looked over quickly. The driver was intent on the task of getting off the ferry and did not see Rob or Brodie get into the BMW. With the ferry not being too busy and Brodie having positioned the BMW three cars behind the silver van, they should easily be able to keep sight of it.

As they sat waiting to leave the ferry, Rob called Joe Harper and updated him on recent events during the crossing, including the death of one of the kidnappers. Joe listened intently.

In turn, he told Rob and Brodie that Kovac had arrived in Yarmouth on the previous ferry and had made straight for the Bentley in the car park. He had made a couple of phone calls then driven off.

"Thanks Joe, where are you now?"

"We're close to the car park entrance, we can see everything that passes by on the road and anything that comes into the car park. Basically, we'll see every vehicle that comes off that ferry."

"Excellent, look out for the silver van, Joe. We're only a couple of cars behind at the moment and we've got eyes on it, but that could change when we get off the ferry. I'm not sure what he's going to do because he doesn't know his big pal's dead, so he's going to be looking for him. Let me know if you catch sight of him."

Rob then called Chris Hall. "Chris, Tony said you guys couldn't get involved with our gig but if need be could mobilise a clean-up squad to keep any collateral damage out of the hands of the local police."

"Yeah, what's happened?"

Rob explained the killing of one of Kovac's heavies on the ferry.

"Right, that's way above my paygrade Rob, that's a Tony one, I'll let him know and he can do the needful, won't be a problem though."

Brodie was moving forward slowly out of the ferry with the van just out of sight but only a few cars ahead.

"OK, thanks Chris."

Rob felt his phone vibrate to warn him of an incoming call.

"Joe!"

"We've got the van, he just came into the car park. "

"Just caught sight of the van as he turned in," Brodie informed Rob

"OK, we need to get Magda back, guys. Leave the call open and on hands free Joe."

Brodie stopped at the car park entrance, indicating to turn right, waiting until two cars and a minibus passed, travelling in the opposite direction. He turned slowly into the car park. The silver van was situated near the far end, well away from other cars.

"Guys, we're going to sandwich him, keep him in the front of the van. Joe take the passenger side, Al.."

"Driver's side" the big Scot finished the sentence for Rob

and smiled across at him as both cars headed towards the van, each gathering speed as they went. Rob buzzed the passenger's window fully open, Joe and Brodie turned sharply at the last minute as Rob pulled a Heckler & Koch pistol from under the passenger seat.

The two cars slid to a halt simultaneously, one on each side of the Transit Connect van, inches away from the target vehicle, preventing anyone from opening a door to exit the vehicle. As they stopped, Rob hammered the driver's window of the van with his pistol, shattering the glass and sending shards showering over the driver who had been on his phone, taking him totally by surprise.

Rob pointed the Heckler & Koch at the man, "Hands on the steering wheel, where I can see them."

The man swivelled his head from right to left in total disbelief.

"Hands! now!" Rob shouted at the man, adding to his confusion.

As if a penny had dropped, the driver suddenly seemed to take in his predicament. His hands shot to the steering wheel and he grasped it as if his life depended on it, which at that moment it did.

"Don't shoot, don't shoot" he screamed at Rob, staring straight ahead out of the windscreen.

"Look at me!" Rob shouted to him, "look at me!"

The man's head turned slowly to look at Rob, his knuckles white as he grasped the steering wheel, the expression on his face, one of sheer panic.

"Keep your eyes on me! Don't look away! Eyes on me! With your left hand reach across and take your key out of the ignition. Now, if you drop the key, you're a dead man. Your only hope of still being alive in five minutes time is to do exactly what I tell you. Do you understand?"

The man nodded vigourously, staring at Rob.

"OK, key, left hand, slowly and hold it up where I can see it."

The driver reached over with his left hand and Rob could see him pull the key out of the ignition and hold it aloft, exactly as he had been told.

"OK, take the key in your right hand and put your left hand back on the steering wheel. Now pass the key to me and I meant what I said, drop it, you're dead."

The man handed the key to Rob.

"Right, hands back on the steering wheel"

Again the man did as he was instructed, his arms trembling.

"Al, go and get Magda," Rob said quietly passing the key over his shoulder to Brodie.

Brodie stepped out of the big SUV and strode to the back of the van.

"Now, you better hope this girl is still alive, fella, because if my big pal finds a body in your van you will join your mate at the gates of hell, after you have suffered a slow, painful death from gun shot wounds, not a fast painless death like your partner in crime. Oh yes, did I not say?"

Alan Brodie ran round to the back of the van, unlocked the rear doors and pulled them open. He looked into the van and saw a very frightened and disorientated Magda Petric looking back up at him, her hands and feet taped together, another strip of tape covering her mouth.

"I'm Alan Brodie, Magda, I work for Rob MacLaine. You're safe now, your safe." Brodie spoke reassuringly to the woman as she stared up at him, conscious that she had never met him and might assume he was one of Kovac's men and would therefore be a threat to her.

"Rob, she's alive, she's OK. Looks like she's been drugged but that seems to be wearing off."

"Oh, you lucky man, you lucky, lucky man." Rob sighed.

Brodie sat sideways on the rear floor of the van and reached over to Magda, but she cowered away from him in terror, shuffling as far forward in the vehicle as she could.

Brodie hesitated, not wanting to frighten her any more than necessary.

"Magda, it's OK, you're safe now. I work with Harper MacLaine, Rob MacLaine and Joe Harper are both here with me. Kasia sent us to find you."

At the mention of her sister's name, the girl looked up at Brodie, he smiled at her.

"You're safe Magda, let me take that tape off you," he said, stretching to get to her. This time she didn't cower away but lay still while Brodie firstly removed the tape from her mouth. She gasped for air as her breathing eased without the constriction of the tape. Brodie slowly took out his knife so as not to panic her and cut first the tape around her ankles and then, as Magda at last held out her arms to him, he freed her wrists.

He held out his hand to Magda and very gingerly she took it. He helped her slide to the back of the van and assisted her to her feet as she stood for a moment albeit unsteadily at first. As she steadied herself, Brodie helped her round to the side of the BMW and lifted her onto the rear passenger seat. She looked over and saw Rob, who turned quickly to her and smiled.

"Got you safe and sound now Magda. I have something to do shortly, but we'll have someone take you back to Winchester, no, I'll tell you what, we'll take you back to my house, you'll be safe there."

Rob turned back to the driver of the van, who was still gripping the steering wheel tightly.

"Joe, we're going to move back now, can you take charge of this piece of scum, tie him up and dump him in the back of the van for NCA to pick him up later. First I need him to spook Kovac into moving."

"Sure"

Joe moved the Audi forward so that he was able to get out,

but with the extra length of the estate car, the rear of which still blocked the passenger door of the Transit as an escape route for the driver. He then walked round to the driver's door of the van and opened it, all the time keeping his pistol aimed at the man behind the wheel.

As he did this, Brodie pulled the BMW back from the van and moved to the next parking bay, which allowed him to continue to shield the activity from most of the rest of the car park. He stepped out of the big SUV and stood beside Joe, reaching into a pocket of his jacket and pulling out a handful of strong, thick, black plastic cable ties. Joe looked at the cable ties and then at Brodie.

"Be prepared," Brodie stated, "Boy Scout motto."

Joe looked over at Rob and shook his head, "Don't you start about Boy Scouts, bad enough him."

Joe ushered the driver out of the van and as he stood up Brodie spun him round and grabbing his wrists, tied them together with the cable ties. The two men then pulled him round to the rear of the van and pushed him roughly onto his back. Brodie used another cable tie to secure his ankles together. He picked up a roll of duct tape the two kidnappers used on Magda, tore a strip off and stuck it over the man's mouth. He finally looped the tape tightly between the cable ties securing his wrists and his ankles, leaving him trussed tightly and unable to move either his arms or his legs. Brodie then pushed him as far back into the van as he could and Joe slammed the doors shut.

Rob met them at the rear of the BMW. "I've just spoken to Chris Hall, we reckon that, with the exception of this guy here, all of Kovac's men in the area are either in custody or dead. That means if this guy cries for help, Kovac has no one else to call on, he would need to react himself, so let's get him out in the open and finish this once and for all".

Rob laid out his plan to get Kovac out of his house and away from his wife and children, while they would move away from the area altogether. Joe and Alan Brodie would board the next ferry back to Lymington with Magda and take her to Rob's home in Bourne End. Ryan would remain with Rob to attend to Kovac.

38

Rob walked round to the rear of the van and pulled the doors open. He stood looking at the driver for a moment, then reached in and pulled the tape off his mouth. The man was terrified, visibly shaking, he stared at Rob with wide eyes.

"OK, you have two choices, so listen carefully. Either you do exactly as I tell you and go to prison, or you mess me around and I kill you now and I mean that. I will kill you," Rob spoke in the man's native Bosnian language

"Please don't kill me, please don't kill me. I do anything, please don't kill me" the man pleaded, almost in tears as he lay on his side, his head bowed, shaking from side to side.

"Right. Let me tell you what you need to do to stay alive and as you heard, I speak Bosnian well enough to know what you are saying. I need you to talk to Kovac and if you say one wrong word, your life is over. Do I make myself clear?"

"I say anything, please do not kill me"

"OK, you call Kovac. Tell him you are in the car park at the Yarmouth ferry terminal with the girl, but your friend is not. You have tried to contact him but he does not answer his phone. Tell him you cannot leave the girl, she has come round and is making noise. Tell him you need help as soon as possible before someone hears the girl. Tell him you cannot do it on your own. Tell him that if you do not get help you will leave the van and girl and go back on the ferry.

"What you are to say to him? in Bosnian."

The man repeated what Rob had told him to say.

"Tell me again"

Again the man repeated the message.

"Good," Rob pulled the man's phone out of his pocket and opened up the call history.

"Which is Kovac's number. Is it this one?" Rob highlighted a number.

"Down."

"This one?"

"Down, there, it ends in 790"

"This one?"

"Yes."

"OK, I 'm going to dial the number and put it on speaker. If Kovac does not answer, we have a problem, you and I."

"He will answer, that is his number."

Rob pressed the dial button and hit speaker. The phone rang. Once, twice, three times, just as Rob was starting to worry, it was answered by a gruff Bosnian male.

"Where are you?"

The driver looked at Rob for a second before replying.

"I am in the car park at the ferry, but the girl has gone and they are going to kill me, Zlatan."

Rob grabbed the phone and hit the driver hard with the butt of his pistol.

"Kovac, we know where you are and we're coming to get you. Your friend here has just signed his death warrant and you're next."

He put the phone down on the floor of the van, picked up the tape he had taken off the man's mouth to replace it.

"You kill me anyway," the man sobbed. "If you not kill me, he will"

"I'm not going to kill you," Rob sighed and replaced the tape over the man's mouth. "God knows why, but I'm not going to kill you, you piece of scum. Better that you end your life in prison."

Rob slammed the doors of the van shut, locked them and placed the keys on the rear passenger side wheel, before making his way round to the BMW where Ryan Hughes sat with a laptop on his knee.

"What's happening, Ryan?"

"Got him, he's just come out of the house, pulling on motor-cycle leathers and gone into his garage. He's just brought out a blue and white Kawasaki motorcycle and parked it. He's got to the Bentley and it looks as if he is putting it into the garage. Yeah, that's what he's done and he's pressed something to close the garage door. He's sat on the bike and taken a helmet off the handlebars and put it on. He looks really spooked, Rob, man in a hurry, by the looks of things. He's off now, down the drive and turned left onto the road. Doesn't look like he's heading for Yarmouth."

"No, he won't be, our man with a van told him what's going on down here. He's heading for the hills mate. Take him out."

"OK, will do."

Ryan picked up the control for the hovering drone which had been over Kovac's house watching and waiting for the target to make a move. He followed the route of the motorcycle which was slow and convoluted because of the tight bends in the road. When Kovac reached a long straight, he opened the throttle of the big motorcycle, picking up speed quickly. By that time he was too late. Ryan had already picked a spot on the man's broad back, locked onto it and had pressed the trigger button. The smart bullet followed the motion of the speeding Kawasaki and hit Kovac high up on his back, blasting a large hole in the leathers as it entered his body, tearing a huge exit wound as it left the front of his chest. It continued on its trajectory, entering the almost full fuel tank which exploded into a ball of flame the force of which blasted the already dead Kovac from the bike, covering him with burning fuel. The man's body hit the ground, bounced once then rolled along the tarmac coming to halt almost on top of the stricken motorcycle, both being consumed by fiercely burning fuel.

Ryan took the drone in closer and hovered, the onboard camera recording the scene. He swung the laptop round so that Rob could see the results of his shot.

"Thanks Ryan," Rob said flatly, with no sign of emotion in his voice or his facial expression.

He took his phone out of his pocket and hit speed dial for Tony Urquhart, who answered almost immediately.

"Job done, Tony. I'll send you a video verification when we get back to the office."

"No, it's fine, some walls have eyes instead of ears. Happy to take your word. I just need details for a clean up squad."

Rob and Ryan confirmed the place and the circumstances of Kovac's death and Urquhart said they would liaise with the local police and crematorium to clear up the debris and dispose of the body.

"OK, Ryan, lets not miss the last ferry, mate. Time for home. Bring the aerial assassin back and let's go."

It took only minutes for Ryan to bring the drone back, taking care to keep it out of public view as he landed it beside the BMW parked at the far end of the car park. He and Rob packed it away and thirty minutes later they were boarding a ferry for the return journey to Lymington. Forty minutes after that Rob was driving on to the quayside at the other end.

As they were leaving the town and heading into the New Forrest, Rob's phone played Springsteen's "Dancing in the Dark", Chris Hall's name appeared on the screen.

"Hi Chris"

"Hi Rob, quick call to let you know we've just picked up your kidnapper from his van in the car park at Yarmouth harbour. He's singing like a bird, thinks we're going to kill him. I wonder why! The other matter is being attended to as we speak. The road has just been reopened and an unscheduled cremation will take place tonight in the crematorium at East Cowes. Job well done, Rob, thanks mate."

"No problem, pleasure working with you again, but let's hope it's the last, for a while anyway. If you need me you know where to find me, cheers Chris."

Rob killed the call and looked over at Ryan.

"This wasn't quite what you signed up for, fella."

"No, but there are times when a man's got to do what a man's got to do, as they say, and I volunteered for this little excursion, nobody forced me to come along. Field work's not my strength now, Rob, but under the circumstances, it was the right thing to do. Even before my injury, my software ability was way ahead of my soldiering skills."

"Point taken and I wouldn't want to put you in any more danger than necessary. From my point of view, I would like you to train some of our guys on the use of drones and concentrate on the software and IT side of our business."

"Happy with that, Rob, that's the best use of my skills. You're not going to use drones every day so if we train a few guys that should be enough."

"I meant what I said about splitting Tony Urquhart's "six figure sum of money" four ways, equal shares, so once I get the payment, I'll ask you for an invoice to cover the amount and we'll pay you direct"

"Oh, you've got my attention now!" Ryan said enthusiastically, rubbing his hands.

39

AN HOUR AND A HALF LATER, ROB PULLED INTO THE DRIVE OF HIS house in Bourne End and was surprised to see Sir Andrew Savage's Jaguar parked by the office door along with Joe's Audi, Alan Brodie's rental car and Ryans car.

He and Ryan headed for the office, but before they got there, Justine appeared at the front door of the house.

"We're all in here Rob," Justine waved.

She stood in the doorway as Rob made sure Ryan was organised and they both made their way over to the house entrance. Rob helped Ryan up the steps and turned to Justine.

"Hello gorgeous," he said, taking her in his arms and kissing her.

"Don't think flattery is going to save you. You've been up to no good, I know that because nobody will tell me what you were doing on the Isle of Wight."

"Can't, Official Secrets Act. Seriously, if I told you I would have to kill you immediately, and we can't have that."

"Honestly, you're imposible"

"All joking aside, I *am* bound by the Official Secrets Act. A lot of our work is and we need to have our integrity intact or our business would go down the pan overnight."

"Mm, so you say. Anyway we have guests. Andy and Sharon brought Kasia across when they heard that Magda was coming here and Alan Brodie and Joe are still here"

Justine took his arm and the two walked into the house.

All those Justine had mentioned were waiting for them in the large lounge. Andy and Sharon Savage were sitting with Joe on one of the settees with Kasia and Magda sitting opposite on the other. Joe and Alan Brodie were standing behind them, talking to the newly arrived Ryan.

As Rob and Justine entered the room, Kasia spotted them and rushed over to Rob, throwing her arms around his neck.

"Thank you, Rob, thank you, thank you!" she cried. "I will never be able to thank you enough for what you have done." She turned back to the room, "All of you, thank you."

Magda, was by then trying to struggle to her feet until Brodie laid his hands on her shoulder to stop her.

"Just you sit where you are, lady. You've been through enough without having to kiss that big lump" he said quietly.

Rob crossed the room towards Magda, taking Kasia with him.

"You look better than when I last saw you, Magda. Duct tape really doesn't suit your complexion. How are you now that you're in safe hands?"

Magda smiled up at him, still pale and tired from her ordeal."I am better now, as you say, now that I am safe." She held out her hand to him and Rob took it in his. "You save my life, Mr MacLaine, thank you"

"No problem, Magda, we do these things every day, usually before lunch." he smiled and winked.

Magda looked puzzled.

"Oh, Magda, with this man you never know if he jokes or is serious," Kasia laughed. "Now he is joking."

Justine handed Rob a glass of Malbec and took his arm, "Andy, Sharon, Magda and Kasia are staying over tonight, its been a long day for everyone, so that made sense and Alan needs to sort out another flight, so he's staying over as well."

"OK, sounds good. Has everyone eaten, I'm starved?"

"No, not yet, its in the oven, be ready in about 20 minutes," Justine informed everyone as she made for the kitchen to check that her Lasagne was cooking as expected.

Andy Savage stood and shook Rob's hand. "Well done all of you, you did a fantastic job. I never thought for a minute you would get involved in what you did. I imagined a simple, dropped below the radar situation, when Kasia told us that day."

"Just as well we did get involved, Andy or who knows where Magda would be now. Tell you what, though, your drones were a godsend. We got intel we wouldn't have got otherwise and we used that to good effect."

"OK, you guys, I'm going to head home, see Suzy and the kids," said Joe making for the door as Justine came back into the room.

"Likewise, I need to get back home," Ryan added. Both said their goodbyes and headed out. Justine and Rob waved them off from the front door.

The evening passed with Justine serving her Lasagne and also presenting Rob with a chilled bottle of champagne from the fridge.

"Kasia brought this," Justine announced as she handed it to Rob for him to open.

"You told me the job was not over till Magda and I walked into your office with a bottle of champagne," Kasia reminded Rob, with a laugh.

"She's right Andy. Nothing wrong with her memory," Rob joked as he popped the cork.

During the meal Magda started to tell the others about how

she got a part time job at "Luftballon", met and became friends with Irena, eventually moving into the flat with her in David-strabe. About three months later, Irena disappeared. The management at the club had said they caught her stealing money and sacked her and because the flat belonged to the club they had asked for the keys, there and then.

Magda said that she and Irena had become very good friends and she did not believe that Irena would just walk away from her and the flat. It had not been the first time that girls had left the club without warning or explanation and Magda had begun to suspect a more sinister undertone in the club. She knew that Europol had been sniffing around and contacted a female officer who had visited the club on more that one occasion. She met with this officer in a hotel room one evening and had agreed to help find out what had happened to the missing girls and to Irena. She managed to help Kovac's club managers to cover up the disappearance of some of the girls when Europol appeared to ask questions so they grew to trust her more, involving her in the operation to move girls to the UK.

The night she had met Rob by the quayside in Stade, Kovac's lieutenant attacked her on the boat and asked her to explain why a hidden camera in the office had picked her up searching the office a few nights before. She knew then that her cover had been blown and thought that they would kill her as soon as they could dispose of her body. The rest of the story everyone knew.

"Did you find Irena?" Sharon Savage asked.

"No, she is somewhere in the UK, that is all I know."

"Maybe NCA will be able to trace her," Rob suggested.

"NCA?"

"National Crime Agency, that's who we were working with. They have Kovac's people in custody and they are talking very freely. They are all trying to save their own skins. I'll talk to our senior contact there in the morning. Don't give up on Irena yet."

"Oh, Rob, that is more than I could hope for."

"I'm sure if there is a way of tracing Irena, Rob will find it, Magda" Andrew Savage said.

"Let's talk to NCA in the morning. No promises though," Rob replied.

"Speaking of the morning, might not be a bad idea to get you to bed, Magda. You've been through a lot today, you look very tired, you must be exhausted," Justine suggested.

"Oh, yes please."

Justine showed Kasia and Magda up to one of the spare rooms and made sure they had all the essensials for an overnight stay before returning to the others, who were themselves making noises about heading for bed.

As they all helped to clear the kitchen and dining room, Sharon Savage said to no one in particular, "What lovely girls. After all she's been through, Magda is still thinking about her friend."

She turned to Rob, "Do you think Tony might help you find her, Rob?"

"He certainly won't hinder us and I'd be surprised if he wouldn't give us some kind of help. After everything Magda has been through to help them catch these guys, I don't think it's a lot to ask. We just need to sell it to him the right way."

40

"IRENA LUKIC?" TONT URQUHART MUSED, "I'M NOT SEEING HER name on our lists, Rob. But that only means that I can tell you where she isn't, which in itself is helpful, because it narrows down the options of where she might be. We pretty much know all the houses where they keep their girls and we are finding out almost by the hour where they have taken those they have brought over to the UK. Having said that, it assumes she is in the UK and we don't know if she is even still alive."

"We are learning quite a lot about how the girls are distributed in the UK. We know that they are housed at addresses in London, Manchester, Edinburgh, Glasgow and Aberdeen. They are warned that if they don't do exactly as they are told, their families will be killed, one family member every time they cause trouble. We're told the girls are kept in comfortable accommodation, fed well, looked after so that they always look their best, because they charge big bucks for their services."

"Do you have a photograph or a description of this girl?"

"Yeah, Magda pulled a photo off her social media page, we'll ping it over to you now."

"Joe, can you send that photograph of Irena to Tony."

"OK, Rob, I'll circulate it, see what we get back. We've got the houses under surveillance and the plan is to hit them simultaneously. The girls are all chaperoned when they are out but they are normally all in the houses in the mornings so we'll go in at nine am tomorrow."

"Sounds as if you've got things well under control, Tony. Let me know if you get anything on Irena."

"Will do and thanks again, Rob, you and the others did a first class job yesterday and we've tidied up all the messy bits."

"Oh, by the way, Europol want to talk to Magda. They wanted us to send her back to Hamburg for a debrief but we said no. They should come to us, she's here now and I don't see the need for her to go there, she's been through enough. They eventually agreed, two officers will fly over tomorrow evening to talk to her the next morning. We might be better to put her into a hotel in London tonight and tomorrow so they can meet with her there."

"Why don't we keep her and Kasia here. We can pick up the Europol guys at the airport and bring them out here. They can use our conference room"

"Sounds like a plan, Rob. I'll let you have their flight details when I get them. I'll tell them what we have agreed. Talk to you later."

Tony ended the call and Rob swung round in his chair to where Magda, Kasia and the others were sitting waiting to hear the outcome of the call.

"OK, as soon as Tony hears anything he will get back to us. She is likely to be in one of five houses, anywhere from London to Aberdeen. They're going to hit all of these tomorrow morning when they say there is the best chance of all the girls and their guards being at home. So, fingers crossed."

The others all nodded their understanding, but sat quietly.

Rob explained the arrangement for Europol to interview

Magda at Bourne End. He got Magda's agreement that she was happy for herself and Kasia to stay over for two nights and meet with Europol there.

"I'll get Tom Johnson to pick up these guys in London the morning after next. Let me know when we get their flight details," Joe said.

"Good idea, Joe"

"OK, you guys seem to have everything under control here, so Sharon and I will head for home I think," Andy Savage said, rising to his feet.

"You want I come back to the office in the morning, Sir Andrew?" Kasia asked tentatively.

"No. no, not at all. You take a couple of days and get Magda sorted out. I'll see you when you're ready to come back, Kasia. Magda, I hope you get things sorted out with the authorities and get settled here in the UK, I think you've earned that if nothing else."

Rob followed Sir Andrew through to the house where Justine and Sharon Savage were sitting at the kitchen table with Alan Brodie, looking at some photographs on his laptop.

"Alan's just showing us some photographs of his house in Puerto Ricas," Sharon said, "looks lovely, right on the beach, the lucky devil. I think we should go over for a girlie week, Tina,if these two won't take us."

"You'd be welcome any time, ladies" Brodie laughed, "with or without these guys."

"Come on you," Andy Savage prompted his wife, "time we headed home, your housework and washing will be piling up," he teased.

"Uncle Andy, you chauvinist," Justine prodded his arm playfully.

"You're a braver man than me, Andy," Rob ventured. "I wouldn't dare say things like that when I was in range of my wife's backhand."

All four laughed as they made for the door. Rob and Justine saw the Savages to their car and waved them off before returning to Alan Brodie in the kitchen.

When they got back, Brodie was just finishing a conversation on his phone.

"Sorry guys, just fixing up my flight home."

"So, Almeria's your home now is it, Al?" Rob enquired.

"That's where my hat is for the time being. I haven't stayed in Kenmore for ages and I still haven't decided whether I'm going to keep it or not. I'll probably end up selling it, I think. I used to be indecisive, Rob, now I'm not so sure!

Anyway, my flight's at six twenty, morning after next, so I'm going to head into London, do a bit of shopping and have a few red wines, bottles that is and just stay at one of the airport hotels."

"Sounds like your sorted, mate. You'll stay for lunch though, yeah?"

"OK, why not, I'm a man of leisure now, no great rush to go anywhere, if that's OK with Tina"

"Sure, of course it is, I was just going to do a giant Ploughmans and let everyone help themselves. How does that sound."

Justine got nods and positive noises all round so set to work doing the preparations, with some help from Kasia and Magda. Ham was sliced, cheese was cut, hard boiled eggs quartered, bread sliced, apples cut, Branson pickle and side salad added. All of this was placed in the middle of the kitchen table and everyone sitting around helping themselves. Rob produced a chilled bottle of New Zealand Sauvignon Blanc and a Malbec Reserva.

The conversation was spontaneous and easy, continuing long after the food had gone and coffee cups had been emptied. Kasia had by now become more relaxed in Joe and Rob's company. She was showing great interest in Alan Brodie and his new Spanish, beachfront villa. Magda was also looking more comfortable with her surroundings and was sharing her sisters interest in Brodie, who was in turn relishing, if not encouraging the female attention.

Joe, Justine and Rob slowly became spectators to the conversation of the others and took great delight in silently acknowledging the scenario to each other with nods, smiles and shakes of the head.

Rob and Justine were stacking the dishwasher when Rob's mobile rang. The display showed Tony Urquhart as the caller.

"Got to take this, Tina, he whispered as he made his way back through to the office as he answered the call.

"Tony, twice in one day, I am honoured."

"Don't get used to it mate, very special circumstances"

"OK!"

"Yes, we're pretty sure we know where Irena Lukic is."

"You always did know how to get a man's attention, Tony.

"A house in Northland Square, just off Holland Park Avenue in London. Two separate detainees have given us that address and it's an address we're very much aware of and will be hitting at nine o'clock tomorrow morning. Given your interest in Irena, we wondered if you wanted to head up the Holland Park team?"

"Oh, you better believe it,Tony, of course I do, thanks mate."

"Good, we've got a surveillance team in place at the moment. We've got boots on the ground and we're using a couple of small drone mounted cameras to watch the rear of the property. The guys are live streaming pictures to us and will do so until we are ready to go in. I'll send you over a secure link. The Met were made aware and they've given us a couple of their top armed response units. Have a look at what we're doing. If you think you can improve anything, let me know."

"How do you propose to enter the building in the morning?"

"Take down the front door."

"Do we know how secure that is, it may well be reinforced?"

"Don't know, Rob"

"OK, maybe that's not the best way. If we try to break down a reinforced door and fail, these guys could wreak havock with the girls while we're trying to gain access and we could end up counting bodies instead of rescuing hostages. Maybe we could try delivering a parcel for Mr Kovac. Get them to open the door."

"Yeah, do you think that would work? Are they really just going to open the door, just like that?"

"Don't know, but even if they just show us how secure the door is it would help. We would have a "persuader" standing by if all else fails. I think it might just work. Bear in mind, they are not expecting us and they are all shit scared of Kovac. We try to deliver a package to him, they're not going to tell us to "naff off". Explain that one to Mr Kovac when he asks for his parcel "Oh that parcel Mr Kovac, sorry we told him to stick it!""

"True. OK, sounds like a plan, Rob. I'll send you the relevant files and the link to the live feed. I've told Tom Parker to expect a call from you."

"Oh, you did, did you?" Robb chided.

"Course I did, you were never going to knock this one back." Urquhart laughed and ended the call.

"Cheeky sod!" Rob said to no one in particular, smiling as he tossed his phone onto his desk.

"Who is?" Joe's voice came from the doorway behind Rob.

"Tony Urquhart is."

Rob explained.

41

Rob and Joe talked over the latest development and while Joe downloaded the files, Rob went back through to the house.

As Rob entered the kitchen, the two sisters were still sitting at the table listening intently to Brodie.

Magda looked up as Rob approached and saw the hard expression on his face.

"What is it? Something has happened. Have they found Irena?"

"They think she is being held in a house in London."

"How sure are they?"

"Sure enough, they have confirmation from more than one source. NCA has asked us to front the strike to get the girls out and shut down their operation at that house."

"We should go now!" Magda jumped to her feet.

"No. The strike is planned for tomorrow morning. All their houses are being hit simultaneously and there is no "we". You are going nowhere young lady."

"I am coming with you. She is my friend, I need to know she is safe. It is why I got involved with Europol."

"Absolutly not Magda," Rob was adamant.

"Tell you what," Brodie's soft West Perthshire accent interjected. " If you let Magda come along, at a distance of course, I'll pop round before I head to the airport, just to make sure you're OK, you understand."

Rob, thought for a moment, "You'll come with us?"

"Sure!"

"OK, if you want to 'pop round' on your way to the airport, I'm sure we could find something for you to do."

"Magda, you can come along but stay well out of the way. It's going to be difficult to get this done without friendly casualties and with all due respect, I won't have time to babysit anyone. Is that clear."

"Clear." Magda replied quickly, taken aback by the sudden change in Rob's attitude.

"OK, Al, you better come through and see the stuff Tony Urquhart has sent."

The two men strode through to the office where Joe was saving files and connecting to live feeds from the NCA surveillance team.

Northland Square was a three sided street with a one way system in operation. The fourth side of the square was Holland Park Rd.

Rob brought up streetview on his computer screen and they did a virtual drive around the square. They discussed what they were seeing, then did a couple more circuits to get a better picture of the surroundings.

The house in question was a terraced property close to the northwest corner of the square. It had four wide steps from the pavement to the front door. A narrow lane which ran the length of the square gave access to the rear of the property through a single pedestrian gate. The back garden was enclosed on all three sides by a seven foot high wall.

Rob, Joe and Brodie studied the property and the surrounding area and made numerous calls to Tom Parker, who was on site. Rob told Parker of his plan to gain access to the house and between the four of them, they developed a plan to access the property and release the girls held hostage within.

Parker's team had established a utilities contractor's site on the opposite side of the Square from the target house and had men working under a manhole cover surrounded by yellow waterproof screens. The area adjacent to the manhole had orange and white, "no parking cones" along the kerbside. Their white Transit van was also the hub for the electronic surveillance, co-ordinating the data being sent to it by the cameras and microphones sited in the van itself. A Volkswagen Passat, sitting close to the northwest corner, was manned by two NCA officers and a small device which had been secreted via the back gate of the property.

"OK, Tom, lets break down the works site tonight, ditch the Passat and replace it with something else. I need you to drive round to the front of the house and put out a line of your "no parking" cones and disappear. Tomorrow morning, about 8.45, go back in the van, park up where your cones are and make as if you're about to set up a work site opposite the house. We'll arrive with a yellow Sprinter van at nine o'clock sharp to attempt to gain access to the house. At that time have your guys ready to follow us in on my command."

The team spent the next hour going over "what ifs", carrying out a risk assessment of the plan to throw up danger areas and ways to manage the risks. Rob then hung up and looked at his two friends.

"That went well. Looks like we have two Met officers plus an Armed Response Team covering the back, four NCA officers plus us three hitting the front of the house."

"I thought it was just you and me, mate, I was lookin' forward to some real fisticuffs tomorrow, but all these guys'll take the fun out of it," Brodie complained bitterly.

"Do you know what, Al, I could almost believe you," Rob laughed.

Joe shook his head at the two men, gathered his things and said that he was going to head for home to see Suzi and his family, agreeing to meet the other two back at the house at six o'clock the next morning.

"Let's go and see if we can get something to eat, Al. You'd be as well to stay over again tonight." Rob suggested, shutting down his laptop. The two were met by a barrage of questions from Magda who wanted to know the ins and outs of the operation.

"Magda, all you need to know is that Joe and I will be driving over in the morning with a big yellow van. Al will take you in his car, park away from the action and you will stay in that car until we come back to you, hopefully with Irena. You will take no part in the operation itself, you will stay there in Al's car. Is that clear Magda?"

"Yes, that is clear."

"Good."

Rob's mood changed. As if someone had flicked a switch, the hard, professional, determined Rob became the Rob that most people knew - amiable, funny and likeable, the Rob that Justine lived with and had married, but she had witnessd the other Rob before and was still frightened by it.

"Man could starve to death in this house, Al, nobody would care, I tell you"

"Surrounded by all these beautiful women, Rob, I could think of worse ways to die."

"Very funny, Mr Brodie and don't encourage my husband, he doesn't need you at his back. As it happens, we three have just ordered a selection of pizzas and they should be here soon. So you, Mr MacLaine, I think, owe us all an apology, so you can do the honours with some drinks to make amends."

"Did you see that ladies, the secret to a happy marriage, always let you wife's friends think she's the boss."

Justine turned and slapped his arm, "Don't you..."

"Saved by the bell," Rob laughed, retrieving a corkscrew from a drawer and handing that and a bottle of wine to Brodie, as he went to answer the doorbell, returning with an armful of pizza boxes.

The group scoffed the pizzas as if they hadn't seen food for a week and washed them down with a few glasses of wine. Rob and Brodie, conscious of their task in the morning, drank very little.

"Best thing about a meal like this, is that all we need to wash up is a pizza cutter and a few wine glasses" Justine remarked as she stacked the empty pizza boxes and took them out to the recycle bin.

The five sat for a while, their discussion eventually turning to Magda's hopes and plans for the future. She would like to stay with Kasia at her flat in London, provided she was able to get a visa and was allowed to stay in the country. Her hope was to look for a job and get her life back on track. Although she had been through a terrible ordeal with the people smugglers she came across as a very resilient young woman.

As they all made moves for bed, Magda turned to Rob, who was lingering in the kitchen.

"What if Kovac is at the house in the morning, Rob?"

"He won't be, Magda. You don't need to worry about that."

"But, what if he is?"

"Trust me, he won't be."

"How do you know that, you cannot be sure that he will not be." Magda began to sound agitated.

"Yes, I can."

"How? How can you be so sure?"

"Because Zlatan Kovac is dead, Magda."

"What? How.." A look of total disbelief crossed her face.

"He was killed in a motorcycle accident yesterday."

"Yesterday, why did you not tell me?"

"He was killed during an operation we were undertaking for the National Crime Agency which is covered by the Official Secrets Act. I shouldn't even be telling you this now, I would get into big trouble if you repeat what I have just told you. I mean it, Magda, I could go to prison for contravening the act or at best lose my business."

Magda, shocked raised her hands to her face,

"Dead! You are sure?"

"Yes, I saw the incident myself and his body was cremated last night. I can assure you, he is dead."

Magda began to visibly shake, tears running down her face.

"Then I am safe. I can live again as normal person."

"Rob?" Justine, stood by the kitchen door, "What's wrong?"

"I've just told Magda that Zlatan Kovac, who was the boss of the people smuggling network and who had Magda kidnapped from the hospital is dead. He was killed in a motorcycle incident yesterday and, Justine, this goes no further than us three. Official Secrets and all that. Not even Kasia or Andy Savage should be told or I could get into real trouble."

"Oh my God, Rob. How, what happened?"

"If I told you, I would need to kill you," Rob smiled, "and I don't want to do that. Seriously, Tina, I'm not at liberty to say"

"Are you OK, Magda," Justine put her arms round her, she was starting to gather herslf from the shock of hearing of Kovac's death.

"Go and sleep well, knowing what you know. All we need to do now is get your friend back tomorrow and it's happy ever after time," Rob suggested to Magda.

Kasia appeared at Magda's side. "What is wrong?" she asked with a worried frown.

"Rob was just telling me how dangerous tomorrow could be

for Irena. I didn't think of it that way. It upset me, Kasia." Magda, looked over at Rob, who nodded slightly.

With everyone off to bed, Justine and Rob finally switched off the lights and went up to their bedroom.

As they got ready for bed, Justine turned to Rob.

"Did you kill Kovac, Rob?"

"I was nowhere near him when he died, none of us were."

"So, you had nothing to do with his death."

"Justine, you know I can't talk about work issues like this. Suffice to say that none of us were anywhere near him when he came off his motorbike."

Justine thought for a moment as Rob kissed her goodnight then stroked his head as he lay beside her.

"The end justifies the means once more."

Rob snuggled in, "You may say that, but I couldn't possibly comment. Goodnight darling."

42

At six thirty the next morning, Joe and Rob reversed their yellow Mercedes Sprinter, which they had acquired second hand from one of the major van rental companies, out of one of the garages at the side of the house. They used this as a surveillance vehicle when required and had embellished it with dark grey HMC logos on both sides.

They packed the operational equipment they knew they would need, including a large, heavy cardboard box which Joe would attempt to deliver to the house in Northland Square

Brodie and Magda watched as they got the van ready.

"What is HMC?" Magda enquired.

"Harper MacLaine Couriers," Rob replied.

"Or, Harper MacLaine Construction," Joe suggested.

"Or Harper MacLaine Contracting," Rob added."But today, we're Harper MacLaine Couriers. Joe is going to deliver a parcel to Zlatan Kovac."

"Al's going to park at some shops, just round the corner from Northland Square, we'll pick him up from there and he and I will travel to Northland Square in the back of the van with Joe driving. You, young lady, will stay in the car. It that understood?"

"Yes, understood."

"Good, we've got plenty of time so we will have a recce of the area when we get there Just to make sure everything is as it should be and we all understand the operation. You travel with Al and we'll see you both in Holland Park."

At six forty, Rob watched as Magda and Brodie left in his rental car and jumped into the van with Joe.

"OK, lets go get the bad guys."

The drive to Holland Park was relatively quiet and uneventful, the M40/A40 traffic was kind to them and by quarter to eight, they were parked outside a row of shops on Holland Park Avenue, behind Brodie's hired Audi.

"Magda, you stay here, we're going to have a look at the house and see how the NCA guys are getting on with their roadworks and parking cones, We won't be long."

Magda nodded silently.

The three men walked along to Northland Square, crossing to the far side of the gardens and using the mature chestnut trees and rhododendron bushes as partial cover. They walked up the opposite side of Northland Square from where the target house was situated. The big trees swayed slightly as the fresh breeze rustled through their upper branches. As they walked, taking care not to stare at the property when they were exposed, rather than hidden by the rhododendron bushes. The white NCA van was parked almost opposite the target house by the north west corner of the Square, the section of road outside the house had been cleared of parked cars by the orange and white traffic cones laid out as instructed by Rob. Four men dressed in Hi-Viz waistcoats over blue coveralls were milling noisily around the area near the van. All looked normal to the three men surveying the scene through the bushes and should not cause any unrest or suspicion to watchers in the target house.

Satisfied that all was ready for the nine o'clock arrival of the parcel delivery van, Rob led the others back to the parked van and Brodie's rental car where a very agitated Magda was sitting.

Rob called Tom Parker. "Tom, Rob MacLaine. Just been round to Northland Square to have a look at the target house. Everything looks pretty normal with your guys. Is the plan still to hit all the properties at 9am?"

"Yes, no change to that, Rob."

"OK, can we agree that it is now, 8.34?"

"Agreed."

"From 5 minutes to nine, can you ensure that traffic is not allowed into your "no parking" area. At one minute to nine you will see a bright yellow Mercedes Sprinter van with the grey logo HMC on the sides of it, turn into Northland Square and it will stop outside the premises. At that point Joe Harper will get out of the van, walk round to the side door and extract a large box which he will attempt to deliver to the house. The minute the door opens we will be out of the side door of the van and up those steps to the front door, you guys need to be right there with us. The door opens, you move, fast. Once in the house, your guys clear the ground floor and basement, you and I will take the first floor and Joe Harper and Alan Brodie the second. Can you repeat that to me please, Tom."

Parker repeated Rob's instructions almost word for word.

"Excellent, thanks, Tom. OK, we'll see you in a few minutes."

The next fifteen minutes passed slowly. The three men made their final preparations, watched by a very nervous Magda. Rob made sure that they all understood their roles and the roles of the others, finally tucking supressed Heckler & Koch pistols into the waistband of their trousers. Rob and Brodie got into the rear of the van and Joe closed the large sliding door. He looked across at Magda, nodded to her and gave her a thumbs up before pointing at Brodie's car as he walked round the van and turned to step into the driver's seat of the yellow van. He didn't fasten his seat belt, delivery drivers rarely did. He began to watch the flow of traffic in his wing mirror, ensuring that he was able to pull out out from the kerb and safely join the traffic when necessary.

Rob checked with Tom Parker that everything was as planned at their end and no nasty surprises were in store for them just around the corner.

Ninety seconds before nine o'clock, he pulled the van away from the kerb and approached Northland Square.

43

ROB AND BRODIE CROUCHED UNCOMFORTABLY IN THE BACK OF THE van as it turned quickly into Northlands Square as Joe accelerated toward the target house, slowing as he approached, making a play of checking the house numbers, eventually stopping outside the correct house. He switched off the engine, leaving the radio playing loudly in the cab, ran round to the nearside of the van and slid the large side door open. He said nothing to his colleagues as he scooped up the bulky box addressed to Kovac and made his way to the front door of the house, taking great care not to drop the box.

He rang the doorbell, then knocked loudly on the door. Rob and Brodie braced themselves for action, waiting for the door to open.

For a minute there was no response. Joe rang the bell again and as he made to knock on the door, a voice could be heard from the intercom.

"Who is it, what do you want?"

"Got a parcel for Mr Kovac, mate."

"For who?"

"Mr Kovac."

"Just leave it on the doorstep"

"Sorry, mate, can't do that, man wants a signature. I need someone to sign for it or I need to take it away. Any time your ready mate, it's a bit on the 'eavy side, know what I mean?"

"OK, I come"

Joe heard the rattle of a door chain and the turning of keys in locks and the door swung open. Joe had leant the box against the door and as it opened, Joe and the box almost literally fell into the front hall, knocking the man on the other side off his feet and sending him sprawling to the floor. The man had a firearm but before he could bring it to bear, Joe pulled the Heckler Koch from his waistband and shot him twice in the chest.

As he did this, Joe was conscious of Brodie, Rob and then others running past him into the house. The NCA officers began to clear the ground floor and basement of the house, Rob and Tom Parker headed to the first floor. As Joe regained his footing he quickly followed Alan Brodie to the second floor where they began to clear the house, room by room.

There were shouts of "Armed Police, everyone on the floor!", from all floors of the house. Other loud voices were heard, in what Rob recognised in the melee to be Eastern European. Rob could hear skuffles and gunshots as the rooms were accessed and cleared. He could hear screams and banging of doors as they were sent crashing hard against the walls of the rooms they belonged to, having been kicked open by the NCA officers or Harper MacLaine personnel.

Tom Parker kicked open the last room door on the first floor, Rob stepped into the entrance, knelt in the doorway his handgun held in both hands, arms outstretched. The room looked empty as Tom Parker strode past him. Suddenly a man appeared from behind the unmade double bed, fired at Parker hitting him in the right shoulder and spinning him round. Rob fired twice at the man, hitting him just above his right eye, the second bullet passing through his throat. The man fell back and disappeared behind the bed, dead before he hit the floor.

Rob looked down at the wounded Parker, who was holding his shoulder moaning in pain.

"Tom, how badly are you hit?

"I'll live," Parker replied wincing in pain as he tried to rise.

Rob bent to help him to his feet, "Easy, mate."

Suddenly the doors of a built-in wardrobe burst open and a tall man, dressed only in a pair of garish shorts stood, aiming a pistol at Rob, catching him unawares trying to help Parker. Rob pushed Parker back to the floor and swung round to fire at the man, knowing he was too late to get his shot off first.

Rob heard the shot, but was amazed not to be feeling pain. Suddenly the man's gun fell and he slumped back into the wardrobe, blood oozing from a large hole in his left upper chest. Rob turned in disbelief, there holding a Glock pistol in both outstretched hands was Magda Petric.

"Thought I told you to stay in the car!"

"I stay in car, maybe you be dead now"

"Where the hell did you get a gun?"

"On floor downstairs, nobody else want it. I know how to use guns. Europol give me small arms training. They said I was good." Magda explained.

Rob looked over at the dead man in the wardrobe. "Can't argue with that!"

During this exchange Joe and Brodie arrived on the scene.

"Second floor clear Rob, Joe advised, "we have two men cable tied and one dead. No girls though."

"We got two dead and one of ours walking wounded." Rob reported.

"Let's check the ground and basement, Al. Joe can you see to Tom, don't think its too serious but best to get him proper medical attention.

"What about 'Annie Get Your Gun' here? " Brodie gestured

at Magda. "Looks like any girls must be down stairs. It would make sense, no windows overlooking other property or the street."

"Come on Magda, lets see if we can find your mate" Rob suggested.

"Might be an idea if I take the gun, Magda," he added

Magda handed Rob the Glock, which he slid into the waistband of his jeans, then followed the two men down the wide stairway to the ground floor.

"What is 'Annie Get Your Gun'?" she asked Rob on the way down.

"Famous American musical, he's just trying to be funny." Rob laughed.

At the bottom of the stairs, Rob encountered two Metropolitan Police firearms officers.

"We got two of them trying to get away through the rear exit, but we had it covered and they're in the room over there cuffed and awaiting NCA instructions," the smaller of the two officers reported.

"Great, thanks, for your support, guys"

"Oh, you might want to take charge of this, " Rob added, retrieving the Glock and handing it to one of the officers. " Magda found it on the floor

"Did you find any of the girls?" Magda asked.

"Far as I know, they're all down in the basement, miss"

Without any hesitation, Magda headed for the stairs leading down to the basement, Rob and Brodie followed.

The basement had been divided into two good sized rooms, each had four single beds, three small bedside cabinets, a dressing table and little other furniture except for a set of built-in wardrobes. Both rooms had en-suite toilets and showers. The small, high level, barred windows with opaque glass panels allowed no views to the outside and very little light into the rooms.

There were six young women either standing or sitting in the first of the two rooms, all looking very distraught and disorientated by the events of the past ten or fifteen minutes.

Magda stood at the doorway searching for her friend, without success. She looked at Brodie, standing beside her.

"She's not here, Al"

"You sure?"

Before Magda could answer, the door to the toilet opened and a tall, slim, dark haired girl walked into the room.

She looked toward the door and her hands flew to her mouth. "Magda?"

Magda, ran across the room, "Irena, I thought we had lost you."

The two girls hugged each other, tears of joy streaming down their faces.

"Magda, they told me you were working for them, I told them no, but they were so sure that you were." Irena sobbed.

"I was working for the Police, Irena, to try to trap them and to find you. Everything that happened, I reported back to Europol, then somehow they found out what I was doing. They drugged me and brought me to the UK. They try to kill me, but these men, they save me and found out where you were. We are all free now, free and safe."

Irena Lukic looked over at Rob and Brodie, disbelief on her face.

"Free and safe?"

"Free and safe, Irena. The gang who brought you here is no more. Most of them have been arrested, others are dead, including the man at the top. All we need to do is get everyone's details for immigration and either you should be able to stay here if you want, or you can go back to Hamburg, or wherever." Rob promised all the young women in the room.

Rob's phone rang, "Tony, has Tom debriefed you?"

"Yes, he has, Rob, congratulations. Tells me he has a large scratch on his upper arm. Did you find Irena Petric?"

"Yeah, about five minutes ago."

"Good. Other good news is that we hit all the other houses at nine o'clock this morning as planned. You guys in London plus Manchester, Edinburgh, Glasgow and Aberdeen, we got the lot, they all came up trumps. Looks like it was only you guys and Edinburgh that came up against armed resistance. We've arrested thirty four of their people and freed thirty six girls, all unharmed. We're bringing them down to one of our training centres in Surrey for processing. I know that sounds all very cold and impersonal, Rob, but is the best way to do this. We find out who they all are, where they're from, family details and what they want to do from here then try to make that happen for them. We'll also have them checked out medically, make sure they are all clean and clear. That includes Irena Petric. It would be helpful if Magda would come too, she knows some of the girls, Irena included, obviously."

"I'll ask, I'm pretty sure she will though."

"Thanks for looking after Tom, Rob. He's a good guy, I wouldn't want to lose him, so thanks for being there for him."

"He'd do the same for me, Tony. That's what these situations are all about, having people with you that you can rely on."

"I know, but thanks anyway. Listen, need to go, but we'll talk later."

Joe Harper joined his colleagues in the basement as Rob was ending the call to Tony Urquhart.

"All OK down here?"

"Yeah, that was Tony. All the houses were hit this morning and all the girls have been accounted for and are OK. The bad guys are all in custody, so it's job done. How's Tom?"

"He's a lucky boy, the Paramedics say, there's no major damage to his arm and he should make a full recovery. They've just now taken him to A&E as a precautionary measure and to get a permanent dressing on the wound."

"Just spoke to Charlie Best from NCA, we met him on Achravie. He said they have a minibus on it's way here to pick up the girls and the Met guys are taking their prisoners to the local nick for processing."

Rob explained the plan to take all the girls to the NCA training centre in Surrey and the reasons behind that decision. He told Magda that Irena would need to go with the others and suggested that she might want to go with her. She agreed enthusiastically, seemingly unwilling to be parted from her friend and former flatmate.

Over the next hour or so, the house in Northland square was a hive of activity as the Metropolitan Police gathered all the uninjured prisoners together and shipped them out to a police station of the NCA's choice. An ambulance took two others with gunshot wounds to hospital under police escort and the two bodies from the first floor of the house were removed in a black van.

The NCA's minibus arrived amidst all of the activity and the girls were shepherded on board with as much of their belongings as they could manage.

Rob had allowed Magda to call Kasia to let her know that everything had gone well and that they had found Irena Petric safe and well. She was also able to tell her that she was going to go to the the NCA training centre with Irena for a few days to lend support to her friend.

"I take it you don't need me any more?" Alan Brodie's voice brought Rob back into the room.

"Sorry? Yes, I mean no, no I don't, if you need to get off Al. I think we've put all this to bed, once and for all and I appreciate your sticking around. We'd have struggled without you, to be fair."

"Speaking of which, I told Tony Urquhart that the big fat

cheque he promised for dealing with the man we can't talk about, would be split equally between, Ryan, Joe, you and me, so once we settle on a figure, Joe'll send you a contract for some consultancy work and if you send him an invoice, he'll pay your share into the bank account you state on your invoice."

"Oh brilliant, that'll help to buy me my bar in Spain."

"What bar in Spain?"

"I fancy a bar somewhere close to where I've bought the house. There's a couple of nice sites fairly close by and I'm keeping an eye open for the right opportunity."

"Oh, hey, house by the sea, your own bar on your doorstep, we're definitely gonn'a visit you now, big buddy. Let me know how you get on."

"Yeah, will do and you keep in touch. Right, I better get this rental back to the car hire company, I'm sure they must think I've nicked it."

"OK, go for it big pal, see you again soon."

Rob and Brodie met in a giant bearhug before Brodie waved across to Joe and strode off down Northland Square to retrieve his rented Audi.

"One of life's real characters is Captain Brodie!" Joe appeared at Rob's shoulder.

"Oh yes. He's all that and more, Joe."

"So, we going to take the yellow peril back to the ranch before we get a parking ticket?"

"Good thinking Batman, lets hit the road."

Rob and Joe said their goodbyes to Magda, checked out with the NCA team and left.

44

Joe drove the yellow van into the spacious garage at the side of the Harper MacLaine office, tossed the keys over to Rob, who closed then locked the roller shutter door.

The two men walked across to the office and went inside, Rob carrying a large holdall containing the guns and unused ammunition. Ryan Hughes looked up as they entered.

"So all went well then?"

"All pretty much as planned, Ryan."

"Good"

Ryan waved then returned to his computer monitor. Rob put the holdall into the large office safe, wandered over to the coffee machine in the office's small kitchen area, popped in a capsule, then pressed the button for a cup of strong, black coffee. As the coffee filtered through, he gestured over to the other two, both shook their heads at Rob's offer.

"I didn't see Justine's car outside when we drove in." Rob remarked.

Ryan replied without lifting his head from his screen, "She's taken Kasia back to her flat, left a couple of hours ago."

"OK, I'll give her a call."

Rob strolled out to the car park, phone in one hand, coffee in the other.

Justine's phone rang ten times then went to voicemail. Rob didn't need to count, he'd set it up to give Justine time to find her phone at the bottom of her handbag then answer it.

"Hi this is Justine, sorry I can't take your call just now but if you leave a number, I'll get back to you as soon as I can," Rob smiled as he listened.

"Hey you! Where are you hiding now? Give me a call back when you can. Love you."

Rob ended the call, walked back toward the office, stopped at the doorway and turned back to the car parking area and front gardens of the house. He looked over the extensive gardens and thought how easily he has settled into the lifestyle he and Justine now enjoyed. He had never envisaged living in a semi-rural environment like Bourne End, but the minute they had walked into her parents' house, as it was then, he just fell in love with it, the area and its riverside location.

He sat at his desk and booted up his laptop. As the screen came to life, his phone started to play Derek and the Dominoes "Layla", Justine's ringtone.

"Hey gorgeous, how you doin'?"

"Hi, where are you?"

"In the office. You?"

"M40, about 20 minutes away."

"Did you get Kasia home OK?"

"Yes, no problem, she's a lot happier now that Magda and her friend are safe. Listen, your timing is spot on as usual, I've had a call from Lorna. She says the contractors have just finished the landscaping on Kintyre View and they'll finish Arran View by the end of the week. We both wondered if you fancied a weekend on Achravie? "

"Actually, that's not a bad idea, after the week I've had, I could do with a bit of R and R. OK, I'll book us flights, we could go up on Friday and back down Sunday."

"OK, I'll leave that to you. See you shortly" Justine ended the call as Rob swung round in his highback chair and logged into the BA website to book the flights to Glasgow, the ferry to Arran and a rental car.

Joe updated Ryan on the days events before he packed up his laptop, said his good nights and made his way out to his wheelchair adapted car.

"We were lucky today, Rob. I always hated clearing buildings like that. Too many unknowns. Too many men hiding in wardrobes."

"Yeah, you're right, we were lucky, I was lucky. If Magda hadn't been behind me, who knows"

Joe winked and smiled, "I won't tell Tina if you don't," he said heading for the door.

Rob smiled back at his friend, "Deal."

"Oh, by the way, Joe, speaking of Tina, we're heading up to Achravie this weekend. Flying up to Glasgow on Friday, heading back Sunday."

"OK. How are things progressing with the chalets?"

"Pretty well, that's what we're going up to see. The chalets are all finished and they're just completing the landscaping, Tina wants to have a look before the contractors disappear off site"

"Oh, right, so you're not going up for a holiday, you're going to be working hard all weekend. Oh, look Ryan's taken the violin with him, what a shame!"

"Sod off home and annoy that poor wife and Scottish child of your's," Rob laughed.

"My wife's lucky and she knows it."

"Not what she told me, pal."

Joe laughed and waved as he walked out of the office.

45

Friday early afternoon, BA flight1484 rose into the air from the runway at Heathrow airport and in what seemed like no time at all, the captain announced that they had started their descent into Glasgow. One hour and ten minutes terminal to terminal.

Both had decided to carry only cabin luggage, so came straight downstairs to the car rental office, collected a white Mercedes C Class and headed for the ferry at Ardrossan.

Weather in the west of Scotland around May time can be some of the best of the year and the journey from Ardrossan to Achravie was blessed with bright blue skys and a slight breeze. The sleeping warrior, as the profile of the island of Arran has been described, closed in on the ferry as it approached the island, only to be replaced by the grandure of Goat Fell. The scenery was resplendent in the late Spring sunshine as they sailed and drove from Ardrossan to Hillcrest House, arriving as the sun was setting behind the Mull of Kintyre, turning the skyline a burnt orange tinted red, topped by a narrow strip of bright duck-egg blue.

Justine had texted Lorna to let her know they were on the

Achravie ferry, so both she and Fraser were waiting at the front entrance to the house to greet Justine and Rob as they drew up on the gravel at the front of the house.

Lorna ran down the steps to meet them as Justine jumped out of the car, the two women hugged and greeted each other. Fraser walked down behind Lorna and Rob got out of the car to meet Fraser. Rob gave Fraser a brief hug and shook his hand, then turned to Lorna.

"This is becoming a habit Rob MacLaine." She threw her arms around him as Rob lifted her off her feet.

"A good habit," Rob replied, laughing, "your're looking good, the pair of you."

Rob moved to the back of the car to retrieve their weekend bags as Fraser and Justine greeted each other with a hug, Fraser now blushing slightly with mild embarrasment.

Despite her protestations, Justine had managed to persuade Lorna not to go to the trouble of cooking dinner at Hillcrest but to book a table for them all that evening at the Red Lion.

"When's dinner booked for, Lorna" Rob enquired as they walked, chatting as they went, up the front steps and into the spacious entrance hall of the house.

"Half past seven, is that OK?"

"Yeah, ideal. That gives us a bit of time for a quick freshen up before we head down, eh Tina?"

"Fine by me. I'll put on something a bit warmer, I think. That clear sky probably means it'll probably get chillier tonight."

Forty minutes later, the four climbed into one of the Hillcrest Land Cruisers with Lorna at the wheel heading for the Red Lion. The car buzzed with enthusiastic conversation as Justine and Rob were given the headline news of the progress with the project.

The Red Lion was relatively busy, as the group walked in. The atmosphere was convivial and welcoming as allways, the hum of conversation and sounds of laughter emanating from all corners of the building. The tall figure of Hamish Allen stood behind the bar pouring a pint of Guinness for one of his customers whilst regailing him for his choice of jacket, in his usual jocular manner.

"That's a really nice jacket yer wearing, Moray, I'd hang on to that, it'll come back into fashion eventually,"

Rob stood looking around while Lorna went to find their table. "Good to be home," he thought with a degree of satisfaction, "Good to be home!"

His thoughts were interrupted as Lorna returned with Lizzie Allen. Lizzie threw her arms around Rob's neck and pulled him to her. "Oh Robbie, it's so good to see you. How long are you here for?"

"Just the weekend Lizzie, we head back on Sunday."

"For goodness sake, Lizzie pit the man doon, ye dinnae ken where he's bin!" Hamish shouted, laughing, as he crossed the room to welcome Rob and Justine.

Lizzie slapped her father's arm as he approached, "I tell you, Dad, someone's goin' to punch your nose for your cheek one day. What's he like Robbie?"

"He's just the same old curmudgeon he was when we were just kids Lizzie. But he's like most old dogs, his bark's worse than his bite."

"How are you, you old dog?" Rob shook Hamish's hand.

"Oh, Lizzie did ye see that, he's squashed ma' fingers. I'll no be able to serve him any drinks, now."

"That fine, Dad, he can just serve himself, then."

"Oh, wait a minute, no, ma hand's getting' better as we speak. I might just be able to pour a glass o' Rioja."

"Just ignore him, come on I'll show you to your table." Lizzie chuckled, leading the way to a corner table away from the hustle and bustle of the main bar area. The reserved table was set for four.

Lizzie brought over menus and handed them round. "Usual for drinks is it?" she enquired.

"Yes, please."

"So," Rob started, "What's been happening that I should know about?"

"Well, as I said to Tina on the phone, the contractors have just finished the landscaping on Kintyre View and Arran View should be finished over the weekend. The two sites are looking good. We had a lot of rain a couple of weeks ago, really heavy and lasted for almost the whole week. That held the contractors up, but the upside was that we know that the drainage and soak-aways on both sites are more than adequate, we had no flooding at all. We can go and have a look tomorrow, I'm sure you'll both be impressed."

"The golf course is coming along well. All the landscaping, such as it was, is complete. The designer used the natural flow of the ground as much as possible so the fairways are all done. The tees and greens are being formed and then its mostly reseeding and cultivating the grass."

"When are you looking at completion, Lorna?" Justine asked.

"The contractor thinks It could be playable by about the turn of the year, although he says that we run the risk of damaging the new grass if it gets overplayed too early, so he would rather see it delayed till Easter time to be on the safe side."

"So we could open the course for Easter next year?" Rob suggested.

"No reason why not from what the contractor says."

"OK, so why don't we aim for an Easter opening. Let's see if there are any problems or hiccups with the course and do an official opening in May. When I was up last time, I spoke to the contractor about an Open Day and he suggested a tournament of some sort. Bring a few local digitaries over, some low handicap amateurs and he says he might be able to get a handful of lower ranking pros to join in for a small fee." Justine suggested.

"Are ye haen a golf shop?" Fraser asked.

"A golf shop?" Lorna repeated

"Aye, a golf shop, ye need a golf shop. Sellin' balls and tees and sweaters and bunnets wi' "Achravie Golf Club" on them. Ye could hire golf clubs and buggies maybe."

The others looked at Fraser open mouthed.

"Am a bein' daft?"

"No, your not Fraser. I think we've all been so focused on the chalets and the course itself, none of us had thought about a shop on the site, but you're right, we should have one. We may only have a par three course here but it's a good one and the two sites are both quality, so we need that to be reflected in the golfing amenities as well. It might not make us a lot of money but it should be there as a service to our golfers," Justine said.

Lorna and Rob nodded in agreement. Fraser smiled with satisfaction.

Just then, Lizzie brought their drinks and took their food orders.

"OK, so who's going to look at our golf shop?" Rob asked

"I can do that, Fraser and I can look at the site for the starters office and see if it would take a bigger building. That would be better than a separate unit." Lorna offered.

"OK, good."

46

THE TABLE THE FOUR WERE SITTING AT WAS IN A QUIET CORNER OF the bar, but still afforded a good, uninterrupted view of the room and Rob became distracted by a small group of five men standing just back from the bar. They were obviously enjoying a lads night out and were in good spirits judging by the laughter and good natured banter he could almost overhear. He was paticulaarly intrigued by a slighty overweight man, with a slight paunch and close cropped hair, who, with a pint of Guinness in hand, was sharing a tale with his companions. They were all listening intently and then burst into loud laughter.

"Lorna, is that the guy you bollocked for dropping the lodge in the wrong place the last time we were up?"

"Yeah, Andy Mackie. You spoke to him. In fact you did more than speak to him, you almost pulled his arm off, if you remember."

"Mm, I thought it was him, but he looks to have lost a bit of weight since then. What's he doing here though, surely all the heavy deliveries have been made?"

"Oh yeah, he's working with the site contractors now. The driving gig was just an agency temp thing and they paid him off once they had delivered all the units. He asked the contractors if they had any work going and they took him on, temporary again.

Don't know what you said to him that day, but he's a different man, I tell you. He works like a Trojan, turns his hand to just about anything on the site. He and Matt Smith, the site manager, get on really well apparently, it was Matt who was telling me about him. He's extremely polite and friendly to me as well, any time I come across him. It's very hard to imagine him as the surly individual we met that day."

"Really, give me a minute, guys." Rob rose from the table and walked towards the group of men. As he drew near, one or two of them turned to stare at him and Andy Mackie, who had not noticed Rob looked over at him, recognising him instantly.

"Mr MacLaine!"

Rob smiled.

"You might not remember me, Mr MacLaine, Andy..."

"Mackie, sergeant. Yes, I remember you and just came over to say hello. I was surprised to see you in here but I understand you're working up at the Arran View site."

Andy Mackie looked over at the table where Justine, Fraser and Lorna were sitting, unsure of Rob's intention.

"Oh, yes, Ms Cameron would tell you. It's OK though I'm finished this weekend, then I'm away. I hope that's not a problem, Mr MacLaine, sir."

"What would be a problem, Andy, the fact that you were working on the site or that you're finished this weekend?"

"Working on the site, sir"

"No, Andy, you working on the site isn't a problem. From what I hear you've been doin' a damned good job."

"Doin' ma best, sir. Look I'm awfa' sorry about the last time we met, really sorry, I get really embarrassed when a think aboot it. I've bin praying we wouldnae meet again. A was going through a really low time and things were getting' on top of me a bit, but that's no excuse…"

"Andy, you don't need to explain. I know first hand what places like Afghanistan can do to people. Listen, looks like my dinner's waiting for me. Good luck for the future Andy, if there's anything I can do for you, let me know."

Rob held out his hand to Mackie, who took it with an embarrassed smile and the two men shook hands.

"Thanks, Sir. A reference from you would help, Sir. I know it's a lot to ask but.."

"I'll write one out for you, bring it up to the site tomorrow, I'll leave it with Matt Smith in the office, if you're not around and stop calling me,"Sir", or I'll pull your other arm off," Rob smiled over his shoulder as he made his way back to the table.

Andy Mackie, looked at Rob unsure for a second, then laughed.

"What was all that about? What are you going to leave at the site office tomorrow?" Justine asked as Rob sat down beside her.

"Andy Mackie tonight isn't the Andy Mackie we encountered that day at the site. He apologised profusely for his behaviour that day, said he was hoping not to have to meet me again he was so embarrassed. He finishes up with the contractors this weekend and he asked if I would give him a reference for another employer. I said I would and drop it off with Matt if he wasn't around tomorrow. I feel for him, Tina, I've seen so many guys come back from war zones with severe behavioural issues, find it difficult to settle back into civilian life and hold down a proper job. Some of them end up losing their families, sleeping rough and there's not a lot of support for them."

"As I said, Matt thinks quite highly of him and his work

ethic. I've spoken to him a few times up at the site and, your right, he is very embarrassed by that day, keeps apologising to me as well. Loves it here by all accounts, brought his wife and kids over for weekends a couple of times." Lorna added.

"He's the same wi me, Robbie. Matt says he's a good worker, attention tae detail, always there tae help" Fraser added, picking up his knife and fork and addressing his plate of hot food, "I'm ready for this."

All four started eating and the conversation took second place to their meals till everyone's plate was emply. Another round of drinks helped to wash down the excellent food and as their glasses were nearing empty, Lizzie approached the table, followed closely by Calum.

"Hi, good to see you again, you're here for the weekend I hear." Calum said.

"Yes, back Sunday."

"Well, I hope you enjoyed your dinner."

"Really good, Calum, thoroughly enjoyed it. In fact we might even come back again tomorrow."

"Good," said Lizzie, "We've got something for you and a favour to ask."

"OK, you've got our attention."

"Well, this thing we've got for you, its kind of virtual, because we can't do the real bit till we get an answer to the favour we want to ask. So, we would like to invite you all to our wedding, its in the Achravie church on 3rd October at 2pm. That's the "got something for you," and the favour is, can we hire Hillcrest House for our reception?"

The four all laughed and simultaneously agreed they would attend the wedding.

"Can you *hire* Hillcrest House though? Sorry, but that's got to be a no,no." Rob looked up at the couple.

Their faces fell in disappointment.

"You can *have* Hillcrest House, you don't need to hire it for goodness sake. Just let us know what you need." Rob stood and walked round the table. He wrapped his arms around Lizzie who hugged him tightly. As the others joined in, Rob shook hands with Calum, "Welcome to the Achravie family, Calum."

47

THE NEXT MORNING WAS CHILLY. AS JUSTINE HAD ALLUDED TO the previous evening, the clear skies overnight had resulted in a sharp drop in temperature leaving a coating of shimmering, white frost glistening in the morning sun. Lorna and Fraser had met Rob and Justine at Hillcrest House for breakfast and the four had sat round the table going over plans and sketches of the Arran View and Kintyre View sites as a precursor to their planned visits.

By the time they arrived at Kintyre View, the frost was evaporating under the new warmth of the mid morning sun, creating a mist which rose in whisps from the exposed surfaces. The site was deserted, as all works had been completed by the contractors more than a week previously and their equipment had now gone, leaving only their Portakabin site office to be removed.

Lorna explained a number of points they had discussed earlier as Rob led the others on an inspection tour of the site. Standing on a raised area at the far end of Kintyre View, Rob looked down at an unfinished play area.

"This is the only part of the site that isn't finished," Lorna explained. "We made changes to this area the last time you were here. You thought that it would be a good idea to add some equipment that older children would use, rather than just swings, slides and roundabouts for young kids. We spoke to the suppliers and they suggested, climbing frames, a rope bridge and a zip slide, a kind of adventure playground. Justine and I went over their suggestions and we ordered the extra equipment from them. There was a bit of a lead time for manufacture because some of the stuff is bespoke. They reckon they will be here to install the equipment and finish the landscaping, week after next."

"Yeah, I remember we talked about that. Great, sounds good, look forward to trying it out." Rob winked. "OK, this all looks good, lets go and look at Arran View."

Twenty minutes later they climbed out of the Land Cruiser in the car park by the site office in Arran View.

This site was a hive of activity as the contractors worked to have it completed by that weekend. There were a dozen or so men still on site putting finishing touches to the development. As they approached the Portakabin office, Matt Smith came out to greet them.

"Hi folks, I heard you and Rob were here, Justine. Good to see you both again. Can I get you guys a coffee or a cup of tea?" he asked.

"Yeah, that would be good, Matt," Rob replied.

Rob looked out of the office window, checking over the site as Matt Smith prepared mugs of coffee.

"So, are they going to finish everything this weekend, Matt?" Lorna asked.

"Oh, yes, they just need to tidy up a few things and finish that run of fence at the entrance and that's it all done. We've checked the build quality of all the units. Electricity and water are all connected and working as they should. All the portable appliances have been tested, satellite TV, internet connections are all good, nice strong signals, hot-tubs are all working and the doors and windows open and lock properly. Outside, everything has been signed off as meeting all the specifications. So, yeah, good to go, which is what I'll be doing tomorrow morning."

"Oh, your leaving tomorrow?" Lorna asked.

"Yes, I'm at home till Tuesday then off to the Lake District to another site."

"OK, I hadn't realised you were away so soon."

"No, this job came up at the last minute."

"Well, it's been a pleasure working with you, Matt." Lorna replied.

"Pleasure's all mine Lorna, I've really enjoyed this project."

"Tell me about Andy Mackie, Matt." Rob asked putting down his mug.

"You know we had problems with him when he was delivering and offloading some of the units. You got involved at one stage. He made his last delivery for that company and apparently told the groundworks contractor that he was being paid off and was looking for another job. These guys were low on bodies at the time and the foreman said he would take him on, temporarily, if he came back on the Monday. He did and straight away he came in here and apologised for kicking off the way he had. He sounded genuinely sorry, but I thought, lets wait and see. Well, he's been like a different person. He works really hard, Rob. He does what he's asked, when he's asked, quite often goes the extra mile. He turns his hand to all sorts with no problem. He's apologised to Lorna, goodness knows how many times, says you and he had a chat when you were last here."

"We did have a chat, that's true. He asked me last night if I would give him a reference because he needed to find another job. I wrote him one this morning before we left Hillcrest but I wanted to check with you before I gave it to him."

"I'd have no problem giving *this* Andy Mackie a reference, in fact I was thinking I might offer him something on the site I'm going to. Better the devil you know and all that."

Lorna folded her arms and turned to Rob.

"Actually, Rob, I've been thinking about our Mr Mackie since we spoke about him last night. We're going to need a maintenance man for the sites when they're up and running, which won't be long now, not much more than a couple of months. I wondered how you would feel about offering him the job." Lorna suggested.

"A could gie him a bit o' work till he wis needed here." Fraser added.

Rob looked over at Justine. "What do you think, Tina?"

"It's not a subject I've given much thought to, but I did wonder if we could offer him something, bearing in mind what you said last night. But from what these guys are saying, it might just work for all of us, so it's a yes from me."

"OK, let's talk to him."

Rob had seen Andy Mackie working on the fence at the site entrance as they had driven in, so they made his way back there to find him.

"Andy," he shouted above the noise of the machinery, "Got a minute?" he gestured at the office and walked back toward it with Andy Mackie following.

"Eh, mornin'. I'm no in any trouble am I?" he asked on entering the office , scanning their faces.

"You asked me last night if I would give you a reference for a new employer, Andy."

"Aye, look, A'm sorry about that Mr MacLaine, I shouldn't have done that, I'd had a couple o' pints.."

"Andy, it's fine." Rob interrupted. "I've written you a reference, we all deserve a second chance." He pulled an envelope out of his jacket pocket.

"Here's your reference. But, I've another offer for you before

I give it you." Rob gestured to the others in the room." These guys have been giving me glowing reports about your application and attitude since you came to work here. They also tell me they're going to need a maintenance guy for these sites and they reckon you could do the job, if you're interested. If not I'll give you your reference and say, good luck to you."

Andy Mackie, stared at Rob, then looked at the others and back to Rob.

"What, you're offering me a job?"

"Yeah, full time and permanent, after a six months trial period."

Mackie looked at Lorna, "Seriously?"

"Seriously."

"I don't believe you." He said to Rob, a look of total incredulity on his unshaven face. "Why would you do that?"

"Cause I'm a big softie!"

"No you're not, so why would you do that?"

"Andy, I've invested a lot of time and money into this estate, but I need help from people I can rely on to make it work. I'm not sure why exactly, but based on what these guys have told me about you, I don't think you would let me down. Would you?"

"No sir, A wouldn't."

"Good, so is that a yes?"

"Yes, sir, Yes! Can I bring my wife and kids with me?"

"Of course you can, I'm sure we can get you a cottage on the estate at a reasonable rent."

"They just love it here, sir. They'll be over the moon."

"OK, so that's it, settled. Talk to Lorna and Fraser over the next few days and they'll sort out a contract and all the other details with you. Welcome on board, Andy."

"Thank you, sir." Mackie stood to attention and had to stop himself from saluting.

"Andy, what did I tell you, if you didn't stop calling me "sir?"

"You said you'd pull my other arm off."

"Right, well you're lucky, I need to get going and you've not finished that fence yet and I've already blown up one Land Cruiser." Rob nodded to Justine.

"See you next time, Andy."" Rob laughed as he turned away.

48

ROB DROVE THEM BACK TO HILLCREST HOUSE AND WHILE JUSTINE and Lorna made up a tray of sandwiches, Fraser and Rob set out some plates on the kitchen table and made a pot of tea. They then laid out some of the plans and drawings on the table and started to look at where the starter's office would be sited. They looked at whether this could be increased in size or a new, separate structure was needed to house a golf shop. Once the two ladies joined them, they discussed the options and eventually decided that the best way forward was to initially increase the size of the starters office to accommodate the shop. If the shop proved popular and needed more space another cabin similar to the originally planned office could be procured and sited adjacent to the shop.

As they worked their way through the sandwiches and tea, they looked at the printer's proofs for the sales brochures and other marketing materials. Justine also showed the others the latest version of the website, which included an online booking and payment system, together with the work she had done on preparing social media pages.

"OK, so lets talk about timescales," Rob suggested.

"We've been taking bookings through the website, for Cabins from Easter onwards, how is that coming on?"

"Doing well, both are about two thirds full at Easter, then it dips a bit until July and we are about eighty ppercent full in July, August and September. It dips to about half full from then through untill Christmas then we fill up again over the holiday period." Lorna read from her spreadsheet.

"Great, that's more than we had budgeted for. I'll come up at Easter just to make sure there's an extra pair of hands if needed." Rob suggested

"Speaking of hands, what staff are we going to need?"

Lorna and Justine looked at each other. "We've had a chat about this," Lorna said, "We need cleaners, someone to book people in and out of the cabins and we did need a maintenance/handyman, but we've got that covered now with Andy Mackie. These will be part-time and I have some locals in mind. Staffing won't be a problem."

"OK, sounds like you've got it covered. What's happening with the smokery?" Rob enquired about his pet project."

"Ah, we had a wee delay there," Fraser interjected, "the building's ready, as you know, but the equipment that Tina's father put us onto got a bit tangled up wi' the receiver o' the place that was closing down. We needed to get a bit heavy and threaten to walk away from it if they wouldnae release it to us."

"So where is it now?"

"They've still got it in their warehouse in Basingstoke."

"Have we paid them for it?"

"Yes, I checked the bank account before we came up here and the payment went through about ten days ago," Justine said.

"Then it's ours, they've no legal right to deny us the equipment. Maybe we need to just go and get it, not wait for them to arrange shipping. Leave that with me." Rob said thoughtfully.

"Anything else we need to talk about, while we're here?"

"No, I think that's about it," Lorna said, shutting her Filofax and buff folder. "Unless you've got anything else, Fraser?"

"No, I'm fine with what we've already talked about."

"Good," Rob said looking out of the window. "Hey, it's getting dark already, I didn't realise it was that late. Why don't we head for the Red Lion, grab a drink and some food?"

"Sounds good to me," Justine replied, the others nodded in agreement.

"OK, can we meet here in about, what, half an hour?" Rob suggested and again everyone agreed.

Forty five minutes later the four walked into the Red Lion and were shown to an empty table by Lizzie Allen, who fussed around them, making sure they had menues and relating a list of chef's specials of the evening, before taking drinks orders and disappearing behind the bar.

She reappeared a few minutes later with a tray of drinks, her father Hamish at her elbow.

Hamish leaned in conspiratorially, "A hear your away the morn, Robbie, Justine, so I thought you might want to know, we got our planning permission through for the new restaurant through this mornin'."

"That's brilliant, Hamish." Rob and Justine responded, in unison.

"I spoke tae Boab the Builder and he can start the work in about two to three weeks. He'll start in the old coachhouse so that he's no in the road over Easter, then he'll do the work to break through from here after the May weekend. He says he'll be finished by the middle o' June. Just perfect!"

"Even better, Hamish. Are you guys still sure about all this, it's a big step?"

"Sure about it? I'm petrified, lad, but aye, I'm sure it's the right thing, if no for me then for the young ones. It should set them up for the future, Robbie. We've a busy night, the night, so if A dinnae get the chance to say cherrio, you hae a good trip back down to your southern softies."

"Eh, excuse me," Justine interrupted, I'm one of these southern softies, Hamish Allen."

"Aye, but *you're* the Lady Laird, Tina, that makes you *oor* southern softie," Hamish winked and waved as he left them to order their food with Lizzie.

The food came and was duly enjoyed by one and all. The four were enjoying another round of drinks, when a group of men from the site contractors came in to the bar and having tolerated the usual good natured abuse from Hamish, ordered drinks. One of the men was Andy Mackie, who acknowledged the group with a quick wave and a wide grin.

"I've just had an idea," Rob stated.

Rising from his seat, he crossed the bar and tapped Mackie on the shoulder, gesturing him to a quiet corner of the room. Mackie shook his head as Rob spoke to him, then nodded a couple of times, a smile growing as he listened. Rod tapped his shoulder, smiled at Mackie then walked back to his table.

As he sat down, Justine frowned at him, " You're up to something, Rob MacLaine,I know that look."

"I think I've just solved our smokehouse problem, Tina."

"Fraser, can you talk with Andy Mackie on Monday morning. I queried if he was busy next week and he said no, so I asked him if he fancied coming with me to collect the smokehouse equipment from this warehouse in Basingstoke and he said yes.

What you guys need to do is figure out what size of truck we would need to take and if you and Lorna can arrange the hire of a truck, Mackie will drive down to Basingstoke, I'll meet him at Beaconsfield services on the M40, we'll drive down to Basingstoke, pick up the equipment and bring it up here, job done!"

"And they'll just give you this equipment?" Justine asked.

"Yes, we'll tell them we are coming and won't take no for an answer. It's ours, we've paid for it." Rob beamed.

49

The next day was Sunday, and as the contractors were due to leave site that day, Lorna and Fraser had gone up to Arran View early to do a handover with their foreman and Matt Smith the site manager.

Rob and Justine had a leisurely breakfast, which Rob cooked, while Justine prepared for their journey back to Bourne End.

After breakfast, Rob suggested they go for a walk, saying that he wanted to show Justine parts of the island she had never seen.

Driving one of the Land Cruisers, Rob turned out of the gates of Hillcrest Estate and followed the coast road toward the southwest corner of the island. Leaving the main road he followed a rough, unfinished track down a steep hill and on to a long, narrow, beach. A mile of beautiful, white sand, interrupted only by the odd large rock protruding from the otherwise flawless, fine sand.

"Oh, Rob, this is beautiful, absolutely gorgeous. If there were palm trees, you would swear you were in the Cabbibean." Justine climbed down from the vehicle.

Rob switched off the engine and joined her on the beach.

"Not bad, is it?"

The beach was deserted, the only sound, that of the waves lapping gently on the sand, the sea was like a millpond, hardly a ripple.

"Is that water cold?" Justine asked mischieviously.

"The words Scotland, May and Atlantic Ocean spring readily to mind, so, yes, it'll be freezing.

What you're looking at is called the Kilbrannan Sound and that's the Kintyre peninsula." Rob pointed to the landmass beyond the water.

"On a clear day like this, you can just make out Saddell Castle, it's 16th-century, sits just above Saddell Bay. I remembered spotting it in Paul McCartney's Mull of Kintyre video, with the Campbeltown Pipe Band marching along the beach and thinking, "I recognise that"."

"I'm going for a paddle," Justine announced, pulling off her boots and socks and tossing them into the Land Cruiser. Before Rob could stop her she was running down the beach and into the shallow water.

"Aaargh, it's freezing." Justine squealed as she ran along the waters edge, splashing through the ankle deep water. She ran out of the sea and back over the soft, fine, white sand to Rob, laughing and stamping her feet as she came. She threw her arms round Rob's neck and kissed him, then ran over to the Land Cruiser and opened the rear door.

She turned with a mischievous look on her face, pulled her heavy woollen sweater over her head and slowly began to unzip her jeans.

"Tina?"

"Well, if you won't take me skinny dipping, the least you can do is join me in the back seat of a Land Cruiser."

An hour later, they pulled up in the cobbled courtyard at the rear of Hillcrest House. They ran laughing into the rear hallway and made their way up to their bedroom to pick up their bags ready to leave for their journey back to Bourne End.

As they came down the wide, heavy wooden staircase, bags in hand, Lorna and Fraser arrived in the other Land Cruiser, having spent the morning with the contractors at Arran View.

"Hi guys," Rob greeted them, "perfect timing, we were just going to come and find you. We need to get going if we want to catch the ferry at Brodick. Miss that one and we don't get back to Ardrosssan in time for our flight."

"We were getting a bit worried we'd miss you, but the contractors took a little longer than we thought. Anyway, that's them finished with the two lodge sites and they're off home, probably on the same ferry as you."

"Good, another milestone, guys. We're actually keeping well on schedule and a lot of that is down to both of you," Justine said, "Well done."

"So, whit did you folks get up to this morning?" Fraser enquired.

Rob and Justine looked at each other and laughed.

"Oh, we just enjoyed the pleasure of a deserted beach," Rob replied.

"That sounds interesting. But ye'd best get off tae catch yer ferry, or ye'll miss it."

"OK, now you'll liaise with Andy Mackie about the truck?"

"Yes, we will," Fraser nodded.

"OK, I'll wait to hear from you."

The four said their goodbyes before Rob and Justine headed back to the village to board the ferry from Achravie to Blackwaterfoot. They then had to drive across Arran to Brodick and a further Ferry to Ardrossan, before driving to Glasgow airport for their flight back to Heathrow.

At eleven o'clock that evening, Rob turned the key in the door of Achravie, as Justine had renamed her parent's house in

Bourne End while the couple had been getting married, a few months earlier.

Rob pulled the door closed behind them and Justine dropped her bag on the floor in the hallway and turning to Rob, reached up and wound her arms round his neck.

"Oh well, that's that then Mr MacLaine. Looks as if we're on for an Easter opening for the two lodge sites and a tournament to open the golf course next Easter. Hamish and Lizzie seem to be on the ball with the Red Lion Coachhouse."

"Yeah, good for Hamish, he's doing this for Lizzie and Calum, even if the prospect scares the living daylights out of him."

"Looks like you'll be back up there sometime this week, if Fraser and Andy Mackie get themselves sorted out."

"Yeah, could do without that but we need to get the smokehouse finished and we need this equipment to do that."

"I'll ask Dad to talk to someone, he knows the people who owned the smokehouse in Cornwall."

"That would be good, they might be able to get the log-jam moving."

Rob bent to kiss Justine. "Bed?"

Justine smiled up at him, "Bed!"

50

THE NEXT MORNING, FRASER, LORNA AND ANDY MACKIE HAD agreed that a five tonne truck would be big enough to take the smokehouse equipment. After Lorna had sorted out the financial side Mackie picked up the truck in Glasgow just after lunch time.

He would drive down to Beaconsfield Services on the M40, stay overnight, then meet up with Rob next morning and drive both of them to Basingstoke to collect the equipment from the warehouse. By late morning, he would begin the drive back up to Ardrossan then catch ferries back to Achravie.

First thing that morning, Justine drove Rob over to Beaconsfield, where she joined the two men in Mackie's hotel for breakfast. As they sat eating, Justine's phone rang.

"Hi Dad."

Justine listened for a few minutes, occasionally nodding her head.

"OK that sounds positive, can you text me his name and phone number?"

"Great, thanks Dad, yes, I'll let you know how it goes. Bye, love you."

"Right, good news. Dad has spoken to the guy who owned the smokehouse and he in turn called the administrator. He confirmed that they have received our payment and are just waiting for the paperwork to catch up with the process."

"So we shouldn't have a problem at the warehouse?"

"Well, he didn't quite say that. The release of the equipment is basically down to the storage company, but he says there shouldn't be a problem."

"Yeah, I've heard that one before. The storage company will be getting paid to store this kit and every day they hang on to it, their bill to the administrator goes up by a few hundred quid. Anyway, Fraser's sent me all the paperwork and you've given me the bank statement showing that the money has been paid, so as you say there shouldn't be a problem."

"OK then, we should go, the sooner we get off the sooner we get back to Achravie."

Justine said goodbye to the two men as they clinbed into the hire truck and headed for Basingstoke.

The traffic was light as they drove down the M40, it became much more conjested as they hit the M25

"That's some woman you've got there, sir."

"You keep your beady eyes off my woman," Rob countered with a smile.

"On, no I didn't mean that,sir. She's way out of my league."

"She way out of my league as well, Andy, truth be told. I just got lucky."

"Yeah, me too. I've got an absolute gem of a wife, sir. Two crackin' kids as well. Still you and her, you're good together, anyone can see that."

"Andy, will you stop calling me "sir". Everyone calls me Rob. "Sir" disappeared when I left the military."

"Sorry, sir, I mean, Rob. Old habits die hard I guess."

"When did you leave the regiment?" Mackie asked eventually.

"Just after Afghanistan, I'd had enough. Seen too many of my mates killed and it was taking longer to count the scars in the shower in the mornings. I reckoned it was only a matter of time before my number would come up, so I thought I would move on while I still could. I'd met Joe Harper and we talked about setting up our own security business. We both left about the same time, so we went for it."

"Yeah. I left about the same time. Different story though, I saw some of my mates go down. Of course you do, you're in a war zone. I thought I could take it, though. One morning we were out on patrol in a Foxhound. We came under heavy fire, Foxhound broke down, just died on us. We were trapped, sitting ducks. Driver called for backup but, we took a hit from an RPG, killed the crew outright. We knew we couldn't just sit there, so the guys tried to get out, I jumped over to the driver's seat, went out the driver's door and got cover behind the vehicle. That was when they hit the Foxhound with another RPG, but from the back as the guys were trying to get out. Seven guys, gone."

Rob noticed a tear course down Mackie's cheek.

"Ten seconds later, one of our Apache gunships took the enemy out. How ironic is that?"

"Hard to bear, Andy."

"Finished me off, sir..Rob. I was gone, a gibbering wreck. Shipped back here, discharged and just left to get on with it."

"You didn't get any counselling?"

"Yeah, got some, not a lot. Didn't do any good. Wife and kids have kept me sane, she didn't need to, she could have walked, I wouldn't have blamed her, but she didn't. My old mates at home all think I'm a right nutter, keep well clear of me.

Hm, not sure why I'm telling you any of that. This job, if you keep me on, It'll give us all a fresh start, away from the past."

"It'll be up to you whether or not we keep you on Andy. I've invested a lot of money in Achravie estate, I need to make it work. I offered you a job because I don't think you'll let me down. I think you'll put your all into the job, that's the kind of feedback I was getting about you, so the rest is up to you."

"I won't let you down, Rob."

"Good."

The men chatted about their pasts, their families and their aspirations for the future, until Mackie saw the turnoff they needed for Basingstoke.

Once off the motorway, Rob began giving Mackie Fraser's directions from his phone. Soon they turned into a large industrial estate. They followed the road round until Mackie pointed out a sign on the front of a large building which read "Clarke Storage".

"That's it, Rob."

Mackie pulled the truck into the entrance to the yard area in front of the warehouse, stopping at the security barrier.

A short, slim, almost skinny, security guard came out of the small gatehouse and approached the driver's window, which Mackie had opened on seeing the man approaching.

"Morning," Mackie greeted the man, who was wearing a black uniform consisting of cargo trousers and a bomber jacket with "Clarke Storage" sewn onto the front.

"What can I do for you?"

"We're here to collect some equipment you've got stored here."

"You, got a manifest?"

"No, it was only arranged yesterday so the paperwork might not have caught up yet, but we've got proof of ownership of the goods."

"Won't do you any good, son. No manifest, no entry, so if I were you, I'd turn around and head back to where you came from till you get a manifest."

"We've just driven down from Scotland, so we're hardly

going to do that, like I say, we've got proof of ownership of the equipment."

"I don't care if you've just beamed down from Mars. Like I say, no manifest, no entry, now, why don't you just do one."

Andy Mackie was starting to get angry, so Rob placed his right hand on his shoulder.

"Wait here, Andy," he said climbing down from the cab.

He walked round the truck to face the security guard.

"Why don't you call your boss and tell him we're here to collect the equipment for Achravie Estate. He knows we're coming today."

"Mr Clarke will tell you the same as I just told your driver, no manifest, no entry."

"Maybe he won't, ask him," Rob stood a full head taller than the guard and stared down at him.

A second security guard appeared from the gatehouse. He was taller and much more portly than his counterpart.

"Everything OK, George?" the larger man asked.

"Oh God, it's Laurel and Hardy," Rob mused.

"Everything's just fine. Your colleague here was just about to give Mr Clarke a call to inform him that we're here to pick up some equipment, weren't you George."

"No chance, now, why don't you just get back in your truck and disappear."

"OK, if you won't ask Mr Clarke then I will," Rob said stepping past the smaller man who suddenly grabbed Rob's arm.

Rob turned, grabbed the man's wrist and twisted his arm viciously against the joint. The man howled in pain as his large friend stepped forward to intervene.

"Don't even think about it big boy," Andy Mackie advised, having jumped down from the truck.

"You try anything, my friend will pull your mate's arm off. Not literally you understand, but he won't be back at work for a few weeks and its going to be really painfull. I've seen him do it before, its not a pretty sight."

"What's going on?" an angry voice demanded from behind Rob.

Rob turned, still holding the smaller security guard's arm to see a middle aged man, short, broad build and well groomed, wearing a navy suit and a coat. He was accompanied by another security guard.

"Mr Clarke, I presume." Rob enquired.

"Who's asking?" the man replied with a sneer.

"I am and I'm here to pick up my equipment, which your company has been good enough to store for the last few weeks."

"You the bloke about the smokehouse stuff?"

"That's me."

"Got a message from the administrators to say you'd be here today, but I haven't agreed to release the goods as yet."

"Well you better do it soon or this man's going to lose the use of his arm and I don't think any of us want that, do we Mr Clarke?"

"OK, OK, let's not get carried away, Joe, let them in and we'll sort things out in the warehouse."

Rob let the man's arm go, as the Hardy of Laurel and Hardy raised the barrier and Mackie got into the truck and drove to the warehouse doors as Rob walked across the yard to join him.

The roller shutter door which was the main entry into the warehouse opened slowly and Mackie was directed to reverse into the building and the door was closed again.

Clarke gave instructions to two men in overalls and with the aid of a gas powered forklift truck, the equipment was extracted from the heavy duty racking loaded on to the truck and the side curtain made secure for the journey back to Achravie.

Rob noticed that the roller shutter door remained closed and as he and Mackie made to return to their truck, they found themselves faced with three security guards, who had been joined by the two warehousemen and Clarke, who had removed his coat and jacket.

"Before you lads leave, we're going to give you a little lesson in manners, teach you that you don't just come in here demanding things, aren't we boys."

This got a murmur of agreement from Clarke's men, who had started to advance toward Rob and Mackie.

"I think you may be getting your ambitions mixed up with you capabilities, wee man." Rob unzipped his jacket and opened it to show the compact Glock automatic pistol tucked into the waistband of his jeans.

"Why don't you guys just open that door and the barrier at the gate, so that we can go home all happy and content. Trust me, you don't want to make me angry."

Andy Mackie looked at the Glock, in surprise and then relief.

"He's right, he gets nasty when he's angry and gunshot wounds take ages to heal"

Clarke's exression showed a mixture of surprise and fear, he looked from Mackie back to Rob. The colour drained from his face. He nodded slowly, "Do what he says, let them go, this time. But don't ever come back here."

The door and barrier were opened, allowing the truck to leave the warehouse and Mackie drove out on to the industrial estate. From there he turned on to Winchester Road and headed back towards the M3 motorway.

They had said nothing to each other until they turned on to the motorway.

Mackie suddenly burst out laughing, "I think I'm going to like working for you!"

"Not every day's going to be like today, Andy, thankfully." Rob replied with a laugh.

"I thought we were in for a real kicking back there."

"Yeah, well, you know that old song "Glock Changes Everything."

"Eh, I think you'll find it's love, "Love Changes Everything.""

"Not today, it didn't!"

Both men laughed,

51

THE REST OF THE JOURNEY BACK TO ACHRAVIE WAS UNEVENTFUL. They stopped for lunch at Norton Canes Services on the M6. Using the toll section of the motorway saved some time, keeping them away from the Birmingham area and they eventually reached the ferry terminal at Ardrossan with time to spare

Mackie parked the truck close to the terminal and they went in search of the fish suppers they had discussed on the way. They sat on a bench beside the truck, overlooking the Firth of Clyde and ate them, before boarding the ferry at the allotted time. It seemed as if they had just driven on to the ferry when it was time to drive off and they were driving across Arran to Blackwaterfoot. They caught the last ferry to Achravie, arriving back at Hillcrest House just before nine o'clock that evening.

Although tired from the journey, both men were aware that they needed to get the smokehouse equipment offloaded that night, as they were booked on the first ferry out in the morning. With the help of Fraser and two of the estate employees they lifted the equipment into the smokehouse building using the estate's fork lift truck, making sure to deposit it close to where it would eventually be required.

"So, did you have any trouble getting them to part wi' the stuff?" Fraser asked as they watched the fork lift driver lift the last pallet of equipment off the truck.

"Took a bit of persuasion, but you know how persuasive two lads from the Regiment can be when they need to be." Mackie answered, with a wink to Rob.

"Oh aye, that A do, Andy." Fraser replied with a knowing look at Rob, who smiled and shrugged.

"Lorna said to tell you she was sorry to miss ye, Robbie, but she's been booked onto this course in Glasgow for weeks and she knows you'll be back up pretty soon."

After that it was bed, as both Mackie and Rob were feeling the effects of the journey.

Having showered Rob decided to call Justine.

"Hello you, thought you'd forgotten about me. I was just off to bed." Justine teased.

"We've just finished offloading the smokehouse equipment. Didn't feel much like doing it tonight, but we're booked on the first ferry in the morning, so we didn't have much choice."

"How did you get on with Andy Mackie?"

"Fine, he's a good guy Tina, been through a lot and not had much support, but he seems to be getting his life back together. I think Achravie 'll be the making of him."

"How're Lorna and Fraser?"

Fraser's doing well, he's just been helping us offload the truck. Lorna's on a course in Glasgow, but Fraser says she's fine."

"Well, I've started planning for the opening . Lorna and I had a good discussion about staff yesterday. She's got that well in hand and we've talked about coming back up for things opening up at Easter."

"So what's next on your agenda?"

"What's next, Mrs MacLaine? Getting ready for Senator Grant's visit in September is what's next."

"You not expecting that to be troublesome though, are you?"

"Nah, walk in the park!"

ACKNOWLEDGMENTS

If you are reading this, it probably means that you have taken the time to read both *The Prodigal Son* and *The Good Samaritan*. I thank you for taking the time to do that. If you haven't read Book I, *The Prodigal Son* I hope you are now compelled to do so.

I have enjoyed writing these books and trust that you enjoyed reading them. If you have, please leave a review on Amazon; in this very competitive market, good reviews sell books.

The Good Samaritan has been the fruit of not just my labour, I would like to acknowledge the patience, time and effort that my good friend, Diana has very kindly put into proof reading and editing my words. A very special thanks to you, Diana.

My thanks also to my wife, Val for not only putting up with me while writing these books, but for taking time to proof read and edit The Good Samaritan in conjunction with Diana. Thanks for your help and support, Val.

ABOUT THE AUTHOR

Les Haswell was born in Glasgow and spent his early years in Ayrshire, in South-West Scotland. Having been educated there and served an engineering apprenticeship he embarking on a world tour of Scotland, living in Ayrshire, Perthshire, Morayshire, Aberdeenshire and Stirlingshire, before ending up in Aberdeen.

Working in the offshore oil & gas industry for much of his business life, Les has travelled the world and visit places as culturally diverse as Latin America and USA, West & East Africa, the Middle & Far East.

Les now lives with his wife in Winchester in Hampshire.

———

To learn more about Les Haswell and discover more Next Chapter authors, visit our website at www.nextchapter.pub.

The Good Samaritan
ISBN: 978-4-82414-093-7

Published by
Next Chapter
1-60-20 Minami-Otsuka
170-0005 Toshima-Ku, Tokyo
+818035793528

31st March 2022

CPSIA information can be obtained
at www.ICGtesting.com
Printed in the USA
LVHW100552240622
722033LV00003B/78